RUINED WINGS

 SEVERED FLAMES
BOOK ONE

ANNIE ANDERSON

RUINED WINGS

Severed Flames Book One

Annie Anderson

Published by Annie Anderson

Copyright © 2024 Annie Anderson

Edited by: Angela Sanders

Cover Art by: Tattered Quill Designs

All rights reserved.

Paperback ISBN: 978-1-960315-46-5

Hardcover ISBN: 978-1-960315-50-2

For all my girlies who were traumatized by the plethora of early 2000s love triangles that ripped our hearts out. This one's for us.

We have to continually be jumping off cliffs and developing our wings on the way down.

— KURT VONNEGUT

CHAPTER 1

VALE

The deadliest part of my day was this stone staircase.

Hunger clawed at my stomach as I trudged up the uneven catwalk toward the overseer behind the line of other miners. The weight of my pack turned my knees to jelly as my muscles threatened to dump me on my ass down the stone steps to the back of the line.

That was if I even survived. Nausea warred with hunger as I lifted my gaze from my feet to the gaping hole in the mountain, the coming night a warning more than anything else. The night brought monsters—great winged beasts that threatened to pick us off if we strayed too close to the surface.

Beasts that breathed fire and pummeled us without mercy.

Beasts that made leaving this place impossible.

Or so the *Perder Lucem* said. I still thought the catwalk was deadlier than any beast outside of this mountain.

Roughly, I was shoved forward, my foot knocking a loose pebble off the edge of the step to the gorge below, which was enough to prove me right. If I didn't pay attention, I'd slip off this skeletal stone staircase that wound toward the top of the mountain and fall to my end like so many had before me.

Last week, a young girl fell from the top—the fraying joke of a rope lining the catwalk unable to stop her from going over the edge.

Some say she was pushed.

Some say she jumped.

But I'd bet she simply fell like so many had before her, not that it mattered. Life under the mountain went on as if we hadn't lost another one of us, as if she meant nothing.

Maybe none of us did to them.

Gritting my teeth, I kept my eyes trained forward, ignoring the burn of my thighs as I took another step. If I didn't fall, I'd hopefully get something to eat. Though, if the expression on the overseer's face meant anything, today wouldn't be a good day.

It never was.

Filthy and sour, Darren was just as tired as the rest of us, but at least when he was doling out rations in exchange for the magic-stealing ore mined from this very mountain, *he* got a seat. I envied that spindly chair and contemplated what I'd give for a cushioned spot to rest my weary bones.

But more?

I'd commit murder for a real meal. It didn't even need to be a real meal, either. It could be broth and a hunk of bread—anything more than the scant bricklike rations they used as payment for *Lumentium*.

Those iridescent rocks poisoned me with every hammer, every breath, every second I spent under this mountain, but they were also my savior. Without them, there would be no way to keep the magic brewing beneath my skin a secret. No way to sneak under the noses of the *Perder Lucem* guild without a death sentence.

Because that was exactly what magic was here.

Death.

But it wasn't just death for me. It was also death for the winged beasts that kept us here. It was our one weapon against the kingdom pinning us inside this mountain. A kingdom I planned on fleeing to, even as much as I hated it.

Each day, I snuck one of those hunks of poison into my pocket, hoping it would temper the cursed power that had awoken on my twentieth birthday. For the last five years, I'd hung onto one of those rocks tight, praying no one ever noticed me lining my pockets with them.

Praying no one tried to take them from me.

Praying I'd still had enough strength to get us out of here, even though I poisoned myself.

Praying the magic-abhorring guild didn't look too closely at what was left of my family.

The three people ahead, a man I didn't recognize slipped on the steps, his pack too heavy for him to carry up the deathtrap that was the catwalk. His shout echoed off the rock walls as his pack knocked into the two men in front of us, nearly taking us all out. My head spun as I let my gaze fall to the bottom of the crevasse. Bones littered the jagged slate, the rest washed away in the trickling stream—all that remained of the dead.

It had been six years since my parents had fallen, trying to escape the fire-breathing beasts that pinned us here, the dragons ferrying them into the afterlife without so much as a warning. I cursed Orrus daily for stealing them from us, but a part of me worried cursing the god of death would have me meeting him sooner rather than later.

At least they'd died before they could see what I'd become.

Crouching so I wouldn't fall, I latched onto my sister's hand, yanking her to the relative safety of my position while my stomach turned end over end. I tried to peel my gaze from the poor man scrambling for purchase on the edge, his pack nowhere to be seen. Someone must have ripped it from his back, and now he dangled above the wide-open crevasse, his death almost assured.

If I were brave enough, I'd run to help him. But instead, I was frozen, squeezing Nyrah's hand so hard she gasped in pain. I met wide green eyes as he realized no one would come to his aid, no one would help, and then I was helpless to watch as he lost his fight with gravity, his body falling to the jagged rocks below.

Closing my eyes, I cursed Orrus yet again for taking another life so needlessly—for making his presence known with every heartbeat, every step, every waking second.

Then the line moved on as if we hadn't just

watched someone take their last breath—as if we hadn't just become closer to our own end.

As if tomorrow it wouldn't be one of us.

Ignoring the burn of tears in my throat, I forced myself to stand up, to move forward, to take another step. Nyrah peeled my hand off of hers, her mumbled chiding barely a murmur over the ringing in my ears.

Ten years my junior, it had been a challenge to keep her safe—to keep her from following our parents in death. If it wasn't the stairs, then it was the lack of food or the cut-throat miners trying to rip off our haul. And that was just what was under the mountain.

Outside brought its own dangers.

Each day was a new delicate dance of survival, worse now that she'd caught the eye of the guild leader's son.

Thane Ashbourne was attractive enough, with a square jaw, bright-blue eyes, and hair as blond as my sister's. But his muscular shoulders hadn't seen a day of mining, and he lacked all humanity, all warmth. He saw my sister as a prize simply because he couldn't have her.

And he *couldn't* have her.

I didn't care who his father was.

All we needed was two more days—maybe a week—and we'd have hoarded enough supplies to carry us to Credour. From there, I didn't know what I'd do to feed us, but it mattered less to me than getting us from underneath the guild's thumb.

"Half a ration," Darren barked to the man in front of us, his haul twice the size of Nyrah's.

My little sister grumbled in affront as she readjusted her grip on her pack, her knees likely trembling harder than mine. We'd worked from sunup until nearly sundown with no breaks, no food, and no water—wasting away as our quotas rose day by day.

That's how they keep you docile.

That's how they keep you under their thumb.

You can't look around and see the cracks if you can't even breathe.

Momma's words echoed in my head, the truth of them just as bitter as the loss of her.

The *Perder Lucem* had been at war with Credour since before I was born—the magic-wielders keeping us locked under this mountain in a conflict which seemed to have no logical end. Other than "our" side being against magic and Credour being the home of it, much of the start of the war was a mystery.

Well, other than the Luxa, but I tried not to think about them.

The deadly fire witches had haunted my nightmares since the day my power rose to the surface, my mother's dire warnings almost like premonitions of what I would become. And her book on the subject did little to ease my fears.

A Luxa will wake the Beast...

A Luxa will unbind him...

A Luxa will destroy us all...

But it was tough to give a fuck about what kind of magic-user I may or may not be—especially from a book so old it might as well have been a fairytale. Credour was the only place that might accept me— the only place I could keep us alive.

Dragons be damned.

If we remained here, one of two things would happen. One, I'd lose my tenuous hold on the magic beneath my skin, get thrust before the guild, and summarily executed. Or two? We would starve to death like River and Jonas had, their withered bodies just giving out on them, even though they were so young.

And for what?

So we could mine more poison rocks?

So we could produce more weapons for the *Perder Lucem's* war?

So we could live and die by a creed likely none of us believed in?

A Luxa hadn't been heard of in two hundred years. The race had probably died out just like the rest of us. And the magic under my skin could be fire. It could also be light, or energy, or...

Acid churned in my belly, the gnawing ache of hunger mingling with the heat of my anger as I stared at the back of the man in front of me. I dreamt of a day when I didn't have to hide, when merely breathing didn't hurt. When I didn't have to fear that every single breath would be my last. When I didn't curse the god of death for taking so many away from us.

But acting on my rage wouldn't serve me—it wouldn't give me bread. It wouldn't give us a real home.

All it would do was get me killed—get *us* killed.

I slipped a hand in my pocket, squeezing the poisonous rock hard enough to split my skin.

Two more days. Maybe a week. Quit being a baby and get yourself together.

The heat of my blood warmed the rock in my

palm as flecks of the stone sizzled against the open wound.

Ignoring Nyrah's grumbles and my own desires, I kept my face carefully blank, feigning patience for my turn. Just last week, this same haul would have given us five rations. Either the food supply was dwindling, or someone had gathered the strength to step out of line.

Because if it wasn't the insurmountable quotas, it was cut rations when we were all practically starving. The guild would do just about anything to keep us from asking questions—to keep us from rising up, from ripping them from their cozy beds and tossing them into the crevasse along with the miners they let die. It was getting to the point where most of us would rather face the dragons ourselves than live in the darkness for one more day.

My gaze slid to my sister as I mentally willed her not to say anything. Her shining blue eyes met mine, and I wondered where I got my features. Nyrah was waif-thin—like all of us—but with an ethereal beauty like a sprite or a Fae. She was all long limbs on her tiny frame, with a button nose and gorgeous in an obvious way even though they worked us damn near to death.

Where she was blonde and blue-eyed like our

parents, I resembled no one. My hair was dark as coal, my eyes the green of the treetops. My little sister barely reached my shoulder and likely wouldn't get much taller, but neither of us were very tall. It was the one thing we had in common.

Just as we reached Darren, Thane seemed to materialize out of the shadows, his gaze locked on Nyrah as she handed her pack to the overseer.

Thane didn't mine like the rest of us. No, he stayed with his father to learn how to lead this guild one day—though if I were to guess, there wouldn't be a guild for him to lead by the time it was his turn. We were barely hanging on by a thread.

The only time he deigned to poke his head out of his plush battle rooms was when Nyrah was close to the guild headquarters. Then he would somehow find my sister, somehow know she was near, seeking her out like she was a beacon.

If he were anyone else, I'd think it was romantic. I'd encourage her to gain his favor. But he wasn't.

"Beautiful as ever, Miss Tenebris." He rubbed at the blond stubble at his jaw, avarice in his cold stare. "Care to share a meal with me?"

Nyrah tried to ignore him, focusing on Darren as we waited for his judgment on her haul. "How many rations today?"

Darren looked up from her haul, slid his cool black gaze to Thane, and then returned to her. "Quarter ration. This is the third day in a row you missed your quota. Don't make it a fourth."

He slapped the ration into her hand, his filthy fingers all over our only food, effectively dismissing her to the clutches of Thane.

And there wasn't a damn thing I could do about it.

I barely registered when Darren took my pack, too busy staring at Thane's menacing hand wrapped around her bicep as he yanked her closer. Swallowing my fear, I clutched the rock tighter in my palm.

Don't. She can handle him. She's not stupid. Just two more days, and we're out of here.

Guilt stabbed me in the chest. If I were braver, we would have left already. If I were smarter, I would have figured out a way to get us out of here and to Credour as soon as my power manifested. If I were a better sister, I would have slammed my fist into his stupid, smug face.

But I was none of those things, and my sister was suffering for it.

"Quarter ration," Darren rumbled, his beady eyes alight with a sick sort of glee as they met mine.

I wondered if he ate the excess, the bastard. All of us were starving, but Darren wasn't as gaunt as the rest of us, and it pissed me off.

"I have four times what my sister carried," I reminded him, forcing myself not to kick his chair over and watch him tumble to the gorge below. "That should at least buy me a whole ration."

Arguing wouldn't do me any good, but I had to try. We couldn't keep going on nothing. I couldn't make it out of here without more food in my belly or...

Two more days. Just two more days.

"This is your third day not meeting your quota, as well. If you want to eat, you have to do the work."

Like he would know anything about work.

He slapped the ration onto my palm, the tiny morsel of food barely two bites. An entire day of work was only worth crumbs. I fought off the urge to scream in his face as I swallowed my rage. Because screaming led to other things. Things like setting my power free just to see if I could watch his head explode.

Squeezing the rock in my pocket tighter, the poison tempered my magic just enough for me to move on and save my sister from the creepy affections of a man it would hurt to piss off. Hooking my sister's elbow with my own, I tugged her toward our sleeping quarters.

Two more days.

Thane stared at my arm like he'd enjoy cutting it off my body, the twist of a sneer a threat all on its own. His grip tightened on my sister's arm hard enough for her to whimper before he let her go.

"Remember what I said, Nyrah." Thane's sneer fell to a sinister smile, as though whatever he'd said was already a foregone conclusion. "I'll expect your answer within the week."

A pit as wide as the gorge yawned wide in my belly, sending me into a proverbial freefall.

One more day.

Because we wouldn't make it two.

CHAPTER 2
VALE

Don't fall asleep.

One would think it was the nights that were the shortest, but they weren't. Even as hard as we worked in the daylight, in the darkness in this labyrinth of a cave system, the nights seemed to stretch on forever until the sun rose again.

Nights brought the monsters—both above and below.

In the darkness with a faint and fleeting flicker of torches, I would wonder if each night would be my last—if they'd somehow found out about the magic under my skin, if they would come for me just as I fell into fitful dreams.

If they'd rip me from Nyrah, leaving her to the clutches of Thane.

Any other night, I'd force myself to close my eyes, to rest for a few hours in the rags we'd cobbled together to form a pallet on the rocky ground. Instead, I was barely keeping them open, hoping I didn't fail us again.

The second Thane's fingers closed around Nyrah's arm, my timetable crumbled to dust. She'd sworn it wasn't bruised, but I knew better. I'd seen her hurt more than once, and her shoulders hit her ears every time I asked about it.

It took everything I had to not divert my plans just a little and seek the bastard out. In my wildest dreams, I stalked him like a hunter in the darkness, taking the blade my mother forced into my palm the fateful day of my parents' death and raking it across his throat. If I wouldn't get caught in an instant, I would do it, too.

I'd do just about anything to keep Nyrah free—do anything to keep my promise to my father before he left that morning. It was as if he knew they wouldn't be coming back.

Watch out for your sister, Vale. Don't let anything happen to her. Promise me.

His order had been a resonant demand, almost

as if he could wield magic himself to compel me to do his bidding.

I would have done it without the order, but something about it still grated, as much as it drove me to be better. The last thing he ever said to me wasn't kindness or comfort—not that there was much of either to be had here. It was of obligation—one I would have taken regardless. It was one I'd taken so many times before.

One I would always take.

We wouldn't be safe until Thane was dealt with or we managed to leave. Nyrah's rebuff embarrassed him, and now we'd be looking around every corner to ensure he wasn't lurking in the shadows.

Peeling myself away from my sister's warmth, I stood, careful not to wake her. Of the two of us, Nyrah hadn't ever been as good at keeping her thoughts off her face or out of her mouth, nor was she as skilled at thievery. The last time she tried stealing, it ended in disaster in more ways than one. Unbidden, my fingers brushed the raised scars at the top of my shoulder where I paid the price for her crimes.

If we were ever to make it out of here, I had to make sure she stayed in the dark, had to make sure she knew nothing, had to keep the majority of my thievery to myself. Because if we were caught hoarding, it wouldn't be the blade or the whip this time.

It would be the gorge.

My gut twisted as I hesitated at the opening in our sleeping chamber—a roughly carved hole in the cave system barely big enough for the both of us. I glanced back at the small lump that was my sister, the golden hair so opposite of mine peeking from underneath the covers. I tried to remember when the last time we'd had a bed or a stick of furniture— tried to remember a time before all we were hadn't been whittled down to scraps of fabric and a sad little hole in the mountain.

It had to be before Momma and Father passed. When our sleeping chamber was larger, when we had beds and a small kitchenette and... *parents*. The day they'd whispered about them falling was still etched into my mind—the way no one would look us in the eye.

It hadn't been until Thane's father—the guild leader of the *Perder Lucem*—graced the entrance to our sleeping chamber did their loss hit home, did he tell me how they ran from the dragons, choosing the gorge over the fire. In the blink of an eye, I'd transitioned from a thoughtless teenager to a mother.

In a single breath, it had become my job to keep Nyrah safe.

In a single moment, we'd lost everything.

And I was failing—at keeping her fed, at keeping her safe, at keeping her alive. We were one hairsbreadth away from death every single day, and now, with my golden sister in Thane's crosshairs...

Somehow, I had to steal enough supplies for the six days we needed instead of only one, and the thought alone gave me enough heartburn that the meager ration I choked down hours ago threatened to come up. My nighttime strolls to the kitchens had stayed undetected this long because I didn't take too much. Just a ration here or there, a skin to hold water, a blade or two.

Nothing from the front of the stores, nothing too flashy.

Nothing that would be missed.

I'd been so careful.

Tonight, I would need to be careful *and* excessive, and those two did not mix.

I'd never been brave a day in my life, but each time I went out into the tunnels, I thought about it being my last. I thought of her waking up alone and scared, about her being left to defend herself under this mountain without anyone at her back.

A part of me wished I was brave—wished I was a person who would run forward to prevent a stranger from falling off the catwalk. Wished I was brave enough to hit Thane with the unruly magic in my veins to make sure he knew never to touch my sister again.

But I wasn't.

I was only me. And the only thing I could do was keep my sister alive.

The best way to accomplish this would be to sneak around in the dark and steal food like a rat—jumping the ship as one of those rodents would, praying we didn't get caught by either side of this never-ending war.

This section of the tunnel was lit with flickering torches, their fuel likely to run out in the next hour or so. At least I had a deadline I could stick to this time. Hugging the walls, I refused to let my cowardice steal what few seconds I had. The carved earth widened, opening to another catwalk, this one only a bit wider than the treacherous stone steps that would take us to the overseer. At least with this one, I had a side wall to hang onto should I stumble.

But I didn't lose my balance. Stealing down those steps, I followed the path into the belly of the mountain, the warmth of being so close to the earth easing some of the pain in my joints. I could pretend it was simply the warmth which made it so I could breathe again, but that wasn't the case. The closer I got to the ground, the farther away I was from the poisoned ore that kept my magic contained.

Here, I could almost breathe easy.

And easy here was dangerous.

If it weren't for the rock clutched so tightly in my palm, the searing magic trapped beneath my skin would burst free, shining like a beacon in the night.

Squeezing my hand tighter on the ore, I swept through the deserted tunnel into the kitchens, my feet silent on the rocky ground, only because I'd done this so many times before.

I minced through the third tunnel on the right, the loose rocks littering the ground easy to trip over if I wasn't ready for them. Jumping to the slight rise in the wall, I leapt from one side to the other over the sharp stones, soundlessly landing on the other side before twirling into a slight person-sized depression in the rock.

There had never been a guard on the door to these kitchens, but I didn't take any chances. Holding my breath, I waited, listening for the sound of feet shuffling or a blade being drawn, anticipating a trick, even though there had never been one before. The central kitchen where our rations were made and stored was just a little farther down the corridor, tucked away as if it were always meant to be hidden. As if the basic necessity of food had always been a bargaining chip, even though there was nothing of importance here.

The leadership kitchen was three levels up, guarded so heavily it was as if they were hiding riches and secrets, not just fresh fruit and meat. I'd never bothered to breach that space, preferring not to revisit my punishment for Nylah's transgressions. There was nothing fresh in these kitchens. Only the dried bricks of rations and a few kitchen utensils.

Nothing worth guarding, nothing worth anything at all.

Except to me.

After several moments of holding my breath, I risked peering around the corner. Just like always, there was no one standing in my way. As quickly as I could without risking the noise, I slipped into the kitchen, skirting the stoves and racks to make my way to dry storage.

Nicking the full bricks, I wordlessly cursed Darren. There was plenty of food for everyone— always had been. Racks and racks of it. But some of the older bricks were mottled with mold, spoiling because they refused to keep us fed. My whole body boiled with the injustice of it.

People were dying, and they let food go to waste.

Swallowing the bile of hatred clawing up my throat, I squeezed my eyes shut. I couldn't decide who I hated more—the dragons who had taken my parents or the leadership who'd tried to kill us with every passing of the sun.

The power roiling underneath my skin surged, trying to break free. My flesh heated, nearly bubbling, as the blaze of magic searched for a way out. I scrambled for the *Lumentium*, latching onto the poisoned rock as the first rays of power seeped from the open cut on my forearm. My skin sizzled from contact with the stone, but it had done its job. Just as suddenly as the light appeared, it flickered and died, retreating from where it came.

Rage wouldn't get these supplies so we could leave.

Rage wouldn't get my sister out of here.

Rage wouldn't help me.

Focus would.

Gritting my teeth, I stuffed the bricks into the pockets of my trousers. The billowing fabric easily concealed my haul, even if it pulled my waistband too low. Hastily, I cinched the belt tighter, hoping it held as I reformed our escape plan in my mind.

We couldn't wait for sunrise, no matter how much easier it would make our exit on the crumbling catwalks leading to the forest. If the leadership was willing to let food spoil to keep us in line, there would be little stopping them from killing us outright. The time to leave had passed a long time ago.

If I woke Nyrah when I got back, I could get us out between the shift change at the entrance. We could make it to the forest before the sun crested the horizon. I'd heard rumors of the dangers in the wood, but the cover would help on the way to Credour. Dragons weren't known to burn the trees searching for prey.

The trek back to our sleeping chamber was quick. My steps may not have been as careful as they could have been, but excitement thrummed in my veins. We were getting out of here as quickly as our feet could carry us. We had enough food, supplies, and the rest we could make up as we went along.

Nyrah would be free from this place as our parents intended.

But the closer I got to our carved hole of a home, the more the little hairs on my arms stood at attention, a frisson of warning snaking down my spine as the flickering torches slowly died. The catwalk beneath me nearly disappeared from view as I took the last few steps to safety.

But the tunnel didn't *feel* safe.

Nothing felt safe.

It took a few precious moments for my vision to adjust to the darkness, but the sound hit my ears long before then. A whimper. Nearly silent, but as known to me as my own mind.

Nyrah.

Before my eyes fully adjusted, I ran, streaking down the corridor because I knew what I'd find. Light poured from the cut on my arm, the hunk of *Lumentium* not enough to stop the surge of power from erupting from my skin. It was so bright it seared my eyes, but I couldn't care about anything but that whimper.

Skidding to a halt outside our sleeping chamber, the brightness marking me as a magic-user illuminated the room, telling me what I knew as soon as I heard my sister's distress.

Thane said she had a week, but he lied.

His big body held her in place, his beefy hand pinning her wrists to the ground as the other snaked into her trousers.

Without hesitation, I dropped the *Lumentium* in my hand, the surge of hatred, bile, and fear calling the barely contained magic forth faster than I ever thought possible.

He shielded his eyes from the light pouring from my skin, taking his hand from my sister, and she lunged, scrabbling for the knife just out of her reach.

"*Luxa*," Thane hissed, the truth from his lips barely a whisper, but it may as well have been a scream.

Yes, I was exactly who he said I was. Not that he'd get a chance to tell anyone.

"Get the *fuck* away from my sister."

He stood, his cruel smile widening. "What are you going to do about it?"

Even I didn't know what this power could actually do, but I didn't have to worry. He didn't take a single step before Nyrah plunged the dagger into his thigh. She ripped it out and jabbed it into his gut. He bellowed, backhanding my sister into the stone wall.

I loosened the reins on the rage I'd been holding onto—years and years of it—pouring it into my limbs, setting it free. Light flowed from my body, spearing like daggers through the gloom, burning

Thane as the bolts of power ran him through worse than my sister had.

His flesh burned, his screams echoing off the walls before they withered and died, the light going out of his eyes as he fell to the ground.

And though I knew he would *never* touch my sister again, I knew worse things still. The sound of running feet hit my ears, and the truth of it settled into my bones.

We wouldn't make it out of here—not the both of us.

But she would.

Thane twitched, his sizzling flesh a miasma of awful filling the room as I yanked my sister to her feet.

I tore the blade from her grip and gave myself a shallow cut across my belly and another on my arm. This needed to look real.

"Scream, Nyrah. Call me a witch. Point the blade at me. Make it look real."

Nyrah just blinked at me.

"We don't have much time. I have rations stashed in the hole in the wall over there." I pointed to the corner. "As soon as you can make it out of here, head to the forest. Go to Credour like we planned. Promise me."

Tears filled her eyes. "I c-can't. Please don't make me."

I gripped her hands before forcing the blade into them. "You have to. Now scream. Make it look real."

She didn't move, so I hauled back and slapped her. "Do it. I love you, little one. Now survive. For me. *Please*."

And even though I'd asked her to, it was still a tiny betrayal when she actually followed through.

"*Luxa*," she screamed at the top of her lungs. "*Witch*."

The thunder of feet moved faster, shouts of angry men growing louder.

But I didn't see them before lightning flashed behind my eyes. Nyrah's face was the last thing I saw before the light beneath my skin flickered.

Died.

And darkness pulled me under.

CHAPTER 3

VALE

M y shoulders screamed in protest as consciousness finally found me. The poison metal of *Lumentium* bit into my wrists as I hung suspended from what I knew was a rough-hewn hook screwed into the craggy carved ceiling of the Judgment Room.

My bare toes narrowly touched the floor, my scant slippers gone. The little blood that wasn't leaking from my head pooled in my legs, making them ache and my hands numb. My skull throbbed as I hazarded a dry swallow, the coppery tang on my tongue enough to make me gag.

Death would be better than where I was now.

Death would be a mercy.

Because I knew what was waiting for me, and none of it was good.

I should know. I'd been here before.

The Judgment Room was little more than a large meeting space carved into the mountain, barely big enough to house us all. But each experience wrought in this room was still burned into my memories like a brand. As an adult, I'd swung from this very hook, paying the price for Nyrah's actions —the whip cracking against my skin still echoing in my ears even then.

At least I knew better than to ask for mercy this time. Because there was none to be found here. This hook had always been the consequence for murderers and food-stealers.

And now I was both.

But I couldn't seem to regret taking Thane's life, even if it meant I'd die hanging from this hook like so many before me. I couldn't regret saving my sister —couldn't regret anything except for leaving her alone in the clutches of that monster.

If I'd been smart, I would have killed him at the first sign of danger—would have pulled us out of here and braved the forest, dragons and all. I should have protected her like our father told me to, and now...

But I couldn't change what I'd done. All I could do was endure for as long as possible to give my sister enough time to escape. She had to escape. It was the only way any of this would be worth it.

Because I would never make it out of this room.

Keeping my eyes closed, I tried to assess just how bad off I was. By the scent of death and the murmurs of the crowd around me, I'd be willing to guess I was a step *beyond* fucked. And above it all, Nyrah's sobs hit me the hardest.

She shouldn't be here.

My lids flashed open, and my gaze unerringly found hers in the gloom. The flickering torches barely illuminated the blackened blood stains on the floor or the faces of my judge and jury. But I could see my sister just fine.

Her temple was bloody, her lip split, eyes wide with fear as the stink of it filled the room over the unwashed bodies of the mostly male audience. I told her to stay alive—whichever way she could—and my only hope was she obeyed me just this once.

But the man towering over her could make that difficult.

Arden Ashbourne, the guild leader, loomed in the shadows, his stark, tattooed face blending into the darkness as his piercing gaze sought me out.

Unlike his bastard of a son, his eyes were an unearthly gold, shining like one of the iridescent rocks we pulled from this very mountain.

If I didn't know better, I'd think he had just as much magic as I did—not that it would do me any good now. In fact, I was pretty sure my magic would be my downfall.

As soon as my eyes made contact with his, Arden's paw of a hand gripped my sister by the back of the neck, forcing her in front of him as he cut through the crowd to where I hung. My sister winced, his hold likely as bruising as his son's had been before I killed him.

Firming my mouth, I refused to let him see my fear. The last time I'd been on this hook, I'd nearly wet myself I was so scared. And the fucker had gotten off on it. It was as if he could taste it in the air, scent it on my skin. But I already knew my fate this time. It would be agony and death, screaming and pain. It would be fire and blood, which somehow took all the fear away.

And I would be damned if he got anything else from me. Or from her.

"Oh, good," he cooed. "You're awake. I thought we'd have to start interrogating your sister if you took much longer to rouse."

Arden's voice was calm yet booming, vibrating through my chest like a drum as my bravado wavered. I'd killed his son.

He should be furious.

Inconsolable.

But he wasn't.

And that was so much worse.

His grip tightened on Nyrah's neck, and her face twisted, her knees buckling. But he held her up as he turned, almost as if he was putting us both on trial here.

"My son is dead—not by blade or axe but by the use of magic. One or both of these women are *Luxa*. This trial is to find the truth."

No, this trial was a witch hunt, only I was making sure my sister didn't go down with me.

Nyrah glanced regretfully in my direction, our eyes meeting in the scant space between us. She would do exactly what I told her to do—she would call me a witch in front of all these people. And just like before, when I told her to save herself, the betrayal still stung.

"She's the witch. She is the *Luxa*," Nyrah hissed, a feigned mask of hatred slipping over her features, the falseness of it only visible to me and me alone. "*She* is the one who killed him."

And she wasn't wrong. I was a witch, a magic-user with no control over my power, and I'd killed Thane. If I had the chance to do it all over again, the only thing I would have changed was getting there before he could hurt my sister.

I didn't deny any of it, my silence ringing out louder than the murmurs of shock rippling through the crowd. A witch hadn't been discovered in these caverns in a long time—not publicly, anyway. Before my power had risen to the surface, before I was marked as a witch, I would have been just as shocked as they were now.

Arden released my sister, and her knees buckled, dropping her to the rough stone ground. Shifting on a foot, his big body loomed over me, the gold in his eyes shining in the dim.

"Do you deny her allegations?" he whispered, the heat of his breath against my face, his threat clear.

"That's not the question you should be asking," I barked, so much louder than either of them spoke. I needed the crowd to hear me. It was the only way Nyrah would make it out of this. "The question you should be asking is why your twenty-five-year-old son was alone with my fifteen-year-old sister in her sleeping chamber."

The shocked murmurs of the older adults helped my case a bit, but the guild leader's eyes only narrowed.

"The question you should be asking is how I found him. The question you should be asking is why his hand was down her pants as she tried and failed to get away from him. The question you should be asking isn't if I killed him. The question you should be asking is if it was just."

But Arden didn't actually give a shit why I'd killed his son—that much was evident by the loathing seeming to darken the runes on his face, the tattoos which marked him as our leader. They also illustrated his vow—to eliminate all *Luxa*. Arden only cared that the murder was done by magic, his feeble mind only latching on to me to perpetuate his own hate.

Might as well give him more of a reason to hate me.

"Your son attacked my baby sister—a *child* under my protection, her safety entrusted to me by my parents before they died. Of course I killed him. Your son was a predator, and I put him down like the rabid dog he was." A ghost of a smile lifted the edges of my lips. "And I'm not sorry."

Let him defend that.

But the gold in his irises only grew brighter

before calming, the hate twisting his expression melting away. Then his hand whipped like a lightning strike, his backhand lashing my face with the force of his bottled rage.

A copper tang flooded my mouth as my vision went white and my ears rang like a gong, the heat of the hit fading only slightly as the pain made itself known.

"Painting my son as the villain in your story won't change the facts. It's possible he could have been attacking your sister. Or *maybe* he was catching you stealing."

Arden tore at my pockets, dumping out the rations I had stolen for us. All six days of them we needed to leave—*our freedom*—were tossed to the ground like trash.

I spat the blood pooling in my mouth at his feet.

"Stealing? I worked for every ration." My lip curled, and I figured I might as well give him a reason to kill me right there and then. Because once I did, I wouldn't be the only one going down.

Starving people were rarely ever rational.

"There's so much food in the kitchens, the rations are spoiling," I shouted, my voice clear over the murmur of the crowd. "They are keeping it from us—making us starve on purpose. There is plenty of food. They just won—"

I expected the next hit, but it still made me swing from my bonds as my knees buckled, the poisoned metal cutting into my wrists. My lungs begged for air as I struggled to take a single breath.

Arden grabbed my face, his grip on my jaw hard enough to crush the bones underneath. "As if anyone would believe a word from a thief. You do still have your brand, don't you? Marking you as the criminal you are?"

Feebly, I kicked my legs out, but he didn't loosen his grip, even as they made contact. I couldn't speak even if I wanted to.

"I showed you mercy last time because you had another mouth to feed. Now I see the error of my ways. I should have run you through with my blade and tossed you to the dragons. Maybe then my son would still be alive."

But there was no sorrow there, only hatred for what I was. It was no secret Thane was an embarrassment to his father—an heir in name only. Arden would never give up the guild leader seat, and now he never had to. I'd done him a favor.

And I would burn for it.

"Your own sister branded you as a *Luxa*. Do you deny it?"

Of course I didn't deny it—not that it mattered. Arden still held my face in his grip, clutching my jaw in such a way, it was impossible to utter a single word.

What's worse, the crowd knew it, too. They saw him hold my mouth shut, but I'd already sown the seeds of dissent. Starving people hated the fat and happy. Starving people hated excess, which was all the guild leadership was—excess. Fancy clothes and full bellies and nice cushioned places to sleep.

And power. Lots and lots of power.

Satisfaction filled me because I knew I was dying here, but maybe after I was gone, the mob of starving men would rip Arden limb from limb. Then he'd rot under this mountain with me.

Arden saw the glee on my face because he shoved me away, my feet scrambling for purchase as I swung back and forth from the hook. His muscles tightened right before he struck, his meaty fist burying itself into my middle. I gagged, the air leaving me in a rush as I fought to suck in a single breath.

"She killed my son with her power," he thundered, trying to quell the buzz of discord. "She will be burned by the dragons as all witches are." The decree echoed off the craggy walls, but it fell on deaf ears—not met with silence or respect but with an uproar of starving men more concerned with their bellies than whether or not I was a witch.

I spat blood at his feet, the insult implied. "You should have fed them when you had a chance," I croaked, my bloody smile stretched wide. "Now you're just as dead as I am. You just don't know it yet."

Arden snarled as he lunged for me, gripping my chain and ripping it from the hook. Unceremoniously, he tossed me over his shoulder, pushing through the emaciated men barring his way.

I met Nyrah's eyes in the crowd, hers filled with tears. This would be the last time I saw her, so I tried to memorize what I could while holding back the hot wetness aching to leak out. Silently, I willed her to leave, hoping that through all of this, she could steal away and save herself.

Arden turned a corner, and I lost her.

But as he stole through the tunnels, climbing to the surface, taking me to the one place I never wanted to be, I knew in my heart I lost her the second I'd killed Thane.

Saving her from him would kill me.

And I was good with that.

We emerged from the mouth of the cave system, the freezing winds biting at my skin as the wooden planks groaned underneath our weight. Arden dumped me to the catwalk like a sack of grain, my battered body catching on the too-thin ropes, which scarcely served as railing. I could only stare at the sharp cliff face below as I scrambled for purchase.

My vision tunneled as my breath stuttered in my chest, but I couldn't will my limbs to move—not even to pull myself to safety. The wind howled, but I could hardly hear it over the thundering of my heart in my ears. I was almost grateful when Arden pulled me from the edge, but my relief disappeared the second my back slammed into the side of the mountain.

His fingers wrapped around my throat as he lifted me from the catwalk, half-dragging me, half-carrying me up the narrow path to the top of the mountain. Something in my brain kicked on, and I started fighting his hold, biting, scratching, kicking, but it did little more than piss him off.

We made it to the top of the catwalk, the artificially flattened plane only decorated by the charred pillar in its center, the abused wood just as black as the mountain. The coming dawn barely lit our way, but it was enough for me to make out the full lantern and rope.

He would tie me to that stake and set me on fire.

My fight became frenzied, but it wasn't until I spied the dagger hidden in his boot that hope made a fool out of me.

"Grab the dagger and get free." Those thoughts weren't my inner voice, but I couldn't stop myself from latching onto the words and following their lead. My fingers darted out, snatching the blade from his boot, and I slashed his wrist. Instantly, Arden let me go, and I sucked in fresh air.

Hobbling to my feet, I faced off against my guild leader, his features twisted into a snarl.

"I'll make you pay for that."

With my hands chained together and his hundred-plus pounds on me, I had no doubt. But I would make him bleed first.

"Put it on my tab," I croaked, baring my teeth in a bloody smile.

"That's it, my brave one. Fight."

I'd never been brave a day in my life, but the closer I got to death, the bolder I felt. Or maybe it was the voice—the one that meant I'd finally cracked and gone crazy. Perhaps if I'd have gone crazy earlier, I wouldn't be in this mess. Emboldened by my slipping sanity and that damned voice, it was as if all the obstacles in my way had been knocked over. Now, there was only the blade in my hand and the man hauling me ever closer to the beyond.

One of us had to go, and I wanted it to be him.

I loosened my knees and set my shoulders as I flipped the dagger, pinching the blade just like my father had taught me back when the guild still let us have weapons. My one saving grace was that the blade was plain steel instead of *Lumentium*—at least I had that going for me. I knew I wouldn't win against Arden in hand-to-hand combat, but if I could lodge this blade in his gut, I may have a shot.

But I couldn't give up my blade too soon. If I didn't time it right, I'd be down my only weapon, with nothing more than air and the cliff's edge at my disposal—neither good enough.

Arden charged, striking out, and I'd thought I was ready for him. At the last second, his body moved too fast for my gaze to track, feinting left when I expected him to go right. I realized my error too late, letting the lone blade loose in a throw, missing him by a mile. The guild leader seemed to pluck it from the air, and then I knew I was truly fucked.

One second, the blade was flying end over end, sailing toward him, and the next, he was in my space, driving that blade home in my gut. The shallow cut I gave myself in our sleeping chamber was nothing compared to this. Everything was on fire—everything was blinding-white agony.

Shock fortified me for a single moment, and then I crumpled, the earth hurtling toward me, but just like before, he plucked me from the ground. Arden had no trouble dragging me to the stake and manhandling me into place, wrapping the rough rope around my shoulders.

Hell, the rope was the only thing holding me up. I couldn't even pull the blade free.

"I told you that you'd pay. Now you get to rot. Maybe the dragons will be merciful and burn you to death."

Arden's hot breath made my gut roil—or maybe it was the knife still buried in my gut.

"You're not dead yet. Breathe through it. You can do this."

"You think they won't bury you, too?" I wheezed, struggling to remain conscious. "I told you: you were dead already. Do you think they won't check the rations? You're just as dead as I am once they find out you've been starving us."

The guild leader gave me a gleeful smile, the first time I'd seen that expression on his stoic face. Then he gripped the blade and yanked it out. A scream tore through the air, but I was pretty sure it had come from me.

He tapped the bloody blade against my cheek, the metal still warm from its former home in my middle. "We'll just see about that, witch."

"*I will kill him for that,*" the voice announced, and it made my heart ache over the blood pumping out of me. This really had to be my shattered mental state, giving me all the things I'd missed in my life right at the end of it—protection, softness, encouragement.

No wonder my brain supplied them—it was a comfort I'd never had and always wanted.

Then Arden dumped the lantern, pouring the fuel onto the earth around me before positioning the glass just so. "When the sun comes up, the rays will hit the glass. If the dragons don't get you, the sun will. Have fun waiting to die."

"*You won't die, my brave one. Not you.*"

But the voice was too little too late. I would die —and soon was my guess.

Then Arden did something odd. He took a key

from his pocket and unlocked my chained wrists. "Wouldn't want these to melt, now, would we?"

I had no time to contemplate just how hot the flames had to be for the stone ore to melt before he wrapped the chain around his knuckles and landed a hit to my middle. Gagging, I lost whatever I had in my stomach as blackness darkened my vision. My knees buckled, the rope the only thing holding me up.

Arden's golden eyes flashed with wrath as he backed up a step to look at his handiwork. "Did you think I wouldn't get back at you for that little stunt in the Judgment Room? But we aren't quite even, now, are we? Maybe I'll *interrogate* your baby sister. Or maybe I'll just kill her. It'll save me the trouble of finding out she's a Luxa just like you. A life for a life, and all that."

I wanted to say something—anything—to make him leave her alone, but pain stole my voice, my mind, my strength. My only hope was if Nyrah had already made a break for it.

"Breathe. Just breathe. Help is coming."

A coppery tang filled my mouth as darkness threatened to overtake me. No help was coming here. There was no help for the helpless. The only thing keeping me conscious was the freezing wind, but I couldn't tell if the cold filling my bones was from it or the blood loss. I couldn't hear anything over the ringing in my ears, and soon, I was alone, Arden heading back to his own consequences as I waited for the dawn to come.

A sick part of me hoped the dawn would burn me up so the pain would stop. The other part wondered if I'd last that long. Cooling blood soaked my tunic and breeches, and I knew I didn't have much time.

At least the dragons wouldn't get me.

As that thought streaked across my brain, I started to laugh, the agony of it quelling my mirth just as quickly as it had come. Who knew if dragons even existed? Arden spoke of them as though they were a blight on our very way of life, but... After the rations, I questioned everything I'd ever been told.

Did dragons kill my parents? Or did Arden?

I slowly shook my head. If Arden had killed my parents, he would have rubbed it in my face before he left me up here. He was the type to use everything at his disposal to make me bleed—both emotionally and physically.

Too bad I was tied up. Jumping to my end would be a hell of a lot faster than waiting for the sun or bleeding to death. I doubted the height would even bother me now.

As the first rays of dawn transformed the sky into pale lavender, I fought the darkness moment by moment.

"Don't fall asleep, my brave one. You won't wake again," the deep, silky voice echoed in my head, forcing my eyes open.

But wasn't that the idea? Just falling asleep and never waking up? Still, something about that commanding tone kept my lids from drooping again, and I allowed myself to feel the wind on my face and the pain roiling in my gut.

The sun crested the horizon, shining like a beacon in the east, but a dark form in the distance brought more terror than Arden ever could.

Especially when I realized it wasn't alone.

The dragons were coming just like Arden said they would.

And there was nowhere for me to go.

CHAPTER 4
KIAN

I hated my job.

Everything about it was a test of my patience. There wasn't a single facet of my burden that I enjoyed. For the last two hundred years, I had been the king's right hand, and as the right hand to a bound king, I'd been stuck doing the dirty work.

Served me right, I supposed. Had I stepped in two centuries ago, none of us would be in this mess. But I didn't, and now look where I was—flying off into the unknown for some slip of a thing that would probably die before she could be of any use.

Like always.

While someone had to find a witch that could break his curse—*our curse*—there were only so many Luxa to be had. Each one barely survived the first trial, let alone lived to tell about the rest. And still, as soon as my king sensed another one, I was off to some far reach of the continent to pluck up another witch like a daisy.

And just like those poor, wilted flowers, they died far faster than if I had just left them alone.

That's not to say I didn't love my king—I did. I wanted to fix what was wrong in our kingdom, wanted to break the curse put on him by a self-righteous witch too powerful for her own good.

I just didn't want to watch another one die and not be able to stop it. I didn't want to watch my king suffer any longer.

But most of all?

I just wanted this to be over.

The war between the *Perder Lucem* and Credour had raged since before my king had been bound. The witch who cursed my king thought binding him would end it—that it would save the continent.

If anything, it made the war rage longer—hotter —than it would have if both sides had just killed each other and been done with it. Perhaps all our magic wouldn't be tempered by the king's curse, or refugees wouldn't be pounding at our gates.

Maybe the outlying provinces wouldn't want to

defect with every missive they sent asking for more aid than we could give them.

This mission was one of the worst of them all. A potential Luxa was stuck in the belly of the beast, at the heart of Direveil, right in the guild's clutches. The mountains were crawling with *Lumentium*, so even if I did find her, she was likely poisoned to the brim with the magic-stealing ore mined from the heart of the mountain range that hadn't existed a century ago.

"Stop pouting."

Xavier's taunt echoed through my head as I soared toward the coordinates King Idris gave us. Luckily—or rather, unluckily, given his prying— Xavier could only read my thoughts in this form. The last thing I needed was him snooping around my brain when I was on two legs.

"I'm not pouting. I'm contemplating my life choices. And mind your own thoughts, asshole."

Flicking my tail in his direction, I banked left and gained altitude. Idris had seen her in the belly of the mountain, hanging from a rough hook like she'd already been found. If we got there too late, she wouldn't make it out of that mountain alive. If we tipped our hand, we'd die under that mountain with her.

Our only hope was that Arden continued to be the consummate prick he'd always been and still thought it was funny to burn witches at the stake.

Xavier cut through the air below me, scanning the lower mountain range just in case the coordinates were wrong, his pale-white scales catching the first rays of the coming dawn. But something tugged me to the north, a sense that we might be on the right track this time.

"This way. She's this way. Can you feel her?"

I beat my wings harder, moving faster toward that pulling in my chest. While dragons had always been the most bound of the species, we were also the most drawn to our would-be saviors. My king might be the only one who could see the Luxa in his visions, but he only sent Xavier and I out on these missions because we were the only ones who could feel the pull of the Luxa.

Something akin to hope filled my heart for the first time in a very long time. We were miles away from Direveil, but I could feel her. None before her had been this strong. None before her had summoned us from such a distance.

"I can, but don't get too excited. She's hurt. Bad."

Gnashing my teeth, I pulled forward, streaking through the sky as I followed the invisible thread toward the injured witch. Then the clouds parted, and Direveil came into view. The small woman had been tied to a blackened stake embedded in a roughly flattened peak of the tallest mountain. Even a mile away, I scented her blood on the wind, the heady perfume of it frightening as it called me forward.

"Blood. Too much of it."

I wasn't telling him anything he didn't already know, and my chest squeezed at the thought of what would happen if we couldn't get to her in time. She was our one shot—I could feel it.

"Like I said. Don't get too excited."

It was rare that I was the hopeful one and he was the pessimist, which did not tell me good things about this situation.

"Watch my back and keep a lookout for dragon bolts. I'd like to avoid a Lumentium arrow in my hide."

Xavier peeled off, circling the mountain, his scales nearly disappearing in the growing sunlight as I darted for the mountaintop. The stink of fear was nearly stamped out by the perfume of her blood, but none of it compared to the call of her power.

Midnight hair blew in the howling wind as bright-green eyes speared into my soul. Face twisted in fear, she weakly struggled against her bonds, her feeble thrashings only making the wound in her middle pour more and more blood.

A growl rumbled from my chest, the sound meant to caution her to stop, but it only served to make her struggle more.

Understanding finally dawned. Every Luxa we had ever encountered had been relieved to see a dragon. Each one had looked upon us as a savior, even though they were supposed to be ours. This woman, however, had been raised in the guild's clutches, their propaganda likely poisoning her mind against us.

A dragon wouldn't be a savior here.

A dragon would be death.

Warily, I dropped to the edge of the mountaintop, stilling my wings as I slowly stepped forward. Rage streaked across her beautiful face, and she let loose a guttural, unholy scream as if she were a dragon herself, ready to breathe fire and lay waste to anything in her path.

This was the difference between the witch in front of me and all the others who'd come before her. In the face of death, she screamed, not in fright but in rage, and not backing down an inch.

Honestly, I was a little impressed. She considered me her enemy—as her coming death—and still, she fought against her bonds as if she were ready to take me on, even in this form.

Carefully, I reached out with one single talon and raked the razor-sharp nail against the ropes, freeing her from the stake. Her own people had tied her there, yet she still feared me. She wilted to the ground, the scent of blood blooming like a perfume of death around her, akin to a shroud.

That didn't stop her from grabbing the closest rock and tossing it at my head. It bounced off my hide with little more to show for it than the black dust blending in with my scales. Green eyes blazing, she roared at me again. Trying to scare me off this mountain, maybe? But my mission was her, and she was coming with me one way or another.

My chest rumbled again, and she dug her fingers into the dirt, seeming to hang on as she braced like she was waiting for me to breathe fire or gobble her up. What had those filthy liars told her about dragons? In what world would we attack an already-injured woman? As far as I knew, no one had eaten anyone in centuries.

"That's enough of that. I'm not going to harm you," I thought to her, irritated we couldn't communicate in this form.

Her head whipped up, those brilliant green eyes boring a hole in my chest as though she understood every word I'd said. I reached out to her, cradling her battered body in my claws before clutching her to my chest. Finally, the itching underneath my scales seemed to settle, and I let out another low rumble. It was almost like a purr, which was a sound I'd never made before in my life. The faint scent of fuel followed her, and I realized had I come any later, she would have burned. A second later, the first tangible rays of dawn hit the glass lantern resting on the ground next to the blackened wood.

Instantly, the ground itself ignited. But over the roar of the fire and howling of the wind, the metallic ratcheting of a mechanism being readied to fire reached my ears. I clutched her tighter, careful not to crush the tiny witch, and leapt from the mountain's edge.

Louder than the wind or fire, the witch screamed as I tucked my wings, following the cliff's face to reduce drag, before I banked left. When I leveled out, her screaming stopped, and her petite body slackened.

Probably for the best.

"I've got her, but they're readying the bolts. We need

to get the fuck out of here and get her healed up, or she won't make the trip back."

What I didn't express through my thoughts was I couldn't use my abilities with her in my grasp. Not this Luxa. She was tainted with so much poison I could sense it leeching my power.

This was *not* good.

Xavier knifed through the sky beside me as the screech of a bolt cut through the air on my right. *"They aren't readying anything. They're firing. On your left."*

Listing right, I dove, heading for the trees. I couldn't camouflage, and with the sun streaking through the sky, I would be a giant target. The trees, however, could provide a bit of cover if we could ge—

Searing pain ripped through my left wing, and I clutched the witch to me tighter. That burn would turn into a raging inferno of agony soon enough.

"I'm hit." Fuck.

"Get to cover, dammit."

But I didn't know if I'd *make it* to cover. The air displaced next to me, and I dove faster toward the trees to avoid getting skewered, my entire left side burning from the poison of the bolt. A small clearing barely big enough to land appeared, but I wouldn't make it without damage—either to me or the witch in my clutches.

Not without...

Xavier roared, letting his flaming breath loose on the treetops. The heat of his fire, coupled with the magic in his form, disintegrated this section of forest, a blackened spot on the landscape just big enough for me to land safely.

Flaring my wings felt like I was being turned inside out, but I managed to get to the ground without crashing. Still, the moment I touched down, the shift took me, shrinking my body to that of a regular man. Luckily, I was able to set the witch on the ground before I was lost to the change, my bones snapping and cracking as a new pain took over my body.

Xavier snatched me up, shoving both me and the witch into the cover of the trees. The *Lumentium* turned my shift into one of the most agonizing experiences in the last century, the unhealed wound a problem for later.

If there *was* a later.

Panting in the dirt, my body reformed, if a little broken, the telltale cracks of Xavier's change reaching my ears.

"For the love of the gods, tell me you have your

pack," I groaned when the snapping stopped, hoping he packed an extra pair of clothes. Laying naked on the forest floor with bracken digging into my ass cheek wasn't my ideal way to spend a Saturday morning.

The slap of leathers hitting me in the face was my answer. "You're lucky I came prepared, or you'd be swinging in the wind all the way back to Tarrasca. Now get over here and help me stop this bleed."

I shoved my legs in the leathers and got to her side. The witch didn't rouse as Xavier peeled back her filthy tunic to reveal her wound. The bleeding had slowed a little, which I couldn't help but think was a bad thing.

"She's filled to the brim with *Lumentium*. I don't know how much I'll be able to help her," he rumbled, his brow pulled tight. "Here." He pointed to her hands. "Hang onto her. The healing will hurt."

My eye twitched as I put her small hands in mine, knowing a Luxa's hands were the most dangerous part of them. The witch was so tiny and delicate that it made the pulling twinge in my middle just a touch sharper. Slithering beneath my flesh, the ache for her burned brighter. She was nothing but skin and bones, her cheeks so sharp they could cut glass. How had she survived this long? How had she gone undetected in the belly of the beast?

With power like hers, she should have been killed years ago.

Then Xavier placed his hand over the mottled pale skin of her abdomen, and a spike of rage produced a low growl in my chest.

My closest friend's eyebrows hit his hairline. "She's not ours," he whispered, his pointed gaze on my fingers wrapped around hers, his own dragon shining from his eyes for a split second. "She will belong to him—not us. *Never* us. Get it through your head now before he can smell it on you."

But the animal raging underneath my skin had his own opinions on the matter. Even quieted by the still-not-healed *Lumentium* wound, my dragon wanted to rip her from his hold and clutch her to my chest where she belonged.

But Xavier was right.

This witch would never be mine, no matter what my dragon wanted. And if I still desired our kingdom's survival, I would accept it.

I had to accept it.

A bright, blinding-white light poured from their point of contact. Xavier's magic differed from mine in the same way his scales did. More adept in the healing arts—even with our powers muted by the curse—he poured his power into the witch.

Her eyes flashed wide, the sclera and irises brighter than the sun instead of the brilliant green of before. Her scream tore through the air as her back bowed off the forest floor, the agony from healing something I was acutely familiar with. I held her down while Xavier finished the healing, his hands denting into her flesh as he willed more power into her. His white hair and pale eyes glowed bright with his magic, but it took everything he had.

Then her screams quieted, her eyes closed, and she wilted back to the ground. A part of me thrashed inside at the thought that maybe we were too late. Xavier slowly peeled his hand from the wound as it sluggishly knitted itself back together. But none of her other injuries followed suit, leaving a thick pink scar where smooth flesh should be.

Sweat dotting his brow, Xavier dropped to his ass in the dirt. "I've done all I can. She'll live, but she must heal the rest the old-fashioned way. And we're grounded. It will be a long walk back to Tarrasca if we can't find some horses."

My mission was to find the Luxa, and I had.

Now, I needed to return her to King Idris.

Gritting my teeth, I removed my fingers from her skin, ignoring the ache in my chest that worried over her—her body not so much as twitching.

She wasn't mine. She wasn't ours. She was *his*.

If she could survive the trials.

I *really* hated my job.

CHAPTER 5
VALE

A gentle rocking pulled me from the darkness as a smokey, spicy scent filled my nose. Warm for the first time in forever, I snuggled closer for fear of losing the calming heat that eased the ache in my bones.

As a child, my mother kept a soft hammock in our sleeping quarters for me, padded with goose-down blankets and topped with thick fleece to fight against the cold nights. This felt exactly like that— safe and warm with no worries or cares, like no one or nothing could get to me, no one could harm me.

A sigh gusted from my lips, and I fought to get closer. If this were a dream, I didn't want to wake up. And if this was what death was like, I'd take it and be happy.

The last thing I remembered was screaming at a giant black dragon. The beast, with its fiery amber eyes, who decidedly had *not* burnt me to death, but instead, cut the ropes binding me to the stake and *jumped* off the side of the cliff, holding me in its massive claws.

Then again, I could have made that up.

Most likely, I'd died long before I'd hallucinated that dragon, and I was safe and warm in the afterlife, Orrus forgiving me for all my curses and showing me kindness.

Strong bands tightened around me as a deep chuckle vibrated against my shoulder and through my chest. Eyes popping wide, I realized all too quickly that the gentle rocking was *not* the hammock and blanket of my childhood, nor was it the calm kindness of the afterlife. No, I was on top of a horse with a complete stranger, draped across his lap, snuggling against him like a cat.

Adrenaline pumped through my system as I tried not to dump myself off the animal, while also attempting to get away from the white-haired giant of a man clutching me to his chest.

"Easy," he rumbled, his pale-blue eyes lighting with mirth as his arms tightened around me. "You're safe now."

Safe?

I'd never been safe a day in my life. Plus, "safe" wasn't the word I would use when I found myself draped over a stunningly gorgeous stranger after nearly being burned at the stake. His eyes were as clear as the summer sky, the blue so light it might as well have been gray. Those striking eyes were offset by dark, expressive brows in ultimate contrast to his long, pale hair, the top half of which had been pulled up and away from his perfect face.

The sharp angle of his jaw led to a perfectly sculpted mouth with wide, full lips curving into a gentle smile.

On anyone else, that smile might have seemed patronizing, but on him, it was almost... *genuine*. Not that I'd seen a genuine emotion that wasn't avarice or fear in a very long time. It was the expression on his face that really did me in. I'd seen plenty of beautiful people under the mountain. Thane himself had been technically attractive but was still the ugliest person I'd ever seen, save for his father.

This man was disarmingly gorgeous, and an unbearable heat hit my cheeks as I realized what I must have looked like to him. He'd saved me somehow. Maybe I hadn't dreamt the dragon. Perhaps it had taken me from the mountaintop, only to drop me while I was unconscious. Perhaps it didn't want to eat a dead girl, or I didn't have enough meat on my bones.

The *lack* of blinding agony made me pause my struggles. I'd been dying—blood flowing from a wound that was sure to kill me before the dragon came. My hand found my middle, the unbearable pain of the knife wound somehow gone. Unbidden, I lifted my filthy tunic, the fabric stiff with dried blood. The skin had knitted back together, with only a pink line of a scar to show for it.

Raking a finger over the former wound, I wondered just how long I'd been unconscious.

Weeks?

Days?

"I—I don't understand," I muttered, still staring at the healed skin while trying to place just how this all came about. "How did I get here?"

I had about a hundred more questions, but I hoped this man would take pity on me and start talking.

"Don't you remember?" A deep, sardonic voice drew my attention from the white-haired giant to another man on a horse next to us, his familiar amber eyes on me.

My breath stuttered in my chest at the weight of

his piercing gaze, my heart fluttering at full speed. Just as large as the man holding me, he had tousled black hair and stubble bisected by a long, jagged scar from the edge of his ear, down the line of his strong jaw, reaching for the edge of his full lower lip.

Where the man holding me was in full black leathers, covered from his neck to his wrists, this one had only pants and a tunic, the garb ill-suited for the cold weather. His golden gaze narrowed, the color brilliant against his tawny skin, but I couldn't quite figure out where I knew those eyes from.

He didn't look cold, though. He only seemed pissed off.

At me? What did I do?

"Remember *what*?" Combining my more recent memories, I couldn't find a single one with him or his friend in them. And I trusted I'd remember these two from under the mountain. I'd have to be dead not to remember them.

The cranky one rubbed at the scar on his face as if it still pained him, those intoxicating eyes nearly luring me in.

"Oh, I don't know," he muttered, shrugging. "Being tied to a stake, nearly bleeding to death from a stab wound to your middle, or—"

"Kian, don't," the white-haired one grumbled,

cutting him off. "She's had a rough go of it. Take it easy."

Kian's voice was nearly as familiar as his eyes, but I couldn't seem to place either. It sounded like...

That's enough of that. I'm not going to harm you.

My breath froze in my lungs as I nearly bucked off the back of the horse. Eyes wide, I scratched and kicked, much to the animal's displeasure. Then I was free, slipping to the ground before taking off at a dead run, ignoring the jabs of freezing cold that burned my bare feet.

Kian was a dragon.

The dragon was Kian.

Kian was a *dragon*.

Dragons were *people*.

The bulk of a leather jacket weighed on my shoulders, its length tangling in my legs and tripping me. I landed belly-first on the forest floor, the impact stealing all thought, all plans for escape. Agony ripped through me, and I curled into the fetal position, struggling to breathe through the worst of it.

I had been stabbed. I'd been healed. I'd been taken off that mountaintop by a dragon—a dragon that was *Kian*.

Nothing made sense anymore. How were dragons people? How could I have been healed?

And if dragons were people, how could they kill with such brutality? How could they take innocent lives? And what did that mean for me?

Nyrah. Her name echoed in my mind, the reminder of my sister cutting through the pain and turmoil and shoving me back to sanity.

Get. Up. Breathe through the pain and get on your feet. Find her.

My sister was either in the middle of this very forest or... or...

I couldn't even contemplate the "or" side of the equation. Groaning, I tried to shrug out of the jacket, shedding the layer that had tripped me, only to have a pair of solid hands yank me from the ground as if I weighed nothing.

Without looking, I knew it was Kian, a fact proven a second later when he whispered in my ear. "Careful. It took a lot of effort to keep you breathing, witch. It would be a shame to undo all our hard work now."

My eye twitched as I used a burst of strength to wrench myself from his grip, shifting to face him. I was doubled over and clutching my middle, sure, but I'd be damned if he was the one to hold me up. I would walk on my own two feet if it killed me.

"My name is not *Witch*," I gasped, trying to regulate my breathing, swallowing the pain as I'd done my whole fucking life. Gritting my teeth, I stood tall. "My name is Vale."

Not that he gave a shit what my name was or why I needed to keep moving. Slowly, I backed up a step, shedding the long leather duster that had to be his and dropping it to the ground. If I needed to run again, it would only slow me down.

Still, I couldn't stop the shiver that vibrated my body as the cold seeped into my bones.

His eyes narrowed once again, and I wondered if it was his default expression. He crossed his arms, the muscles in his chest and arms rippling as he stared me down. "I don't give a shit what your name is. You're just another Luxa to be delivered to my king. Now quit being a nuisance and get back on the horse."

Luxa. He knew what I was—or rather what I could be—and he planned on delivering me to his king like a parcel.

A Luxa will wake the Beast...

A Luxa will unbind him...

A Luxa will destroy us all...

My feet drew away from him on their own, realizing quicker than I could that I'd rather burn at the stake than let him turn me over to anyone, but especially the beast of a king bound by a Luxa's power.

Hate and fear warred in my gut in equal measure. "Go fuck yourself, dragon. I'd rather die right here and right now in this forest than help a king who aided the death of my parents."

He nodded as if this was exactly what he'd thought I'd say, pursing his lips into an almost smile. Then his hand whipped out, and Kian gripped me by my throat. Lifting me off my feet for a split second, he tucked me into his side, snagging his jacket as he went in a fluid grace that I couldn't emulate if I'd tried. I hated to even think it, but while the treatment was unkind, it was almost as though he was actively trying not to hurt me.

Somehow, that pissed me off even more.

"No one asked you what you wanted," Kian growled, hauling me like a sack of grain back toward the horses, my escape pitiful against his overpowering strength. "We have a mission, and I aim to see it through. You can go willingly or hog-tied on the back of a horse—either way, we will fulfill our duty. It's your choice."

It wasn't the first time I'd had my will taken

away, my future decided by a high-handed, piece-of-shit asshole with too much power and not enough sense. And just like with the guild, I had no intention of following the leader and every intention of keeping my mouth shut and my eyes open wide for the first chance of escaping.

I might have been freed from the *Perder Lucem*, but Nyrah was still out there. She could be freezing in this forest or still stuck under the mountain—either way, I would find her or die trying.

I only needed an opening.

"You're welcome, by the way," he growled in my ear, his hot breath on my skin sending a shiver down the length of my spine. "If I'd left you there, you would have died—or maybe that was your plan? If so, you sure were doing a bang-up job of it."

A long time ago, I'd learned that silence in the face of arrogant people was a virtue. They couldn't pick you apart if they had nothing to go on. Still, something about him made me want to fight, made me want to rage, so keeping my mouth shut wasn't exactly an option.

"Considering your king needs me far more than I need him, it's tough to feel gratitude. And if you're going to be an asshole about plucking me off that mountain after saving my sister's life, you can save it. I'd rather burn a thousand times than allow my sister to suffer."

Kian dropped me to my feet, the impact jarring the not-quite-healed wound in my middle. Hissing in pain, I forced myself to stand tall, staring *up, up, up* into those contemptuous amber eyes. It didn't matter how big he was, how beautiful, or that he'd nicked me off that mountain as if I were no bigger than a pebble.

He wouldn't win with me—not now, not ever.

"Keep that in mind, dragon. I've killed before, and I'll do it again if I have to. Now, get out of my way. I have a sister to find."

His expression grew skeptical before sharing a look with the white-haired giant I still didn't know the name of.

"How do you plan on finding her?" Kian asked, his tone both reprimanding and kind all at the same time. "Wandering the forest, screaming her name? Are you planning to storm the mountain by yourself? You can barely stand up."

The truth was that I didn't have a plan at all. As callous as his words were, the best I had was combing this stupid expanse of a forest for her. But worse? I had no idea where we were or how far we'd come. I could be as little as miles from her, or

I could be in a completely different province by now.

Defeat filtered through every inch of me. It was my job to keep Nyrah safe. How could I do that if I were headed in the opposite direction? How could I keep her safe if I wasn't there with her?

Inexplicably, my eyes welled with tears. Yes, I'd saved her from Thane, but how would I save her from Arden if I didn't even know if she was still alive? Roughly, I dashed the tears away, firming my jaw.

"Maybe we're getting off on the wrong foot," the white-haired one muttered.

He slipped off the back of his horse, his towering height intimidating enough that I fell back a step. It was one thing for Kian to be that obnoxiously large, but two of them? I couldn't make it out of this forest with both of them on my heels.

An ache swelled in my chest, threatening to burst it wide open. I'd failed my parents. I'd failed Nyrah. She was alone in the world without anyone to protect her—least of all me. And they wanted me to just blindly follow them back to a king that had made that so.

The giant thrust out his hand for me to shake.

"I'm Xavier, and this asshole is Kian. It's nice to meet you, Vale."

My brows pulled together as I stared at that massive paw. If I took it, he could easily overpower me and yank me onto the horse. If I didn't, I'd be the asshole. I wasn't sure I cared about politeness, though.

My gaze cut to Kian, his inscrutable expression telling me absolutely nothing. I didn't know if this was a trick, but something about Xavier loosened the band of heartbreak tightening around my chest. I placed my hand in his, and his fingers closed gently over it.

He could crush it if he wanted to, but he didn't.

"I'm sorry for the abrupt way we met, but saving your life was more important to us than niceties. I couldn't heal you completely, and I fear you'll scar, but I did what I could."

He had been the one who healed me? Obviously, he must not have scanned any other part of my body while doing the job, or else he would have figured out that I owned far more than my fair share.

"I don't care about scars. And..." I swallowed hard, hugging my arms to my chest to preserve the fleeting warmth of my body. I was alive because of them. They may want me for their king, but I owed them—at the *very* least—a bit of gratitude. "Thank you both. But I can't go with you."

Xavier and Kian shared a glance before Xavier gently pulled me to his side, tucking me under his arm to share the heat I desperately needed after shedding Kian's coat. Another band around my chest loosened, and I couldn't help the sigh that fell from my lips.

"I get it," he murmured. "You want to help your sister. But that isn't possible right now. You're hurt, you don't have supplies to get back, or a plan. Maybe we can talk to the king. If you help him, he will likely give you a boon. You could ask him for help in rescuing your sister."

I wasn't an idiot. I knew he was likely just telling me what I wanted to hear to get me back on that horse. They had a job, and that job was procuring me for their king. But I couldn't think of another option that didn't involve me dying in the forest or getting trussed up and forced to go.

Pulling out of Xavier's arms, I considered my options for a single long moment. Swallowing hard, I nodded reluctantly.

The weight of a coat returned to my shoulders, quelling the shivers I hadn't realized were shaking my whole body. I shot a glance over my shoulder, but Kian was already mounting his horse, his back to me.

I had a feeling he didn't want a "thank you" any more than I wanted to give him one.

Xavier graced me with a brilliant—if tired— smile. Then we were back on the horse, his big body surrounding me as he urged the animal closer to the one place I'd never wanted to go and yet was the only place I might be accepted.

His warm arm circled my middle, securing me in such a way, I knew I wouldn't be going anywhere but where they wanted me to.

Heat suffused my cheeks, and I could decide if I was better off here or back on the mountain with a knife in my gut.

I guessed I was about to find out.

CHAPTER 6

VALE

The forest had eyes.

Despite the constant rocking of the horse and the warmth radiating from Xavier at my back, I was on edge as soon as the sun began to set. It wasn't just the noises, but they didn't help. There was so little life in the mountain I used to call home, that each sound from beyond the trees had me jumping out of my skin.

Occasionally, we would glimpse a small, furred mammal peeking out from its den, but that wasn't what had me on edge. Something *else* was in the trees. I could feel it.

And I wasn't the only one.

Kian and Xavier were just as on edge as I was, their shoulders tense as they guided the horses through the thinning forest, the snow starting to fall as we ascended another foothill. Xavier said we were going around the mountain range that separated the Girovian Province from Festia, where the capital city of Credour resided.

"We aren't *technically* in enemy territory," Kian had said, his stony expression belaying his words as he urged his horse into a faster clip, "since we aren't at war, but I wouldn't want us caught in these woods."

From then on, I had been a ball of nerves, afraid of every snapping twig and swaying branch. I'd barely survived my own guild. I had no idea what I would do if we had to go against an army.

I tried to remember the long list of territories Xavier mentioned. The kingdom of Credour was so much larger than I'd originally thought. He'd explained that the *Perder Lucem* was situated in the northernmost mountain range of the Direveil Province—a title I'd never heard uttered anywhere in the guild.

The forest to the south of the range was Girovia, a province that didn't like being the barrier between the capital and the guild, hating both with equal measure. Festia was close, but the mountain pass was blocked by heavy winter blizzards, the elevation so unbearably high that only dragons traversed the skies above it. There were more outlying territories, but I'd already forgotten their names.

In my most detailed of plans, I'd never allowed myself to think past getting Nyrah and I down the jagged ridge of the mountain and to this very forest. Other than knowing that Credour was south, I'd barely had a heading.

A sinking realization in my gut had my shoulders drooping and shame lashing my insides as I swept my gaze left and right. I wouldn't have been able to get Nyrah to safety with my hasty, ill-conceived plan. We'd had no horses, improper clothing, and no way to make shelter. It would have taken us days to get as far as the three of us had come in these long hours.

I hadn't even stolen enough rations.

But there was enough for her alone, and she was smart. If she made it out, she would survive. And if she didn't...

Xavier's arm tightened around my waist, his sharp inhale drawing my gaze to him over my shoulder.

"What?" I murmured, my gaze skirting around the forest before returning to him.

Crystalline eyes glowed in the rapidly growing

darkness, Xavier's mouth set in a firm line. "You're upset," he rumbled, his hold not loosening a millimeter. "You smell of regret. What has you so sad?"

Facing forward, I offered a noncommittal shrug. "It's nothing."

That was a lie. Nyrah was *more* than nothing, but I couldn't do anything about it and talking of escaping put them both on edge. I knew I couldn't get to her, knew my plan was horrible, and the odds of us surviving and getting somewhere that would accept us were damn near nil. Obsessing over it wouldn't change the facts.

A sigh gusted across the nape of my neck, and I suppressed a shiver. His breath was nearly scalding, almost as if he could breathe fire, and then I realized Xavier was *also* a dragon and most likely could. But that gentle puff of air twisted my insides as did his hold around my middle. It was tender and reassuring, the first comfort anyone had ever given me.

Momma and Father weren't the consoling type, our home and the guild never allowing such things. After they'd passed, Nyrah was mostly the recipient of my hugs, but even I had to admit most of them were awkward and stilted. I didn't know how to give comfort to a grieving child, and no one had ever taught me how to be a mother.

I fought off the urge to settle into Xavier's embrace again and allow myself to be soothed. It would be so easy and so, *so* dangerous.

What good could come from a dragon? These men were not my friends or my family. They didn't care about me any more than what was required to get the job done. Xavier was only playing at being kind because he wanted me to trust him. It didn't matter if every single touch had my heart thundering in my chest or my stomach twisting in knots. It didn't matter that his breath on my neck made me ache.

I knew better.

Didn't I?

Stiffening, I shifted forward, shoving his arm off of me. I would not be lulled into a false sense of security only to have the rug pulled from underneath me again. I wouldn't trust either of them, and I was not safe—not here on the back of this horse, not in Direveil, and I wouldn't be in Credour, either.

Especially not in the domain of the king.

A faint *whooshing* had all the hair on my arms standing at attention, before a thick metal arrow embedded into the trunk of a tree, scarcely a foot from my face. In a blur of speed, Xavier ripped the arrow out of the bark and threw it back from whence it came.

A sharp cry in the darkness told me his aim had struck true.

Then several things seemed to happen at once. A curtain of arrows flew from the tree line, blanketing the darkening space before we were up and off the horse, its big body blocking most of them as I was pulled to safety. The horrific sound of the arrows hitting the animal instead of us had tears hitting my eyes.

I'd cursed Orrus many times over the years, but this...

Xavier let out a low grunt as he drew a sword from his back, blocking the worst of the scene with his large frame. Kian's warmth registered on my right as I was roughly shoved behind the thick width of a tree, its gnarled trunk offering too little cover from the onslaught. The pair of them shielded me, and I could see nothing of the people attacking us.

But I could hear their arrows hitting the bark over and over again.

"Remember how I said we didn't want to get caught in this forest?" Kian muttered, ripping his own twin swords from the scabbards at his back.

I figured the question was rhetorical—either that, or shock had stolen my words completely— and simply blinked at him. I'd never been in battle before, but by the glint in his eye, he'd endured more than his fair share.

"How many?" Xavier growled, his fingers closing around a thick arrow in his side and yanking it out.

"A dozen," Kian muttered, pausing to almost taste the air. "Magically enhanced. Amulets and spells most likely."

Xavier flipped the arrow, volleying it back to the answer of another scream. "Less than a dozen now. Are you able to assist?"

Assist? Did he mean with those giant swords or—

Kian's eyes brightened, his amber irises glowing in the dim as he stood completely still. Then his lips curved into a ruthless smile for one solid moment before it fell. His gaze narrowed on me.

"I *would* help—however, we have the magical equivalent of a cock block with us."

I couldn't figure out what he meant until I remembered the *Lumentium* I always kept in my pocket. Reaching into the baggy fabric, I searched for the rocks that typically weighed me down, coming up empty.

"But I don't have any *Lumentium*," I protested stupidly, my confusion growing by the second.

I didn't want to be in this forest getting shot up with arrows any more than he did. And if he could do magic, I was all for it. I might have been cursing Orrus, but I sure as hell didn't want to meet him personally.

Kian rolled his eyes as his grip tightened on his swords. "You're covered in it. It's in your blood, in your skin. Years and years of breathing it in probably put it in your bones."

I was sure he was right, but...

"I still used my powers under the mountain," I admitted, my voice no louder than a whisper.

But of *course* I had. And using it had signaled them somehow, drawing them to me like a beacon. I was proved right not a moment later.

"You were *under* the mountain when you..." Xavier trailed off, meeting Kian's gaze over my head.

They seemed to be communicating mind to mind, their conversation abruptly halted by another wave of arrows.

Kian's amber gaze landed on me again. "We need an opening so we can end this. Anytime you want to use those amazing *Luxa powers* to help us kill these assholes, we'd be all for it."

But I'd only ever killed Thane, and that had been a time of blind panic and rage. This was... this was... shaping up to be a similar situation.

Firming my mouth, I snatched the dagger at his belt. I had zero desire to help him with anything, nor his king, but I didn't want to die in this stupid, freezing forest any more than he did.

"I'll see what I can do," I growled, slicing into the delicate skin of my wrist, careful not to go too deep.

His dagger was sharper than any I'd ever used, the steel of the highest quality. A thin rivulet of blood welled from the cut before light began to bloom. I'd never used this power on purpose, so harnessing it was impossible, but I could force it out of me. It grew brighter, the tree unable to hide the shining target that I now was.

"Oh, great, now you're a beacon in the dark instead of a weapon."

Gritting my teeth, I shot him a dark glare. "Aren't you a dragon? Why don't you shift and breathe fire on them or something? Isn't that all you're good for?"

Kian's amber gaze began to glow, another beacon in the night as his lips curled into an arrogant smirk. "That's not all I'm good for."

Then he spun out from the cover of the tree,

likely using my light like a distraction as he flitted through the night into the fray.

Closing my eyes, I tried to call upon the tendril of power in my veins. Yes, I was tired and sore, my wounds still aching, but I'd been tired before. I'd been hungry and worn, but I'd still saved Nyrah from a fate worse than death. I could ensure we made it out of this forest.

"That's it, Vale. Call it forth," Xavier rumbled, his voice so close to my ear, I shivered. "Latch onto it and set it free."

It was almost as though he could see that thread of magic inside me, too, encouraging me to latch onto it to save us all. I tried to grab it, but I couldn't move fast enough.

I may have been having trouble accessing the magic, forming it into a weapon, but the people attacking us had no such issues. The tree that had shielded us from their onslaught shivered, quaked, and then its very roots snaked up from the ground, twisting in the air as they snapped, freeing itself from its home.

Xavier curled a hand around my waist, lifting me off my feet before tossing me to the frozen snow-covered ground. A fierce growl rumbled from his throat as white scales grew from his arms, climbing up his neck. His pale-blue eyes glowed brighter than my magic as he ripped his sword through the tree's roots.

Those roots now had foot-long thorns, and I nearly screamed when one swiped at Xavier's middle, catching in the fabric of his tunic before he managed to spin away.

Arrows flew through the air, each loose nearly hitting him, the deadly tips embedding into the ground at his feet. But instead of willing my magic to the surface, I could do little to help, other than back away from the devil tree, hoping my distance would let his power free.

A rough grip wrenched me from the ground, and I was spun to face a gnarled, hooded man with glowing violet eyes. His blackened smile reeked of old rot and death, his crazed expression far scarier than anything I'd ever seen before.

"Credour scum," he hissed as he gripped the front of my tunic in his fist and lifted me off my feet. "You'll die in this forest."

But I'd already been threatened enough in the last twenty-four hours to let this putrid mage kill me now. I tightened my fist around Kian's dagger —the blade still somehow in my hand—and slashed. The too-sharp metal sliced all the way through the bone, taking his head in a single swipe.

Bile rose in my throat as his grip loosened, dropping me from his rapidly shriveling flesh. The tips of his fingers snapped off as I fell to the earth, my backside bearing the brunt of my landing. All at once, the tree ceased its attack, as if my cutting off the mage's head had severed the power linking the two. As the mage melted into ash, the tree plummeted to the earth in a great creaking *crash*.

Xavier ripped a thorn from his thigh, throwing it to the ground as he slowly limped my way. He surveyed what remained of the felled mage, amusement evident in his gaze as he offered me a hand up.

"You didn't use your magic, but a win is a win. Maybe—"

His head snapped up as his glowing crystalline eyes widened a fraction before he jerked me past him, his massive body covering me as arrows pierced the air once again. Only, this time, there wasn't a horse or tree to block the onslaught.

No, the only thing saving me was Xavier.

He crowded me, shoved me against the felled tree as he took arrow after arrow, his body bowing with each strike. His eyes, which seemed so human before, grew slitted as scales sprang from the skin of his neck. Those scales didn't cover all of him, though, and he winced with every hit, every slice, every wound.

But he didn't make a sound until a pained gasp managed to slip from his lips, the noise transforming my insides into a burning ball of fury.

Xavier had done nothing but help me since I'd met him.

Yes, he was a dragon.

Yes, he would deliver me to a king I hated.

Yes, he was technically my enemy, but in that instant, none of it mattered.

Someone was harming him, and they needed to stop. Rage akin to when Thane was hurting Nyrah raced through my veins, igniting the magic I'd tried so hard to keep contained. I'd been suppressing it for so long, maybe it only took an act of fury to call it to me.

They'd wanted a Luxa, right?

Shoving with all my might, I barely moved Xavier off of me. Luckily, I was small. Ducking from underneath him, I allowed the fiery power to rise, to consume, to erupt from me in blinding arrows of my own. Screaming at the agony of it, I ripped that power from my skin and launched bolt after bolt of the flaming magic, knowing with a certainty I didn't understand, that they would hit their marks.

Then, the power that had risen so quickly within me flickered and died, and I collapsed to the ground. The freezing cold of the snow bit into my fevered skin as I sucked in a lungful of air.

A warm grip on my ankle nearly made me scream until I spun to look at the body attached to it, my gaze landing on the mangled horror that was Xavier's back. Knees in the snow, he leaned heavily on the fallen tree, too many arrows piercing his skin. He shouldn't be alive—shouldn't be breathing—but somehow, he was.

"You saved me," I whispered, awe and fear warring in my chest as tears threatened to clog my throat. No one had ever saved me. No one had put their body in harm's way because of me. No one...

My gut twisted with indecision as I considered what someone like me could do to help him. We were in the middle of nowhere with nothing. No water, no thread, no needle. And that was if he didn't bleed out if I managed to remove the arrows embedded deep into his flesh.

If he had been a regular person under the mountain with me, I would be cursing Orrus right about then, the death god likely ready to receive another soul. But Xavier was a dragon, and he had to be stronger than the weak humans trapped in the guild's clutches.

"Just doing my job," he whispered, a faint chuckle making him groan in pain.

And while he'd said it so casually, I knew what he'd done was no small matter. I would have died if he hadn't shielded me.

A snap of a twig had me back on my feet, reaching for my power, but the faint tendril would not come. I'd spent so much of my time pressing it down, shoving it away, and now when I needed it, it was nowhere to be found. My grip tightened on the blade in my hand, realizing I would have to fight our way out of this.

A hooded figure slid into view, violet eyes shining from beneath his cloak as his own magic crackled in the air.

Branches and twigs rose in the sky, felled arrows and rocks and debris following suit. I knew as soon as he gave the order, those objects would pelt us, and it would be all over. The knife in my hand would do little to protect me, but I wouldn't let another fucking thing hit Xavier—not if I could help it.

Bracing myself, I stood my ground, blocking

Xavier much like he had done for me, prepared for the worst.

Suddenly, out of thin air, Kian seemed to appear, his form not there one second and then melting into view the next. His amber gaze locked onto the bevy of arrows protruding from his friend's back. Then those glowing eyes fell on me, clocking the way I was blocking him, before switching that focus to the mage between us.

A faint trickle of hope warmed my chest.

His twin swords at the ready, Kian's lip curled as he moved. With a fluid grace, he spun those blades and took the mage's head. Much like the mage who had once held me, the magic died as his body fell to the ground, the objects following his withering corpse.

But Kian didn't so much as look at the man he'd killed before rushing to Xavier's side.

"Always have to be the hero, huh?" he growled, reaching for the first arrow and ripping it out. His attention flitted to me for a moment, his scowl scalding enough to burn right through me. "So much for that Luxa power bullshit. The least you can do is help, witch. The sooner we get the arrows out, the sooner he can heal."

As much as I wanted to argue, Kian was right.

Whatever power I had beneath my skin hadn't done much, other than make me a target and thrust Xavier in the crossfire only to save me.

Xavier let out a pained grunt as Kian brutally ripped out another arrow, and the shame of each one pierced my heart. Gently, I brought a calming hand to Xavier's cheek, his face blurry as tears welled in my eyes.

Then my fingers closed around the thick metal of an arrow, and I yanked it out.

CHAPTER 7
XAVIER

Thee two were going to be the death of me.

I'd thought this would be a simple retrieval mission for another doomed woman. Instead, it had been dragon bolts, a near-death Luxa, and Girovian mages out for our blood.

And we weren't even to the border yet.

Kian ripped another arrow from my shoulder, and I bit off a curse, doing my best not to take my claws to my best friend.

Yes, each one would need to come out before I could heal properly, but his fear—a scent I'd rarely tasted before—was making his ministrations far more punishing than they needed to be. Still, that was better than Vale's. Her slow, methodical removals were a prolonged agony made worse by her guilt.

She hadn't wanted any of this, and yet she'd still saved my life. She'd used her brilliant magic in my defense, and if I wasn't already half driven mad by the perfume of her skin, I would have fallen for her then. She had been in my arms all day, her poisoned skin completely worth the sting because it meant I could give her my warmth—it meant I was right there as she rested against me, when she slept in my arms.

Still, she would never be ours, but I was having trouble following my own advice. I'd told Kian that fact myself, but the truth of it was almost too bitter of a pill to swallow.

"Gods, witch," Kian growled, his deadly rumble something he usually reserved for the maesters in charge of the libraries and potion hoards. "It's bad enough you nearly got him killed. The least you could do is not draw out the pain."

Kian's harsh reprimand was punctuated by his reaching for an arrow, grasping it tight, and ripping it out with a force that stole my breath. Maybe Vale's technique *was* better. At least she wasn't trying to make it hurt.

Vale shoved up from her knees, her small frame

towering over us as her teeth ground together—a fearsome sight only hindered by the tears swimming in her eyes. Kian was right to be drawn to her. The second I put my hands on her creamy skin, I'd been lost, the war of duty and service with my desires raging before I could get control of it.

She was so tiny, so fragile, so... *doomed* that it made me consider mutiny just this once.

No Luxa had survived thus far, and I didn't want Vale to be another one of the dead. In two hundred years, there had been none to break the curse on our king, none strong enough to free him—and by extension, us—from the shackles likely one of her ancestors placed on the Continent. We were sending her to her slaughter. If she managed to survive the first trial—though over three-quarters did not—she would have to endure the rest.

She would have to be strong enough for our king —strong enough to break the curse.

And that was a feat no one had accomplished in two centuries.

"I didn't ask him to save me," she growled, her voice solid and deadly, just as she had been in battle. "I didn't ask to be here. And I swear to Orrus, if you don't stop criticizing every little thing I do like I've got a choice in the matter, I will show you exactly what I did to get tied to that fucking stake in the first place."

A faint glow flickered from the small cut on her wrist. It seemed rage was the key to making her power shine—that was my hypothesis, at any rate. She'd been enraged when I'd taken the arrows for her, managing to shove my weight off of her to face down a conclave of mages herself.

"That's enough, you two," I groaned, Kian's abrupt removal of another arrow stealing my breath for a moment. "I'd rather not find out the hard way that those mages weren't alone."

At my hiss, she knelt at my side again and put a shushing hand on the back of my neck, her small fingers tickling the fine hairs at my nape. Even bleeding and in pain, her touch sent a thrill of awareness over every inch of my skin. She'd been between my legs all damn day, her lithe body rubbing against mine as she shared my saddle. Every rock and sway of the horse had my cock threatening to bust from my leathers, her scent driving me to madness.

I wanted that touch everywhere.

"There are only a few left," she murmured, her touch just as maddening as her scent. "Do you have clean cloth and supplies in your bag? I can help you bandage the ones that are still bleeding."

Guilt snuffed out my lust like water to a flame. My gaze flitted to the felled horse, its big body still as death. Kian's horse was nowhere to be found. I didn't want her to dig through the animal's corpse to find my pack. "They'll heal. I'm fine."

Kian let out a low rumble, his dragon close to the surface. "They're not. If bandaging your wounds is all she's capable of doing, then—"

"Stop," I commanded, cutting him off before he said something stupid. "Treat her with respect, old friend, or I won't be the only one bleeding."

I knew what he was doing. He was pushing her away because he couldn't have her. Because, like me, he would watch her die just like all the others—this beautiful light of a woman snuffed out once again. It made me wonder if we were the monsters in this scenario. We had sacrificed life after life to free our king in an effort to save every other magical being on the Continent. They had all been willing, of course, the honor of serving the king, of becoming an all-powerful Luxa a draw for so many, but...

Maybe the guild was right.

Maybe we shouldn't have magic.

Maybe the witch had been right to limit all of our power.

Maybe we didn't deserve it.

Kian's amber gaze met mine, and I sensed a faint thread of shame. Unless Vale would win the trials out of spite, I couldn't see how treating her like she was the villain would do anything other than make him feel more guilt after she was gone.

Vale turned, shuffling through the snow on her bare feet to the horse, and that made me wince more than the arrow Kian ripped from my back while I was distracted. I should have thought to bring her shoes. I should have thought to bring her clothes.

She deserved better.

"You have to stop antagonizing her. She hasn't done anything wrong," I muttered, breathing through the pain.

"I'm not antagonizing her. I am giving encouragement in an unorthodox manner."

No, he was lying to himself to save his own heart.

"You know this pressure barely scratches the surface of the first trial, and she can barely handle this. A conclave of mages is hardly worse than what she'll face. She fears dragons, Xavier. If she is going to survive, she cannot fear anything."

And while I knew the truth of his words, they still stung.

"Why do you think I've been drawing this out by taking the long way around the mountain? She needs time to gather her strength, or else she won't make it. I know I put us in danger staying in Girovia too long, but it's for her own good. And if she survives the first trial out of spite, then I'm going to count it as a win."

I shot a scathing glare at my best friend. "Just because spite is the motivation for everything that you do, doesn't mean it will be hers."

Kian's lips curled into a knowing smirk. "She survived Arden and that mountain by sheer force of will. She roared at me like she was a dragon herself. She can do it. I know she can. I just need to push her a little more, and she'll... she'll..."

"Break," I murmured, wincing as I watched her yank the pack from the ruined saddle. "She'll break. You didn't see her face when you put that coat on her. No one has cared for her. Maybe not ever. There is only so much someone can take before there is nothing more left to give. And..." I paused, understanding I didn't want to face forming like lead in my gut.

"I don't think she understands what being a

Luxa is. I—I don't think she knows the risk." Meeting his gaze once more, I knew he'd already come to the same conclusion. "We have to tell her. It wouldn't be right. And as soon as we do, she'll try to escape the first chance she gets."

Kian rolled his eyes, feigning indifference when I knew he was anything but. "Then why don't you pull on the sister heartstring a little more? I'm sure that'll get her motivated. Dangle a carrot in front of her face for all I fucking care. I can't do this anymore. I can't watch another one die."

But I knew what he was really saying. He couldn't watch *her* die. I couldn't understand why she was so important to both of us so quickly. It didn't make any sense. We had brought so many Luxa to the king over the last two centuries.

Why was this one different?

Before I had an answer, Vale returned with my pack, rummaging through it to pilfer what she could for first aid supplies. "There's not much here, but I can make do with this," she said, retrieving a strip of clean cloth. "If I can find some Nightwinter berries, I can make a healing salve."

Kian latched onto the last arrow and yanked, my shoulders easing a bit now that they were free of the blasted things.

"Don't trouble yourself," I murmured. "I should heal soon enough."

Vale's expression drew into a worried frown as she bit her full bottom lip. She nodded, but I could tell she didn't mean it. She'd needle me until she could tend to my wounds, I could sense it.

"You'll see. Bandage them, and then we can be on our way. In a few hours, I'll be just fine."

But even I knew that was a lie—a kind one, but a lie, nonetheless. I wasn't healing like I should, and I had a feeling it had as much to do with the woman next to me as the sheer number of hits I'd taken. If pressed, I could shift and heal fully, but something about Kian's words struck true in my chest.

She needed time to regain her strength. Yes, she'd used her power beautifully, but she wasn't strong enough yet.

Vale went to work, packing and binding my wounds, while Kian left us to retrieve his own horse. Being away from Vale, he could likely use his abilities with less interference. By the time she was done, Kian had returned with a single horse, his rueful expression letting me know I'd be walking for a while.

"Come on, Vale. Up you go," Kian said, his hands outstretched to our little Luxa.

And when had I started to think she was mine? For my own sake as well as hers, I had to stop before it was too late.

Naturally, she frowned, backing away from his touch like he was the devil himself. "I'm not the injured one. Xavier rides. I can walk."

"Barefoot?" he growled, his glowing amber gaze on her shoeless feet. He may be pretending to be an asshole, but I had a feeling this would be where he drew the line.

I stood, testing the weight of my legs. It would be a challenge for a while, but I could easily walk a hundred miles if it meant she didn't.

"Do you think this is the first time I've been without shoes, dragon?" Her smile was bitter as she shook her head.

That smile said she'd been without food, without comfort, without safety for longer than she could remember. Of course she wouldn't balk at walking in the snow. She hadn't made so much as a complaint about it so far. She'd done battle in that snow, killed men in that snow. What was a few more miles to her?

Just the thought of it made me see red, my scales rippling across my flesh. But if I let them argue, we'd be here all night. The last thing we needed was more mages stumbling upon us while I was in this state.

"The only way I'll ride this horse is if you're riding with me, little Luxa. And I'm more stubborn than Kian, so..." I gave her a little shrug, which I instantly regretted.

Gaze narrowed, teeth gritted, she allowed Kian to place her on the horse. I quickly followed her onto the saddle, surrounding her like I'd done all day. Something in my chest eased at being so close to her again. Urging the animal into a gentle trot, Kian easily kept pace beside us, his breath steady, not breaking a sweat. I knew from experience he could run three times as fast without difficulty and still run headlong into battle without blinking an eye.

"There's an inn just beyond the border wards," he supplied, his path cutting off the excess he'd padded the route with and shaved hours off our trip. "We can stay there for a night before we continue on."

He'd been almost helpful, but naturally, he had to ruin it. Because Kian wouldn't be Kian without sticking his foot in his mouth.

"Maybe then you can wash the poison and stench off of you. Honestly, I don't know how you can stand being so close to her."

Vale quietly gasped at the insult, her shoulders curling in on themselves. I'd seen flashes of her memories as I'd healed her—not enough to really know her, but enough to get an idea of how she had lived before us. From what I'd witnessed, she had endured more pain, more turmoil, more death than some of the most seasoned of soldiers.

It didn't matter if Kian was trying to make her survive out of spite. The next time he was within arm's reach, I would pummel him to dust.

Swallowing the hurt I scented, she lifted her chin and straightened her spine. I knew if I offered comfort, she'd just shrug me off, so I tightened my thighs around hers and wrapped my arm around her waist, in likely the only version of a hug she'd accept.

Then I pushed the horse harder, passing my idiot friend toward the inn that would be our refuge for the night.

CHAPTER 8

XAVIER

Crossing the wards into Festia had never felt so right and so wrong at the same time. I didn't want Vale so close to the kingdom—not as unprepared as she was. By the time we reached the inn, night had fallen in earnest, the darkness of the path almost absolute.

Then, like a mirage in Sandgrave, the small town appeared. None of my wounds had healed, and I knew as soon as Vale and Kian found out, I'd be in real trouble. The inn was only half-full, the proprietor happy to have extra unexpected guests. While we could have taken two rooms, the battle against the mages was too close for comfort.

"Just the one room," Kian growled, his train of thought following mine.

Two rooms were harder to secure, but if we all bunked together, there would be fewer surprises. It would be tight, and someone would sleep on the floor, but it would be far more manageable than a blade to the throat.

The Fae innkeeper blanched, the tips of his pointed ears going as red as his bushy beard. "B-but the only room fit for three is the Grand Suite. Surely—"

Brownies were a particular lot, and ensuring a comfortable stay for all their guests was paramount, and sticking two dragon shifters in a room was usually a bad idea. Still, I would not risk Vale's life after she'd nearly died saving me. My eyes narrowed as I dropped a pile of coins on the desk.

"For your trouble. The king bestows his gratitude."

If he hadn't noticed the royal seal woven into the breast of my coat, he did then. The innkeeper's mouth unhinged for a moment before he snapped it shut, swiping the golden coins off the desktop quick as a blink.

Kian's gaze flitted to Vale, her small body half-hidden behind me. "And bring in two bathing tubs and supper."

The innkeeper was nice enough not to balk at

the request. He simply blinked and snapped his fingers. "Consider it done."

Vale's shoulders were like iron, but her eyes flared at the "supper" remark. When had she last eaten? My travel pack didn't have rations, a change that would need to be rectified if Vale ever—

I had to stop thinking of a future with her. She would not ride with me. We would not travel the continent together. She would be King Idris' Luxa, and that was if she even survived.

She *had to* survive.

Vale's gaze tracked every single movement, every guest, every door and window, her wary stare as sharp as a blade, like she was used to watching her own back. While most of me hated the fact she'd been forced to survive that way, it was almost a relief. She would be wary of every corner of the castle, every nook and cranny, and maybe that would keep her breathing.

The three of us were covered in blood, drawing stares from the other patrons, but the proprietor didn't so much as flinch, guiding us to the Grand Suite like his heels were on fire. Considering the small mountain of Festian gold I'd dumped onto his desk, this level of service was not only expected, but required.

I fought off the urge to grab Vale's hand, allowing her to walk behind Kian as I watched her back. She was still wearing his coat, the tails of it slapping each step as she strode up the stairs, her fingers gripping the railing as if her life depended on it. Shoulders bunched, she followed, her breaths only evening out after we reached the landing.

To hear Kian tell it, she had roared at him like she was a dragon herself. She had faced off seemingly by herself against a conclave of mages. All that, and our little Luxa was afraid of heights?

Then the innkeeper swept us into the Grand Suite, pointing out the furnishings of the room as he snapped his fingers, lighting the fire in the grate, as well as the mage lights hanging from the walls, illuminating the space. It was humble compared to the castle, but it would do for the night.

The room was separated into sections as if it were almost a home. To the far right was a small sitting area close to the now-roaring fireplace, the chairs clad in a dark-green brocade fabric too nice for a place like this. Dominating the center of the space was a large four-poster bed, the drapes drawn back. The far left held a bathing area—an uncommon feature in accommodations such as these—and finally, a large screen separating the area, offering privacy should we need it.

Two giant tubs steamed side by side, their crystal-clear water the most welcome of sights in a long time. Beside them was a stack of plush towels and three fur-lined dressing gowns. It took a second to realize that the innkeeper had exited the room, leaving the three of us cocooned in tense silence. Kian was practically climbing the walls, Vale needed to eat and get off her battered feet, and I...

Likely needed stitches.

Blood dripped from my little finger onto the rough-hewn hardwoods, the scent of it drawing Kian's sharp gaze. His growl was barely audible, but I heard it all the same. I should have healed already, and for some odd reason, I hadn't. Hissing, I eased off my coat, wondering where I should put the bloody thing. At Vale's gasp, I figured my tunic must be soaked through—what was left of it, anyway.

She shook herself, drawing up to her full height and planted her small fists on her hips. "You'll need stitches, but you need to get clean first. Gods know what was in those arrows. Kian, find me a needle and thread. And some Nightwinter berries."

Kian scoffed. "Like you're going to be the one to stitch him up? You'd probably be too afraid to hurt him, vomit all over his feet, pass out, and then where will he be?"

But I'd seen glimpses of her memories. She was iron in a tiny little package.

Vale's gaze cut to him, nearly slicing him in half where he stood. "You don't know me," she said, her voice no louder than a whisper. "You have no idea what I'm capable of. Remember that when you close your eyes tonight, dragon."

Kian opened his mouth, but if I let him needle her, we'd be here all night, and I'd bleed to death. "Just get the damn thread," I rumbled, my patience fraying. "And some clothes for all of us. Something a little less royal for tomorrow. If we're walking in, I'd like to be under the radar."

"Fine," he whispered, his gaze pained as he pivoted on a heel, striding out the door to get what we needed. He only wanted to delay, his bickering a feeble stall tactic the only reason I didn't knock him unconscious.

Then Vale and I were alone, but that didn't mean she let her orders slide.

"Get in the tub so I can clean your wounds," she demanded, her small foot beginning to tap with her impatience. "Are you *trying* to bleed to death?"

Grumbling, I struggled to peel the tunic from my

skin, the fabric sticking in places, reopening the bound wounds.

"Bend down," she urged, helping me with bits caught on the bandages.

Her gentle touch sent lightning down my spine, and when the tunic was finally off, I realized just how close we were. We'd been close all day, but something about me being half-naked in a room with a bed made everything that much more intimate.

Straightening, I stared down at those wide green eyes, the irises glowing just slightly in the light. Her lips parted, and I fought the urge to bend down and nibble on them. I wanted to taste her, and it was becoming a distant memory as to why I shouldn't.

Without me telling them to, my fingers found the end of her braid, playing with the silky hair because I had to touch some part of her.

I had to.

She'd been in my arms since dawn, but somehow it never seemed close enough. I didn't particularly care that I was bleeding, either. But she did.

Seeming to shake herself into reality, Vale backed up a step, the bubble of tension somewhat broken as she moved away from me. Immediately, I felt the loss of her, the ache settling in my chest begging me to follow.

But I couldn't follow her. I could get in the water and let her patch up my wounds.

Tugging off my boots and socks, I hissed when my bare feet touched the cold floor. Then I pulled the tie at my waist, shucked my pants, and slid into the blissfully scalding water.

"You need to get in the water, too. You're probably freezing," I said, noticing her flaming cheeks as she avoided looking anywhere in my direction.

The vein at the side of her neck fluttered with her rapid heartbeat, and I had the strongest urge to pull her into the tub with me. If she would have been within reach, I might have. My cock stirred at the thought of her slippery skin rubbing against mine. Of—

"It's warmer than under the mountain," she replied, her gaze now firmly on the floor.

What I wouldn't give to see that flush of hers everywhere. I fought off a groan as warmth seeped into my bones, easing the aches that had cropped up since healing on my own seemed to be off the table. But I didn't close my eyes. No, the woman in front of me was far too entertaining with her blushing cheeks and avoidant gaze.

"I take it you've never been around shifters before," I teased gently, wanting to see a smile on her face just once.

Her gaze finally landed on me, those brilliant green eyes so beautiful, it almost hurt to look at her. But looking away was impossible. I wanted to soak her in.

"And when would a shifter waltz into the *Perder Lucem*? Other than you two, I've never seen another magical person before. Ever."

I couldn't resist teasing her a little more. "Or a naked male before, either."

She pressed her lips together, steeling her shoulders before shrugging off Kian's coat. Her torn tunic was bloody and filthy, and still, she looked like a damn goddess. "No, I haven't. But it's not like it was a conscious choice or anything. There just wasn't time."

"Happy to be your first," I said, my mind drifting to other firsts I'd like to show her.

Rolling those beautiful eyes, she crossed her arms. "I take it shifters are a naked bunch, then? I suppose that's good to know since you'll be taking me to the king of them. I'd hate to blush and lose my big, bad Luxa reputation on the first day."

That sobered me more than anything else ever

could. I had to tell her the truth before it was too late.

Her gaze landed on the water—the hue now pink with my blood. Her lips tightened as she marched to my side before she snatched the washcloth from a nearby stool and sat down. Her small hand reached into the water to wet it, and then she rubbed a thick bar of soap into the fibers.

"Lean forward. I need to get the debris out before Asshole comes back with the needle and thread. The last thing I need is more bullshit for him to gripe at me about."

And even though she was cleaning my wounds, her touch on my skin had my cock thickening despite the pain. She moved my long hair aside, the white tresses likely stained as much as my skin, and it was as if I could feel her fingers all over me. She leaned closer, abrading the cuts to make sure they were clean, but I didn't feel the pain. All I felt was her warmth so close, her breath on my skin.

I had to distract myself. If I didn't, she would be in this water with me.

Tell her the truth. Don't let her walk in there unprepared. If you care about her at all, you'd keep her safe.

Swallowing, I forced myself to calm down. "What do you know about Luxa?" I asked, hoping she'd been prepared—even if it were only in a small way.

Gently, she continued dabbing at my wounds. "Not much. Before my parents died, my mother gave me a book about Luxa and magic, but I didn't get too much into it. It all seemed like a bunch of hokum until the day I turned twenty and my magic started blooming. Had I known what was to come, I might have paid attention, but by the time they died, and I knew it was all real, I didn't want to read about the witches that were supposed to be the end of the world. Especially if it was about me."

Perfect. She knew next to nothing.

"I sort of felt like if I knew too much, it would make it worse, make it come true. Plus, I was too busy working my life away and taking care of Nyrah. There wasn't time to read about my impending doom. That was already staring me in the face."

I peered at her over my shoulder, needing her to keep talking. There was so much I didn't know about her. So much I needed to know. "Nyrah. Is that your sister's name?"

Swallowing hard, she offered a sharp nod. "She's fifteen. Smart as a whip and so stubborn. Once she puts her mind to something, it gets done. Even as a toddler, she was like that." Chuckling, she shook her head. "She never wanted to stay contained, always spoke her mind. It was all I could do to keep her from mouthing off to someone. And once she became a teenager..."

Tears filled her eyes then, and I turned fully, brushing away a wayward tear. "She'll make it out," I reassured her. "And she's young enough that even if she is a Luxa like you, it won't show. She won't be attacked in Girovia. Someone will help her."

Vale's lips curved into a trembling smile, her cheek leaning into my touch. "You think so?" Then her brows pulled together as she straightened. "Wait. A Luxa like me? I thought—"

"It's in the blood," I replied, already knowing I'd said too much as I drew away. "A very specific bloodline spanning back centuries. If you share the same parents, she will likely be a Luxa once she comes of age."

Blood drained from her face, and she wobbled on the stool. Yep, I'd definitely said too much.

"There have been more before me, haven't there? Luxa who have tried to break the curse."

I turned back around, not wanting to meet her gaze when I told her the truth. Because she knew already. She'd figured it out just like I'd wanted her to.

So why did I feel so guilty?

"Yes," I croaked. "There have been many of them." I could feel her heart beating like a drum in her chest, the tripping pulse only stressing just how smart she was.

"I take it by your tone, they didn't make it out alive, did they?"

The searing knife of indecision tore through me. But as much as I wanted to tell her the truth, I owed my kingdom as well. I owed Idris. He'd taken the curse for all of us—he'd endured when so many of us could not. And magic was dying. He was...

I had to help him, but I didn't want her to be a casualty of this war.

Not her.

"When my king feels a Luxa emerge, he sends us out to find her. Usually, it's somewhere within our province or a neighboring one, and they are eager to serve the king. Eager for the honor, for the wealth they could bring their families, for the fame it could bring them, for the power. But in two hundred years, no one has been able to break the curse."

"So it's a death sentence," she murmured, still working on my wounds as if I weren't the harbinger of her doom.

"I think so," I said, shame tearing a brand-new hole in my chest.

"And if I can't help—if I die in the process—someday, my sister could be in my same shoes, trying and failing to do the same thing you're bringing me to the king to do?"

I didn't answer, but she didn't need me to.

"And there's no escape, is there?"

I knew her sister was the string, the carrot to dangle to get her to come with us, but I'd never intended to use her that way. But as much as I wanted to deny her words, I couldn't.

But I could comfort her—even if that meant little. I spun in the tub, reaching for her as tears swam in her eyes. Cupping her cheeks, I brought her forehead to mine. It was a custom of our kind, a way to share breath and warmth and comfort. For fate-born mates, it was a signal that their minds and hearts would always be one. For families, it was a sign of being bound through the bloodline.

Fateborn mates didn't exist anymore, the curse wiping them from our very existence, and Vale wasn't my blood, but it seemed right to touch her this way.

"Magic is dying everywhere. There's only so long he can endure this. If magic dies, so many lives will be lost. I don't want to take you, but we have to go back," I urged, trying to think of anything that would prove me wrong—that she wouldn't die as soon as the king touched her. Then I remembered what Idris had said. "The king said he felt you stronger than he's ever felt any Luxa before. Even as far away as you were. He—"

"He spoke to me," she whispered, her swallow audible as she twisted her hands in the cloth. "In my head. Encouraged me. When Arden stabbed me, he told me you were coming. He told me I just had to stay awake, stay alive, and help would be there."

Shock had me drawing away, letting her go, staring at her like I'd never seen her before in my life.

"That was him, wasn't it? Unless I'm going crazy, and all of this is a dream, which could be completely possible."

A sinking pit of loss replaced my shame for a moment because none of the other women we delivered to the king had ever mentioned anything of Idris speaking to them in their mind. None had bragged about that sort of tie to the king.

Even though the bath was scalding, I was colder than I'd ever been. I'd been right when I told Kian that she would never be ours.

She was his already.

"I don't think you're crazy," I whispered, swallowing the sting of it all. "I think you're strong—maybe stronger than any who've come before you. There are trials coming. Trials you have to be strong for. Half the reason Kian is being such an asshole is because he thinks if he pisses you off enough, you'll survive out of spite."

Her musical laugh was just as beautiful as it was mocking, and it twisted the knife in my chest. I'd wanted to hear that laugh, but now it just highlighted that all this want in my gut would only fester.

"So, his assholery is him being kind? Go figure."

Gritting my teeth, I forced a smile, even though she couldn't see it. "That's just Kian. His main motivator is spite. It's what keeps him breathing when all else fails."

But then her laugh died. "Were you ever going to tell me? Had we not gotten attacked, would you have just let me walk in there unprepared?"

I let my gaze drift to my chest, wondering if there was actually a knife protruding from my heart or if it was simply her phantom clutch squeezing it for all it was worth.

"I was planning on it, though, I'd never had to

tell any of the others before you. They all knew the risks. It wasn't until we realized you knew so little that it became obvious that part of the equation was missing. I wasn't hiding, I swear. I just—"

Was a weakling coward who didn't know how to tell you the truth.

"I understand."

She soaked the rag in the water before squeezing it over my back, rinsing the wounds as best she could. Then she handed me the rag and soap.

"Finish washing. Hopefully, Kian will return with a needle and thread soon so I can suture your wounds."

Incredulously, I swiveled in the tub, the water sloshing over the side. "Why? I just told you I was taking you to your death, and you're still going to help me? You're still going to sew my wounds closed?"

She stood from the stool, skirting around the tub as she moved to the privacy screen. "You've saved my life twice now. I owe you one."

"That doesn't make any sense, Vale," I growled, my words hard as stone. "Why would you help me?"

Those green eyes flashed as she finally looked me in the eye. "Because I'm not going to die in that kingdom, Xavier. Not if my death means my baby sister will be on the chopping block."

Iron. She was made of iron.

"If the only way I can keep my sister alive is to break this fucking curse, then I'll do it. I don't care what it takes."

Then she moved past the screen, and I lost those eyes. And though I'd been gutted, for the first time all day, Vale's words brought me a sliver of hope.

She wouldn't die.

I'd make sure of it.

CHAPTER 9

KIAN

Xavier was right. I was a dick.

It was getting harder and harder to justify my actions, too.

Gritting my teeth, I moved through the inn, the weight of my new pack cutting into my shoulder as I ascended the stairs that had caused Vale to cling to the railing as if her life depended on it. The satchel was full of clothing for the three of us, plus weapons we sorely needed for the trek home. The brownie innkeeper convinced his wife to open the shop next door so I could pick out clothes and supplies, his pile of gold growing bigger and bigger.

It was easy to find them for myself and Xavier, being the same size, I just got two of everything, but when it came to Vale, it was a mission I hadn't expected. Maybe it was the gods punishing me for being an asshole, but every garment I chose, only made me think of her in my arms. Of peeling each layer from her skin, of her sighs in my ear, and moans from my touch.

And I would never have any of that because I'd been nothing but a jerk to her since she'd woken up.

Self-preservation was a fickle bitch sometimes.

I chose a soft indigo dress for her, with long bell sleeves and a matching fur-lined cloak to keep her warm. Whether we shifted or not, her delicate skin would be shielded from the cold. Then I picked up shoes and thick stockings to keep her legs protected from our scales, as well as undergarments and toiletries.

They had been the real challenge, and I'd contemplated the wares for several minutes before I'd been saved by our host. The brownie's magic allowed him to know what his customers needed better than they did, and instead of the leathers I'd wanted for Vale, he'd pulled the dress instead. I'd been tempted to argue with him, but if tomorrow went how it usually did, Vale would want something presentable to wear to the high court.

I may have given her shit the entire ride here, but I wouldn't allow those vultures to embarrass her. It wasn't her fault where she was born, and if she was the one who could break the curse, what did her station in life matter?

Xavier thought we'd lose her immediately, but I knew better. As scared as she was of dragons, she'd still roared like one. She was stronger than all those who'd come before her. And the more I needled her, the more I knew she would fight tooth and nail to survive.

Was she ready? No, she most certainly wasn't.

She was likely the most ill-prepared Luxa to ever grace the kingdom. But something in my gut told me she would survive. I just had to push her a little more. Or maybe I should back off. Let her rest, let her not be so on guard. If she survived the first trial, she'd never have her guard down again.

Striding through the door to our room, I spied a still-filthy Vale pacing behind the privacy partition as Xavier pulled himself from the bath, her tunic stained burgundy from dried blood, her breeches billowing around her legs. I was actually amazed she'd forced him into the tub first, with the scent of her blood in the air, once again proving just how formidable she was.

I'd already washed the toll of the day from my skin, the common baths a workable solution so I didn't have to risk being naked in the same room as Vale. I honestly didn't know how Xavier could stand it. Even filthy and covered in poison, she was still a siren, calling me to my doom.

"Did you get the needle and thread?" she asked, a certain kind of resolve in the line of her shoulders, setting my teeth on edge.

"What about weapons?" Xavier called, donning a towel around his waist.

That was a dumb question, and he knew it. I still had my twin swords, but Xavier had nothing. Of course I would get him weapons.

"Yeah, yeah. I got what you needed. And clothes, toiletries, and *weapons*. You're welcome."

I didn't need to be that snide, but unfortunate jealousy seeped into my tone, making me a petulant fool. Something had happened while I was gone, and I didn't like it one bit.

She opened her mouth, likely to volley a zinger in retort, but she snapped her jaw shut as her eyes tightened at the edges.

"Thank you," she whispered, and the sound of it had me closing my eyes so I didn't fuck up everything and kiss her right there.

I swore to all the gods and goddesses, it was as if she'd run her fingers down my spine and sighed in my ear. She'd only ever yelled at me, so this soft voice had my balls aching and my cock standing at attention. How could she do that with just two simple words?

This was it. This was why I'd been an asshole all damn day. If she managed to weasel her way into my heart, she'd claim all of me, consume all of me, gobble up my very soul and smile while she did it.

And I'd fucking let her.

My jaw was granite as I offloaded the pack to the floor and knelt, removing items to keep my hands busy or else I'd reach for her, poison be damned.

At the top of the pack lay the suture kit, the curved needle and cordage exactly what we needed to close Xavier's wounds. I didn't hand it to her. She needed to get that poison off her skin first, and the thought of her disrobing only a few feet from me, made me certain I'd done something in a past life to be punished this way.

Carefully, I set it on the bed along with her dress, cloak, and Xavier's leathers. Next to them, I placed a wicked dagger with a jeweled inlay, which I thought she'd like, and a silver hairbrush and comb set.

"What about the Nightwinter berries?" she asked softly, likely trying and failing not to alert Xavier that she was worried. "Could you find any?"

Of course she wouldn't care about sundries when Xavier was still bleeding.

I reached into my breast pocket and dumped the berries in a small basin on the side table. "It's the most I could find. I haven't seen them in a century, but then again, I haven't been looking for them, either."

Why would I need them when I could heal in minutes? But something told me she'd needed them far more than I'd have liked her to.

"You need to get in the bath," I reminded her, kinder this time, even though it would likely kill me to be this close to her naked. "I can close him up."

She stopped pacing, but she didn't stop wringing her hands.

"I told him I would do it. I'm the reason they're there in the first place. He wouldn't have gotten them if I—"

Perfect. I'd shoved her away so much, now she felt guilty for Xavier's battle wounds. Gods, I was an asshole.

"I shouldn't have said that to you," I admitted, really looking into her eyes for the first time since the mountaintop. "It wasn't your fault. That battle had nothing to do with you or your magic. Had I been smarter about it, I would have ripped off our royal patches before we traipsed through enemy territory. They weren't attacking because of you. They were attacking because of us. None of it was your fault."

In fact, I'd been the one to paint a target on her back. She'd been wearing my coat, the large royal crest on its back a beacon for attack. I'd thought I'd been so kind, but my kindness had nearly gotten her killed. It seemed even when I was trying not to be an asshole, I still was one.

Her smile was bitter as she shook her head. "That doesn't mean he didn't step in front of those arrows because of me. That he wasn't in the forest because of me. Because he did and he was. I said I would help him, so hand over the damn kit."

No, she'd been in that forest because of me. Because I hadn't kept her safe, because I wanted to stall, because I'd taken a hit with that stupid dragon bolt and nearly gotten us both killed.

Guilt lashed at me like a whip.

Vale reached for the roll of leather, but I snatched it up before she could touch it, holding it out of her grasp. "You have what amounts to poison on your skin," I said gently. "It's hurting you with every passing second. If that's not enough for you, Xavier's not healing like he should because of it. I'm not trying to be an asshole, it's just a fact. He needs stitches, and I need to be the one to do it."

Those searing green eyes seemed to slice right through me like she was waiting for the next insult. I supposed I deserved that. I'd been needling her all damn day. But this time, I swallowed my pride and said a word that hadn't crossed my lips in a century or more.

"*Please*, Vale. Let me do this."

The word seemed to take her by surprise, halting her single-minded focus on getting the kit from me. It felt so good, I said it again.

"Please?"

Eyes wide, her lush, full lips parted, and I nearly lost all my will right then. Naturally, Xavier took that moment to appear, a towel around his waist and a robe in his hand. Vale startled before her gaze went anywhere but in his direction.

Oh, yeah. Something had happened.

"Fine. After you stitch him, mash the berries into a paste and coat the wounds. It should help with the pain and help them clot."

Then she turned away from me, giving Xavier a wide berth as she skirted around the screen.

Her shadow drew my gaze, and I watched as she unwound her braid before she peeled off her filthy tunic and breeches. My heart picked up speed, and my cock thickened in my leathers as a fair bit of shame hit me square in the gut. I turned, refusing to subject myself to the torture of her shadow or invade what little privacy she had.

Gritting my teeth, I yanked the rest of the procured items out of my bag and unrolled the suture kit. Then my desire died a cold death when she hissed in pain as she climbed in. Her poor feet had to have been mangled in that damn forest, not that she'd said anything. Squeezing my eyes shut, I tried not to think about the mage with his hand on her throat, how she'd been forced to fight before she even had her full strength. How she'd put her body between a mage and Xavier after he'd been injured.

Jealousy burned hotter in my gut, but I swallowed it down. She needed food and healing and sleep. I'd have to save some of those berries for her, too.

Once she was submerged, she let out a little moan of pleasure, and it took everything in me not to turn around and knock that damn screen out of my way just so I could listen to her do it again. My cock throbbed, my scales shivered, and my dragon roared in my head, but I swallowed it all down.

Mindlessly, I opened the suture kit, focusing on

the task at hand before I lost the very last vestiges of my control. And all the while, I had to force my dragon back to the depths of my consciousness, his screams for claiming getting harder and harder to ignore.

"Sit down before you fall down," I ordered once Xavier started to sway.

Jaw like granite, he sat on the edge of the bed, his eyes glued to the same damn screen I'd been staring at moments ago. I couldn't do the same—not if I wanted his bleeding to stop. So I settled with listening to the water splash in the tub as I got to work closing the wounds that should have healed almost as soon as he'd gotten them.

"We can't let her go through with this," Xavier whispered, his gaze never leaving the screen, even as I knotted the first stitch and started on the next.

As much as I wanted to agree with him, I couldn't. The problem was that the longer I thought about it, the more evident it was to me that Vale was exactly who we needed to break the curse. She might not have the experience with magic as the witches who came before her, but she had a heart like no other.

She would make it out alive—I knew it.

"And we're just supposed to, what? Abscond

with a witch under our arm and fuck off to parts unknown? Do you honestly think we would get away with that? Idris knows she's alive. He could sense her all the way from Direveil under a mountain of *Lumentium*. There is no such thing as running, Xavier."

He flinched as I tied another stitch, but there was no way he'd let this go.

"You and I both know he can't leave that castle. We could get away if we needed to. I know you've thought about it more than once. Don't lie to me."

He knew damn well I couldn't. I *had* thought about it a time or two when I got low—when I thought this would never end. Dreamt of flying fast and far across the sea, if only to catch a glimpse of what was out there.

"Well, aren't you ready to burn it all down. Let's say she *is* the one. By taking her, you would be condemning every person with magic to a slow, agonizing death. I don't want her to die either, but everything in me is screaming that she is the one."

He shook his head, likely ready to beat me senseless. "But what if she's not? I don't think you understand. She is—"

"Important?" I growled, cutting him off. "Trust me, I know."

"Then how in good conscience could we take her there? How could we sit idly by while she b—"

Fighting off the urge to put my fist in his face, I tied off another stitch. When I moved to the next wound, he hissed, my needle placement not nearly as kind as it should have been. "She. Won't. You didn't see her on that mountaintop. You didn't see how fierce she was. Bloody and dying, and still, she screamed at me like she wasn't afraid but like she was a dragon herself. She's going to make it."

She had to. I didn't think I'd survive if she didn't.

Xavier's shoulders drooped, and all I scented in the room was his sorrow. "If she does, you and I both know she'll never be ours."

But I knew that already.

"She can hear him," he admitted, and the statement seemed to be ripped from his very soul. "I didn't realize how fucking selfish I was until she told me that. On the mountaintop, he told her we were coming. He told her to stay strong. I think we both know what that means."

If he had stabbed me in the gut, it would have hurt less. But then again, Idris wasn't the only one who could speak inside her head. "I don't think he's alone in that one," I muttered, tying off another stitch. "I'm almost certain she understood me when I told her to stop screaming at me."

Xavier's jaw clenched, and I could almost smell his jealousy.

"Because she can hear both of you," he began, his tone measured as if he had to keep it under lock and key, or else he would throw a punch in my face, "then there's a possibility that she could be far more powerful than either of us can even comprehend."

"Exactly. Meaning she will survive this."

His fists clenched as he swiveled to stare at me, nearly knocking the needle out of my hand. That mattered less than the slitted pupil in his eyes or the scales climbing up his neck. He got to his feet, not giving that first shit about the still-bleeding wounds at his back.

"But will she survive the second? Or the third? She stood in front of me, not knowing whether she would live or die, Kian. I can't let her walk into a slaughter. I just can't do it."

And as much as I wanted to agree with him, I just couldn't. "Out of the two of us, I wouldn't have figured you for a fan of high treason."

"Remember when I told you she would never be ours? If we let her walk in there, I'll be right."

I swallowed, knowing he was right, but... "And if

we don't let her walk in there, she's as good as dead, anyway."

His scales started climbing down his arms, over his torso, his body vibrating with rage. I followed his gaze through the top of the screen at the little witch. Her back was to us, her wet hair over her shoulder as she scrubbed at her skin, the flesh pink.

But he wasn't looking at the suds.

No, his eyes were glued to the same damn thing mine were. Thick scars crisscrossed over her whole back, the white color of them telling of their age. Some were jagged as if a whip had ripped her flesh wide. A few were thin, almost surgical. Those had been done with a blade. And at the center of it all, resting between her shoulder blades, was a symbol in old Festian branded into her skin—a symbol that hadn't been used in the kingdom for hundreds of years.

Maybe more.

A long time ago, it was used to shun the worst of us, the ones cursed by the gods, the ones with too much magic, too much power, and too much dark knowledge. Over the years, it became a punishment for minor crimes, a shame that seemed to follow the bloodline, meant to ostracize and condemn. Once branded, those with the mark rarely survived for long.

Once Idris became king, he deemed the punishment barbaric and put an end to it.

But the leader of the *Perder Lucem* was nothing like Idris, and for whatever crime she'd committed, he'd labeled her a heretic.

I didn't have to ask her who it was that had whipped and cut and branded her skin. I knew it was the same man who'd stabbed her, who'd tied her to a stake and left her as bait to burn.

Arden.

"I take it back," I growled, the shift threatening to take me over. "Treason it is."

Because there was no way I would let her walk in there knowing what was to come.

Not her.

Not ever.

CHAPTER 10
VALE

I f I had it my way, I'd live in the bathtub. The decadent water nearly reached my collarbones, encasing me in blissfully scalding heat. It lapped at the sides of the golden tub as I scrubbed my skin pink, the warmth easing the aches in my muscles and bones. The suds of the lemony soap popped and crackled against the water, and even that was a damn delight.

I couldn't recall a time I'd been so clean. I tried not to look at the state of the water beneath the layer of bubbles or feel the nagging whispers of guilt for experiencing something so wonderful when Nyrah couldn't. But since there was a definite possibility I could die in the next twenty-four hours, I figured enjoying it was a far better use of my time than wallowing.

Wallowing wouldn't do anything but make me feel like I didn't deserve this, and dammit, if I was about to break a curse and save a kingdom, I deserved a bath at the very least.

I hadn't forgotten the trials Xavier mentioned— even if he wouldn't tell me what they were. If all the Luxa had died during them, I would hang onto every single little good thing I could before they started. Dunking my head, I rinsed my hair of the blue hair potion that had appeared on the small wooden stool next to the tub. It carried a faint scent of flowers and something I couldn't place, the pleasant perfume another luxury I'd carry with me.

When I couldn't wash another body part, and my fingers got all wrinkled and pale, I pulled myself from the water. Reaching for the same fluffy white cloth Xavier had used to wrap around his waist, I relished the soft glide of it as I dried my skin.

Under the mountain, such luxuries would be considered too good for the miners and lower class. The majority of us only had the frigid pools diverted from the stream to use for bathing. While they were an escape from the heat in the summer months, they were nearly unbearable in the winter. There were a few women who made soaps as well, but their supplies were always limited.

A cream confection of fabric hung over the privacy partition, the thin garment soft and silky as I ran my fingers over it.

"It's a nightgown," Kian said when I didn't grab it, his voice rough with an emotion I couldn't place. "I also have some underclothing as well. And a dress for tomorrow. And some other things I thought you might need."

I swallowed down the tears threatening to fall, covering my mouth so I wouldn't make a noise. Gifts were a new experience for me, and it made me thankful and angry and… confused. Kian and Xavier were dragons, and yet, I couldn't reconcile these men with what the *Perder Lucem* insisted they were. I couldn't imagine them murdering without cause or hurting innocents.

Even Kian, who had been a complete prick to me all day, had still not injured me in any way. Was that just because I was a Luxa? Was it because they needed me? And why did not knowing make me so crazed?

And how could I trust Arden at his word? This was the same man who'd beaten me, stabbed me, whipped me, tied me to a stake to have me burn.

He'd made me pay for Nyrah's actions, even though she'd just been a hungry child. Why would he tell the truth? He and the rest of the guild were starving us, killing us...

It didn't make sense for me to punish Kian and Xavier for Arden's word.

"T-thank you," I choked out, trying not to let my emotions get the better of me. "That was kind of you."

Gently, I plucked the garments from the screen. One had to be the nightgown, but the other two confused me quite a bit. The first was a pair of briefs similar to bloomers, only silkier and smaller, and appeared to fit close to the skin. I'd never seen anything like them, but they didn't seem too complicated. I pulled the silky fabric up my legs, letting it rest against the bony protrusions of my hips.

The next garment was similar to a bustier, but I hadn't seen one since before my parents died. It had strings and fastenings, and it seemed like it would be terribly uncomfortable, so I left it alone. Then I slipped the nightgown over my head and shivered at the creamy texture of it. But the room, in spite of the fire, was slightly chilly, so I grabbed the fluffy robe hanging near the tub and slid my arms into it. The plush fabric was heavy and warm, as if magic had been keeping it ready for me. Maybe it had.

Tying the belt around my waist, I gathered myself enough to round the partition. Kian was still stitching Xavier's wounds, the last of them the shallowest of cuts. Still, his large, half-naked body made my belly dive for my knees. It didn't matter that I'd ridden with him all day, it was different when he'd stripped to the skin for his bath.

I'd never been around a single naked man, let alone a giant dragon shifter who'd saved my life. And then the way he'd cupped my face in his hands? I'd wanted to kiss him then, but I'd been too much of a coward to make that move.

"Am I clean enough to mash the berries?" I asked, holding up my hands for inspection. I'd said it as a joke, but the dirt was gone from under my fingernails, and my skin was about three shades lighter.

Kian abandoned the needle and thread and took my hand in his. His touch was gentle as he looked my fingers over, turning my hand this way and that as if he was looking for the slightest hint of poison. There was nothing I could do about the raised callouses on my palms or the jagged scars on my knuckles from mining. I hated the hardness of them, but they were clean at least.

Then, as if he was giving his seal of approval, Kian bent his head, pressing his soft lips to the tender skin of the inside of my wrist, his kiss placed over the cut I'd given myself with his blade to set my power free. My whole body felt as if a flash fire had ignited along my spine, and I tried and failed to swallow down a gasp.

"You pass inspection," he rumbled, those burning amber eyes meeting mine as his breath gusted over my flesh.

Something about his voice sent a shiver through me, tightening my nipples and making my core clench. If he'd been pushing me away before, he'd definitely changed directions.

"Good," I managed to croak, pulling back my hand and spinning to face the berries.

Nightwinter berries were a small, pink fruit plucked from a night-blooming bush that only grew in the coldest, darkest of places. Naturally, they were everywhere under the mountain, popping up where blood had been spilled. I liked to think the earth was giving some of the lives lost back to us with the fruit, its only real purpose to help heal wounds.

Gently, I mashed the berries with my knuckles, careful not to be too rough. The sweet scent filled my nose, reminding me of Nyrah so much my heart twisted in my chest. She'd tended to me for days while my back healed, attacking my thick wounds with the paste as if it would take back what she'd done. And even though I'd taken her punishment, I'd never blamed her.

She would have died had I not.

Swallowing down the hurt, I spread the paste over the closed cuts on Xavier's back, managing to pretend to ignore both men as I worked. Even the unstitched cuts seemed to be healing faster than before, and I hated that Kian was right about the bath. I had been the reason Xavier was hurt, and the guilt made a home for itself in my middle.

Naturally, my belly took that moment to make my hunger known, grumbling a plaintive yowl that spoke of an entire day without food.

Kian's brow rose as he stared at my middle, a faint smile tipping up the side of his mouth. "And I thought only dragons could roar that loud."

A blush heated my face, and I ducked my head as a fair amount of shame twisted my insides. Xavier elbowed him in the gut as a knock sounded at the door. Kian let out a pained "*oof*," and Xavier rose from the edge of the bed, opening the door to the innkeeper.

A heavily laden tray was in his arms, the precarious balance of the items both tantalizing with their aromas as they were frightening. The sheer thought of losing any of the food had my heart tripping in my chest.

Before it could meet a horrible fate, Xavier saved the day, scooping up the tray as it tipped and depositing it on the small side table beside the fire. I was sure words were said, but I could only stare at the huge hunks of bread and giant bowls of creamy broth with thick curls of steam wafting up from the surface. A hand on my shoulder had me nearly jumping out of my skin as my stomach twisted into hungry knots.

I couldn't remember the last time I'd had anything other than the brick-like rations from the guild—the ones that tasted of dirt and half-spoiled vegetables that likely were the scraps from the leadership's tables.

"Have a seat," Xavier rumbled, the low words almost a command.

But my body didn't so much as twitch as I stared at the feast, afraid that if I moved, I would dive for the tray like the starving woman I was. It wasn't until I was gently but firmly pushed into the chair and Kian handed me the bread that I started devouring the food.

There was no such thing as manners or etiquette. I ripped into the bread with my teeth, the buttery, flakey crust zinging my tastebuds with flavor. I was almost positive I moaned, and I couldn't have cared less. Then, there was the soft, chewy center, and my toes practically curled as I swallowed it down.

Xavier knelt at my side, handing me the bowl of soup, and I fought off the urge to snatch it from him. Taking the bowl with both hands, I relished the heat filtering into my palms for half a second before I drank deep. I knew I moaned then, the savory liquid even better than the bread. It warmed me from the inside out, and I gulped down the broth until there was none left, my belly filled near to bursting.

I couldn't recall the last time I'd been full, the unfamiliar sensation almost uncomfortable but welcome all the same. I stared at the other plates full of braised meat and multicolored vegetables, but I knew if I ate another bite, I would lose it all over the floor. When was the last time I'd eaten meat?

Ten years?

Fifteen?

It had been as a child when we still had hunters in the guild instead of just miners. Back when we had acres of terraced farmland to tend and raised animals for food. It took nearly everything I had not to stuff myself, to not to gorge on the offered decadence. Not to hoard the leftovers just in case I never got food again.

"When was the last time you ate?" Kian asked, his voice no louder than a whisper, but his tone had my head whipping up to look him in the eye.

As soon as I met his amber gaze, I almost wished I hadn't. It was filled with enough knowing that a thread of shame tugged at the small cocoon of comfort I'd managed to wrap myself in.

"I don't know," I admitted, unwilling to lie to him. "It's been a while. And even when we do eat, it's not much."

I thought about the quarter ration that had spurred my trip to the kitchens and set everything into motion. Had we been given the whole ration that day, I doubted I would have pushed the issue. We'd likely still be under the mountain now. Then again, Thane wasn't someone who would let a slight slide, and Nyrah had refused him publicly. I'd likely be right where I was, worrying for Nyrah and wondering how I'd get us out of this.

Kian's large hand closed over my wrist, the joint emaciated from lack of nutrients and too many hours hammering away at the side of the mountain, mining for *Lumentium*. "I can see that. Did they not feed you?"

My chuckle was mirthless as I pulled my wrist from his loose grip. "Not if they could help it."

Xavier's touch on my ankle had me flinching, but that didn't stop the big man from pulling my battered feet into his lap so he could inspect the bottoms. I tried to tuck them back, but his grip was much firmer than Kian's had been. He held out a hand, and Kian passed him the bowl of leftover Nightwinter berries.

"You don't heal as quickly as we do. I'll need to bind these cuts."

"It's fine. I don't—"

"Could you just let me?" he growled, ire making his eyes glow with what I assumed was his dragon.

But it had been a long time since someone had truly taken care of me, and I wasn't used to it.

"If you must," I grumbled, allowing him to inspect my feet.

At the first touch of the paste, I hissed, the healing properties of the fruit working its way into the cuts. It wasn't the first time I'd gone without shoes, so I wasn't worried about the state of my feet, but Xavier was. His brow pulled into a frown as he clucked his tongue.

"Some of these could use stitches, but—"

"No stitches." Stitches meant the skin pulling as I walked and popping into a bigger wound if I ran. I'd take a scar over not being able to run if I needed to. "Just bandage them if you have to."

Xavier's jaw hardened, his gaze seeming to see right through my skin to the heart of my soul. It was as if he knew why I didn't want them, and he was trying to decide whether or not he would listen to me. His warm touch skimmed my ankle as he loosened his hold, but he said nothing.

"Do what she asks, brother," Kian murmured, handing him a roll of cloth.

Xavier didn't move to take it. Instead, he looked at me for one long moment, seeming to come to a decision about something. Only then did he pluck the offered roll, and soon, my soles were expertly bandaged, his tender care nearly bringing tears to my eyes.

"I wish I could have healed you," he whispered as he finished, and my hand instinctively went to my middle, resting over the thick scar from Arden's blade.

"I think you healed me just fine." I swallowed, the day taking its toll as another thread of guilt piled on my shoulders. "I'm sorry I didn't say thank you before—to both of you. I would have died up there had you not saved me." But meeting their gazes was too hard, and my eyes fell to my hands in my lap. "I know I'm just a job to you, but I still appreciate it."

Kian huffed out a mirthless laugh as he turned away, but the heat of Xavier's gaze never left my face, those pale-blue eyes always seeming to see right through me. Still, the weight of the day hit me in earnest, and his gaze fell away, releasing me from the hold they'd had on me all damn day.

Exhaustion tugged at every limb as I pulled my feet from his hold and curled deeper into the chair, tucking the robe around my legs as my eyes slowly drooped and then closed. The cushions were thicker than the thin mat of blankets my sister and I usually slept on, and even though the position was slightly awkward, I could still rest comfortably there.

I was nearly fast asleep before thick arms plucked me from the cushions. My eyelids barely cracked as I caught Kian lifting me into his arms and walking the short distance to the bed. He gently deposited me onto the mattress, and plush blankets and softness stole the rest of my energy.

"If you think I'm going to let you curl up in a chair when there is a perfectly good bed available, you're dreaming."

I wanted to argue, but I didn't even have the energy to part my lips in anything other than a sigh of contentment.

"Sleep well, little witch. Tomorrow will come soon enough."

And even though tomorrow would likely hold more than I could handle, I had a full belly, a soft, comfortable mattress cushioning my aching bones, and a nice firm pillow under my cheek. And that said nothing of the safety that settled over me like the blanket Kian tucked around my shoulders.

No one would get me with Kian and Xavier here, no one could touch me. For the first time since my parents died, I was safe.

With no more fight left in me, I gave in, allowing sleep to have me.

"*Yes,*" a familiar voice rumbled in the deep recesses of my consciousness. "*Sleep well, my brave one. I'll see you soon.*"

CHAPTER 11
VALE

Hard rocks dug into my knees as I scrambled up the narrow staircase to the mountaintop. I had to find Nyrah. She had to be around here somewhere. The frigid, biting wind raked against my flesh as I ignored the steep cliff face, racing up the catwalk.

Of course, the bath and food and the rescue had all been a dream. There was no such thing as dragon shifters, and no one was coming to save me.

No one was coming to save us.

The catwalk ended at the artificially flattened mountaintop, a blackened stake embedded into the ground. But instead of me being tied to the wooden prison, it was Nyrah's small frame, her bloody blonde hair blowing in the wind, her battered face twisted with *fear. She struggled against her bonds, a ragged wound at her middle right where mine had been. The scent of fuel reached my nostrils as the faint first rays of dawn breached the horizon.*

"No, no, no," I whimpered, racing faster toward her but never coming within reach. The rays of light caught the convex glass of the lantern, igniting the fuel. But it was only once the first flames caught that I was able to move.

"Help me," she screamed, fighting against the ropes binding her to the stake.

"No. This is supposed to be me. Not you. Never you. I'm going to get you out of this. I'm going to help you," I promised, but the flames were already licking up my back.

I was already burning, and it didn't matter what I tried, the ropes would not loosen.

I reached for the power inside me, the power I tried so hard to keep hidden while we lived under this mountain. But it wasn't there. I wasn't tethered to anything. I was alone, powerless, weak, and I was failing my sister.

Fire seared my skin, and I screamed at the agony of it.

We would die on the mountain. Because even if I could run—even if I could save myself—I wouldn't leave her to die alone. Accepting my fate, I tried to pull her in my arms, but the closer I got to my baby sister, the more her body faded, turning to smoke and ash as she floated into the distance, the gusts ripping her from me.

"Nyrah," I screamed, but that too was carried away on the bitter wind.

I fell to my knees in the dirt, letting the flames eat at my skin as despair clawed my insides to ribbons.

"Is this what you really see when you close your eyes?" a deep voice asked, and somehow, I spun even though everything was slow and thick, changing in a way I couldn't understand. The fire around me died as did the pain, fading away as if it had never been there in the first place.

The man was sitting in a gilded chair, his posture relaxed as if he didn't have a single care, as if he was in charge of everything and everyone. A crooked crown sat upon his head as golden eyes surveyed me. Dark hair fell over his brow, the wavy tresses windswept as his gaze pinned me to the spot.

"Who are you?" I asked, but I knew.

If there were ever a man who screamed "power," this would be him. Arden often spoke of the king of Credour, claiming he was as ruthless as he was unyielding, ruling his people with an iron fist. How he commanded the dragons to pin us to that mountain to keep us starving and weak.

"You know exactly who I am, Vale."

Of course I did, though, part of me thought he would look much older than the man before me. Dark stubble decorated his sharp jaw, his commanding features so regal in nature that so few men possessed.

"King Idris," I murmured, and he inclined his head. "Am I dreaming? Or are you in my head?"

I looked down at the ragged, filthy clothes billowing around my small frame. My tunic was bloody, the gaping hole where Arden had stabbed me exposing a still-bleeding wound. Bleeding but not painful.

Was I still on that mountain so close to death?

Was I safe in the inn with Xavier and Kian?

I didn't know.

"Here and there, I suppose. But I didn't take us here. You did."

He stood from his throne and part of the sky melted into a darkened bedroom, a faint crackling of fire in a grate next to a four-poster bed, the curtains drawn.

The room was drenched in a blackened scarlet, the fabrics, the tapestries. It was almost as if the walls themselves were drenched in blood. And somehow with the king walking toward me, I would still take that darkened bedroom over this mountaintop.

Then he reached for me, his scalding touch pulling me from the chill of the mountain and into his world, the wind dying as he guided me closer. He was tall, so tall I had to crane my neck to see his face. The shadows of the fire danced over his sharp cheekbones and full lips and strong jaw. His golden eyes glowed in the dim, and a knowing smile tipped the corners of his lips.

"Isn't that better? Don't you prefer my bedroom to that mountain?"

I swallowed thickly, all the tiny hairs standing up on my arms as his voice slid down my spine like honey.

I couldn't quite answer him, so I settled on a nod.

"Now tell me, my brave one, what is taking you so long to come to me? Why are you sleeping in that inn and not in my castle with me?"

With him? He couldn't mean it the way it sounded.

"W-we were attacked on the road. Xavier was injured. His wounds weren't closing so we had to stop."

Shame had me trying to pull my hand from his, but the king only pulled me closer, my chest pressing against him, his warmth seeping into my bones. Heat rose in my cheeks, but when I tried averting my gaze, he put a finger under my chin, making me look at him.

"I-it's my fault. The Lumentium on my skin was hurting him—hurting them. I did what I could, but Xavier still got hurt because of me. I'm sorry."

Understanding dawned in his expression and his arm banded around my back, pressing me closer. But I guessed I wasn't close enough because he lifted me off my feet. My legs had a mind of their own and wound around his back, the scalding heat of his body touching me everywhere.

"No one blames you, my brave one," he rumbled, the honeyed cadence easing my worries as his touch set me on fire. "You've done so well. You don't have to apologize."

His head dipped, and he ran his nose up the side of my neck, drawing in my scent. Just like with Kian and Xavier, my skin pebbled, my nipples tightened, and my core clenched.

"What are you doing?" I gasped, fighting the urge to tip my head back and bare my throat to him.

A rumble, almost like a purr, vibrated in his chest. "Scenting you." His lips followed the line his nose made. "Kissing you." Then his tongue followed suit. "Tasting you."

My brain made a feeble attempt at questioning why he held me so close, why he wanted to taste me, but I ignored the misgivings as his teeth gently bit at my pulse point. If this were a dream, I would gladly hang onto it.

Tilting my head back, I let the moan I was holding in free.

Sharp fangs raked my skin, and as much as they sent

a thread of fear through me, the desire to have them pierce my flesh filled me more.

"Come to me, Vale," he murmured, his voice so soft it was barely a whisper. "Come to me, and I'll give you anything, everything."

His touch became faint as well, almost as if he wasn't holding me anymore. Instead, other touches caressed my skin, the scarlet bedroom fading away as darkness overtook my vision.

"Come to me, my brave one."

Warmth enveloped me on all sides, my body burning as teeth nipped at my neck, my shoulder, my jaw. An arm banded around my middle, holding me tight, nestling me against a hot, hard body. My leg was thrown over someone's hip as my hands roamed over a bare chest.

I couldn't tell where the dream ended and where this began, and I wasn't sure I cared. Soft lips found mine in the darkness, and I parted for them, hungry for touch, for kisses, for all the pleasure I'd been denied my whole life. It felt so good, I didn't care if it was real or fake, I wanted—no, I *needed*—this.

"Fuck, you taste good, my little witch," Kian murmured against my lips before diving back in for another kiss, his tongue sweeping inside at my hungry gasp. His words twisted the knot inside me, igniting a ravenous need that pulsed through every part of my body.

"Let me taste," Xavier demanded, his large hand wrapping around my throat as he guided my chin in his direction.

My pulse hammered under that commanding touch, and I knew he could feel it. Then his mouth claimed mine while Kian's lips moved lower, down my neck, over my collarbone. He pulled my robe open and brushed my nightgown aside, pulling the peak of my nipple into his mouth while he cupped the other breast.

I moaned into Xavier's kiss, that ache between my legs only growing worse. I didn't understand how I could be this needy, this hungry. I'd gone without touch nearly my whole life, but this was just like bread: once I had a taste, I needed more. I wanted to glut myself on it.

Xavier's arm loosened around my middle as he reached to pull up the skirt of my gown, while Kian's hands ran over the exposed skin. His fingers hooked in the silky fabric covering my sex, drawing it down my legs, and I let him—I let *them*. Every errant touch was akin to lightning on my skin.

"Do you taste this good everywhere?" Xavier

asked against my mouth, but I didn't understand the question.

It wasn't until Kian's hands parted my knees and his tongue licked at the lips of my sex, did I manage to comprehend even a little of it. But by then, I was burning, moaning, scrabbling for something to hold onto as Kian set about giving me the sweetest torture while Xavier whispered dirty things in my ear.

"Fuck, you smell sweet," he growled, sharp fangs nipping at my neck. *When did he get fangs?* "When it's my turn, you're going to sit on my face, aren't you? You're going to give me all of you. Fucking drown me."

My hips bucked as Kian lapped at my sex, and when his mouth closed around my clit, I nearly screamed. Xavier cupped my breasts, his fingers gently pinching my peaked nipples as he growled against the skin of my neck. "Come on his tongue, my beautiful witch. Let him make you feel good."

I didn't know what coming was, but if it was this growing pressure that threatened to yank me under, I would gladly do whatever he said. My moans grew louder, my hips moving on their own as I reached for that blissful feeling building in my core, like a bubble about to pop. I didn't exactly know what I was reaching *for*, but I needed it in a way I couldn't describe.

When it broke, I screamed against Xavier's lips until he swallowed it down with his kiss, his tongue claiming me much in the way Kian's mouth had.

"So sensitive," Kian growled, his voice deeper, rougher, drawing my attention, his glowing amber eyes all I could see in the darkness.

His fingers lightly ran over the lips of my sex, pressing but not entering, but I wanted him to. I still ached, even though tiny pulses of pleasure washed over me, and I knew those fingers would cure it. They had to.

Xavier's fingers joined Kian's as they played with me. "So wet."

Kian's fingers gently pushed inside me, pausing for a moment before he pulled them out. Then he rested his cheek on my belly, his stubble delicious as it raked against my oversensitive skin.

"It's my turn to have a taste," Xavier rumbled, his voice making my empty core clench with need, even though I'd just had so much pleasure. "But I want to see you first."

Kian's touch left me for a moment before the dim glow of the bedside lantern flared to life. Light caressed the flat planes of his muscles, making him seem bigger, broader. He slipped two fingers into his mouth, and I knew those were the same ones he'd fit inside me. He licked them clean, and something about the way he'd done it made me want to lick him that way.

My breath hitched as he knelt on the bed, and I moaned when he bent to kiss me, the taste of my desire on his lips. It was salty and sweet and mixed with the heady flavor of Kian's tongue—it was the most delicious thing I'd ever tasted. Xavier pulled at the sleeves of my robe and slipped my nightgown down my hips while Kian took my mouth in a punishing kiss, peeling my layers away as he ran his lips down my spine.

Then he laid flat on his back, and a moment later, they'd positioned me so my sex was over Xavier's mouth. When he'd said he wanted me to sit on his face, he'd actually meant it. I tried not to rest my weight on him fully, but Xavier pulled me down, lapping at my slit like a man starved.

It was almost too much, I couldn't handle the pleasure of it. I bucked, trying to get away, but both of their grips were like iron, holding me in place.

I needed both of them to feel like I did, needed them to be desperate and needy, too. Instinctively, I reached for Kian, running my hands over his pecs, his abs, reaching into the soft breeches encasing his thighs. My hand closed around his length, and he let out the best groan. He was hot and impossibly hard, and I loved the way his whole body vibrated as I ran my fingers over the velvety soft skin.

"Show me what you want," I gasped and then moaned when Xavier sucked on my clit.

Kian's hand closed over mine, guiding my hold as he thrust into my fist. "I want you, little witch. Whatever way I can have you."

Looking down, I saw a bead of his seed glistening at the head of his cock, and I had the strongest urge to lick it, to take him into my mouth like he'd done to me, to explore both of them the way they were exploring me.

I *needed* it.

Never loosening my grip, I kissed my way down his neck, over the planes of his hardened muscles, down his abdomen. He shuddered but held himself still until I swiped my tongue over his thick, pink head. He jerked as if I'd branded him, the salty flavor of his desire driving my need higher as he let out the best groan.

Xavier's hold got tighter, pinpricks of his claws digging into my skin, making me moan as I pulled the head of Kian's cock into my mouth. My hips bucked, and that same instinct had me reaching for Xavier's breeches, needing him to feel the same pleasure Kian and I were. My hand wrapped around him, and he nearly roared into my sex.

His hold constricted, his mouth turned punishing, and he devoured me as he put his hand over mine, tightening my hold on him as he thrust into my fist, taking his pleasure as he gave me mine.

Kian gathered my hair in his fist, the pull of it making a flash fire of need hotter, damn near smoldering as I took him deeper into my mouth. I wanted it all, I wanted more.

I needed more.

My hips bucked as Kian took over, setting the pace for us all as he used my mouth for his pleasure. The hand I'd used to hold him steady fell away, and he thrust deeper into my mouth, touching the back of my throat as I moaned over and over again.

"Fuck, baby. Look at you taking me deep. Swallow me down."

I hollowed my cheeks, swallowing just a little, and he groaned like I'd ripped the very marrow from his bones.

"Yeah, baby. Just like that. Such a good little witch. You're going to make me come, aren't you?"

I wanted to. I wanted him to feel just a little of

what he'd done to me, what Xavier was doing to me. I sucked harder, running my tongue on the underside of his cock as I swallowed again.

Kian roared as he roughly pulled me off of him. His fingers wrapped around my throat as he captured my lips in a punishing kiss. His free hand seized mine, and we fisted his length, the spit slick as he thrust into our hold. What felt like seconds later, hot spurts of his seed splashed my hip, and I bucked, my need driving higher with each lash of it. I'd been marked by him, and I craved every ribbon of his desire that painted my skin.

Xavier groaned as I ground into his lips, my pleasure climbing as Kian's hold loosened just a little. Then I broke the kiss, gasping as he fisted my hair once more.

"You want to suck on Xavier the way you sucked on me, don't you?"

Moaning, I could barely nod, but Kian didn't need me to. He guided my mouth to Xavier's thick cock, the head almost purple as the giant man practically vibrated under me. Xavier's hold on his length fell away as his grip on me tightened. I ran my tongue across the glistening head, catching his seed on my tongue. He tasted just as good as Kian, and I sucked him deep.

Kian's grip on my hair was nearly punishing, but the tiny bite of pain only had me moaning as I hollowed my cheeks, allowing him to set the pace as I laved his friend's cock.

Xavier's moans vibrated through my sex, driving my desire higher and higher as he licked and sucked and twisted me into knots. Then I felt pressure at my opening, and Xavier thrust two fingers into my sex. My walls fluttered around the intrusion as I got used to the sensation, the slight bite of pain only making me suck him harder as my desire nearly reached its peak.

I ground my hips against his mouth, taking his fingers deeper, needing something, I just didn't know what. Then he curled those fingers, hitting something inside me that no one had touched before—over and over until I was a mindless sexual creature, squirming in his hold as the pleasure became too much, too overwhelming. Every part of my body was aware of his tongue between my legs, of his breaths on my sex, of his fingers filling me, stretching me, thrusting into me.

Then it crested, and I screamed around Xavier's cock, my whole body strung tight as wave after wave of the most intense pleasure crashed over me. Xavier roared against my sex, and then thick ribbons of his seed exploded in my mouth. Moaning, I swallowed the salty, sweet liquid as my pleasure continued to pummel me. I couldn't breathe, I couldn't move, all I could do was let it pull me under.

Kian's hold tightened on my hair, and Xavier slipped from my mouth. I sucked in a breath, my heart hammering in my chest as my sex clenched over and over again, the tremors of pleasure washing over me again and again.

I shivered when Xavier gave my sex one last lick, and he gently pulled his fingers from my core. My walls clenched, and I moaned at the loss, even if I couldn't take another ounce of pleasure. Boneless, Kian helped me sit up, pulling me off of Xavier as if I were a pile of rags.

He handed me a cup of water, and I greedily drank it down, draining it in two gulps. Then he ran a cloth over my hip where he'd branded me with his seed. Shivering, I bit my lip, my greedy body almost begging for something it couldn't handle.

Then Kian dropped the most tender of kisses to my lips before pressing his forehead to mine, much like Xavier had done. It felt important and more than just people finding pleasure together. But before I could ask, Kian tucked me back under the covers, sandwiching me between his big body and Xavier's.

Xavier ran gentle kisses up the column of my neck before he wrapped his arm around my middle. Then Kian curled my leg over his hip, resembling the position I'd woken up in, only this time I was very, very naked.

Still, it was beyond comfortable, so I curled into my pillow, nestled in the warmth of their bodies as exhaustion and contentment filtered through my limbs.

But as sleep overtook me, the king's final plea echoed through my brain.

Come to me, my brave one.

Tomorrow. I would go to the king tomorrow.

Tonight, I would enjoy this.

CHAPTER 12
VALE

"*Come to me.*"

The loud demand from King Idris startled me out of a dead sleep as I shoved myself from the plush mattress. Heart thundering in my chest, I took stock and nearly hid my head under a pillow in embarrassment. Naked and alone, my actions from the night before settled into the flaming blush on my cheeks.

A part of me wished it all could have been a *remarkably* good dream, but my lack of clothing and the heady scent of desire perfuming the air told another story. That said nothing of the needy ache between my legs when I remembered Kian's face, Xavier's moans, my screams. My entire body throbbed with equal parts need and

Not shame, but something like it.

I couldn't be sure who had started the heavy petting, but I had a feeling whatever had happened in my dream with Idris threw everything into motion. I was almost positive it had been *me* who'd attacked *them*, leading to the most satisfaction I'd ever had and the best sleep I'd ever gotten. As well as a morning after that had me more confused than anything else.

The dream with Idris was branded into my brain, but I couldn't tell if it had been an actual dream or if it had been something else. And in dissecting it, his insistence that I would be in his bed gave me the tiniest bit of guilt. Well, until I remembered that Idris hadn't bothered to ask me if I wanted to be in his bed at all. He might have assumed, and he might be King, but that didn't mean I had to give him my body on top of breaking the curse.

Plus, I could very well die before the day was over. I had no call to be ashamed of my actions the night before or how I acted *in a dream* of all things. The thought of Idris' lips and fangs at my neck sent a throb of want to my sex.

No. This is how you ended up in between two dragon shifters last night. Get yourself together.

Get myself together. That, I could do.

Shoving myself up from the mattress, I pulled my wild hair out of my face. I hadn't bothered to brush it after my bath, and the wavy mass had likely doubled in size. At first, I'd been embarrassed, but now I was glad I was alone. Lighting the bedside lantern, I searched for my nightgown and underwear.

Both were draped over the foot of the bed along with a pretty vibrantly pink flower and a note in a swooping, barely legible scrawl.

You were too peaceful to wake.
We'll be back soon.
—K&X

A faint smile graced my lips at the sweet scent of the flower, my blush burning my cheeks as the shame dwindled into nothing. I'd needed that comfort last night, and they had gladly obliged. We were all consenting adults, and there was nothing to be ashamed of.

Donning my nightgown, I pulled back the curtain, allowing the rays of sunlight to warm me to the bone. Sunlight wasn't a common commodity under the mountain, and a gust of a sigh fell from my lips as I allowed myself that additional comfort. Beyond the rooftops, a large castle took up most of the eastern sky. The castle rose up like a mountain in the distance, and almost as though Idris was in the room next to me, his order shook me to my knees.

"Come to me, Vale."

The demand got louder, more insistent, and I knew it couldn't be a dream. The king was speaking inside my head just as he had on the mountain, and the order was one I would have to follow.

"Fine. I'm coming. Settle down."

Before long, I had handled my morning business and set out to tame my hair. The wavy tresses fell about my shoulders and down my back, and I attacked the mass of it with a pretty silver brush and comb Kian brought me.

Catching glimpses of myself in the dressing table mirror, I marveled how much difference a day made. After a decent meal and rest in a comfortable bed—not to mention last night's romp—my skin was rosy, my cheeks not so hollow. The creamy fabric caressed my modest curves, and even though my hair was a mass of waves, I felt almost pretty.

Soon, the mass was in a passable braid, and I inspected the pile of undergarments that seemed to go with the beautiful garment that couldn't be called "just a dress." Its color wasn't simply blue, either. It was indigo, rich and almost royal, edged in woven golden flowers and vines that made the color pop. The fabric was heavy and thick, far more luxurious and beautiful than anything I'd ever worn, and I didn't know if it was fit for the likes of me.

Who was I, really? A girl from nowhere with no real family, no money, plucked from a mountaintop, saved from execution. How was I supposed to break a curse? I barely knew how to dress myself. Once upon a time, my mother had taught me the proper way to dress, but it had been so long since I'd had quality clothing that wasn't falling apart, nothing was as I remembered.

But just like with this stupid curse, I'd figure it out. By the time I'd secured my stockings and sheathed the jeweled dagger to my thigh, I felt like a whole new person. I would figure it out.

Lacing the heeled boot up my calf, I made up my mind. I could walk into the kingdom and face the first trial. I would survive it, too. I would make sure Nyrah never had to walk this same path or breathe one day longer in captivity than she had to. I would pass these stupid tests. I would break the curse. And I would do whatever it took to survive.

Somehow.

The door opened, and the nerves I'd been stomping down roared back to life as Kian and Xavier strode through the entrance. The room seemed to shrink as they filled the space, the echoes of last night thrumming through my body as their stares pinned me to the spot. I straightened, standing tall even though I felt anything but confident, waiting to see what their reactions would be in the light of day.

Kian's amber gaze smoldered as he looked me over, his pupils narrowing to the slits of his dragon as a steady rumble vibrated from his chest. In fact, his entire body was vibrating, as if the scent in the room and the memory of what we did was affecting him like it was affecting me.

Just the sight of him reminded me of how he'd yanked my hair, of how the sting of it heated my whole body as Xavier devoured me. Xavier's pale-blue eyes flared, glowing with power as he strode forward, his fingers finding the end of my braid.

"You look beautiful," he murmured, his low growl sending a shiver of desire racing down my spine, even though he wasn't touching anything but the ends of my hair. "And you smell like heaven. Did you miss us?"

I fought off the urge to deny his words and settled on a whispered, "Yes."

Xavier's fingertips lifted my chin, and he slowly lowered his lips to mine, the softest of brushes melting me with its sweetness. "How are you feeling this morning?"

That blush I'd managed to tamp down rose like a brush fire in my cheeks. I swallowed a titter of shyness. "I'm fine."

Kian appeared at my right, his imposing presence not the threat it used to be. Now, it just made me want to climb him like a tree.

"Fine?" he rumbled, his nose dipping down to scent my neck. "The way you screamed should amount to far more than just a '*fine*,' my little witch."

If I let him kiss me like Xavier had, we'd never leave this room. We'd end up doing a hell of a lot more than what we'd done last night. Imagining it had me swallowing a moan, and I squeezed my legs together to stop the ache.

"Don't be rude," I chided, stepping away from the cage their bodies made. Already, their scents, their heat, their presence made it hard to think.

But Kian wasn't one to let me go so easily. He

followed me, stalking me until my back was against the wall. He fit his thick thigh between mine, pressing against the ache as if he knew exactly what I needed.

"I think you like me rude." He tucked a finger into the low neckline of my dress, the tip of his nail transforming into a sharp talon that gently scraped the tender flesh. "Want to see how rude I can be?"

My nipples tightened under my chemise as my skin pebbled, and I nearly gave in. If Xavier hadn't cleared his throat, I would have.

"You know we don't have time for this. The ferry will leave soon."

That brought me up short, my desire cooling instantly. "Ferry? What ferry?"

Kian brought his forehead to mine, seeming to calm himself before stepping away. "The ferry that will take us off this continent," he murmured, gauging my reaction as if he were prepared for me to lose my mind. "After what happened last night, we can't in good conscience take you to the king."

A pit of dread opened up in my belly. "What do you mean?"

This time, Kian's body vibrated for a whole new reason, and he cupped my cheeks in his hands, his touch gentle, although his words were not. "I won't let you put yourself in that kind of danger, Vale. Not a single Luxa has survived the trials, and I'm not going to watch you die. Not you."

My heart twisted in my chest as I pulled away and stared at them both, my gaze shifting from Kian to Xavier and back again. They cared for me. Of that, I was certain. I had no illusions about that. But what they didn't understand was that I wasn't just doing this impossible task just for me. I was doing it for my sister. And taking me off continent wouldn't change the fact that she was still in danger.

That this plan that they had concocted without asking me, never once accounted for her.

Kian's shoulders were set, his jaw like granite, and I knew no amount of talking or pleading would change his mind. He would put me on that ferry whether I wanted him to or not. My gaze fell on Xavier. His jaw was just as hard, his eyes just as determined, his shoulders just as set.

They were immovable, twin mountains of granite. The only thing I could do was nod.

"The boat leaves in an hour," Kian whispered, reaching for my hand. He laced his fingers with mine before kissing the inside of my wrist. "Grab whatever you think you'll need, and we'll go. I promise to take care of you, Vale. We both do."

The hard part was, I believed him. Kian and

Xavier would likely do whatever they had to do to protect me.

But that left Nyrah alone in the world. I swore the day my parents died that I would keep her safe. If I let them have their way, I was sentencing her to either a life of fear or death.

Xavier settled the fur-lined cloak over my shoulders as I got my heart under control, and Kian snatched up the comb and brush before stuffing it into his pack. That was likely everything I owned, and I couldn't stall even a moment to think.

"That's everything I have," I whispered, my mind racing as I plotted how to fix this.

"We'll get breakfast on the way, but we'll have to hurry," Xavier said, and I nodded again, following behind him as we swept down the hall.

I tensed at the stairs, a plan forming in my head as I tried not to think of falling from the top as the heaviness of my skirts tangled in my legs. Kian snatched up my hand, squeezing it reassuringly, and I let out a tense sigh.

Come to me, my brave one.

This time, the words were faint, as if they were a memory rather than Idris speaking inside my head. I had to go to the castle. I couldn't allow them to take me off continent. I had no money to get back, no options.

Kian led us outside, where a porter was finishing saddling two glossy black horses. He handed Xavier the reins and tipped his hat when Kian flipped him a golden coin. Then, a stroke of genius hit me.

I gasped, patting down my body. "I forgot the dagger," I moaned, allowing the distress of the situation to help sell it. "It's so beautiful, I don't want to leave it behind. Can you go back for it?"

Kian dipped his head and nipped at my throat. "Of course."

He hefted to pack off his back, handing it to Xavier. Xavier donned the leather bag and then lifted me onto the back of the first horse. I adjusted the skirt of my dress and smiled as my stomach chose to grace me with another stroke of luck.

Xavier's eyebrows hit his hairline. "How about I get you some bread for the road. I don't want you uncomfortable."

I bent, pressing a kiss to his cheek. "Thank you. I know we're in a hurry, but..."

"It's no problem."

My heart thudded in my chest as he turned his back, afraid he would figure out my plans before I did. The door to the inn closed behind him, and my fingers tightened on the reins. My legs squeezed, and the animal underneath me got the message, taking off as if he knew the way.

I held on for dear life as the horse raced down the lane in the direction of the looming castle. I did little but try not to fall off as we cut through the streets, nearly trampling people as we barreled through the city until the buildings gave way to a wide-open cobblestone lane leading up a sharp incline toward the one place I needed to be.

"Come to me, my Queen."

That voice grew louder, rougher, more insistent. And worse, calling me "my Queen" gave me more than a little bit of pause. I wouldn't be a queen. I would be a curse breaker at best, and at worst, I'd be roadkill trampled under the circumstances of my birth. But not a queen, of that, I was certain.

Once the path was open, the horse picked up speed, galloping as if something was chasing him. It was as if he knew that we only had so much time before Kian and Xavier figured out what I had done and why I'd done it. As if he knew I couldn't let them find me on this road.

I passed several townspeople on the path, their drawn faces full of anger, and it wasn't until I approached a wide bridge leading to the gate bisecting the castle wall, did I see a mob of them shouting at palace guards. They demanded to be let past the gate, tossing perfectly good food at the guards, wasting it.

The starving girl in me wanted to scream at them, but I didn't—couldn't. They had the freedom to rise up, to make their grievances known. I sort of had to admire them for that, and I hoped the people under the mountain had done the same.

There would be no way past them and definitely no way past the guards. Their faces were drawn and fierce, and I knew it would be a lost cause pleading my case to them.

"Come to me, my Queen."

The demand rattled inside my head, nearly knocking me off the horse. It sent a sharp spike of pain right between my eyes as bile raced up my throat.

"I'd love to," I growled through gritted teeth. "How in the hell am I supposed to get past the mob outside your door?"

A man startled next to me, his scrutiny sharp as though I'd been talking to myself. Granted, he didn't realize an angry king was yelling inside my head, so I couldn't exactly fault him for it.

"I will show you the way," he growled, his voice so

much louder than before. *"Get off the road. There's a way around the bridge."*

I pulled the reins to the left, guiding the horse off the path. It veered into the thick brush that led to a dense forest. The trees were wide and tall, blocking out the morning light, and instantly, I shivered at the sudden drop in temperature.

"Lose the horse," he ordered, and a faint thread of trepidation made me pause.

What if this was a trap? What if it wasn't the right way? What if it wasn't Idris inside my head, but someone else? I didn't want to leave the road, and I certainly did not want to leave the horse.

A distant screeching roar hit my ears then, and I knew without a doubt that Kian and Xavier had figured out that I wasn't at the inn anymore. Hastily, I dismounted, slapping the horse's rump so he would run back to the road. Then I drew the dagger from the sheath at my thigh.

If this was a trap, at the very least, I was armed.

"Fine. I'm officially off the road and have lost the horse. Now what?"

"Head in the direction of the castle but remain in the shadows. There are guards patrolling the forests for trespassers. Follow my voice."

A tremble of fear had my knees knocking

together, but I steeled my spine and marched forward, my fingers fisting on the hilt of the dagger. The closer I got to the castle, the darker and denser the forest became, the cold seeping into my bones, even under the fur-lined cloak and thick stockings and boots.

"This way," he called, and it was almost as if I could hear him for real and not just inside my head.

I adjusted my course to the north just a bit, and the ground sloped sharply, plunging into a darkened rocky crevasse that nearly stole every bit of my breath. I caught myself on the trunk of a gnarled tree, its roots clinging precariously to the hillside as I swallowed down a scream.

The last thing I needed was to freeze here, but I was petrified.

I can't. I can't. Tears spilled down my cheeks as I trembled, every death I'd witnessed dancing through my head. Their screams. Their pleas for help. I'd done nothing for them—too scared to lose my own life or my sister's. I cursed Orrus in my head, blaming him for every single needless death. I cursed him for my impending one, too, angry at the god for stealing so much.

It was too easy to lose a life, the fleeting breath of it so ephemeral, so brief.

Nyrah. You do it for Nyrah. One step at a time until it's done.

Whimpering, I hesitantly tucked the jeweled dagger back into the sheath at my thigh. I needed both hands free if I planned on surviving this. Then, I grabbed a thick root, clinging to it as the soft ground abraded away under my feet, the thick layer of fallen leaves and loose soil almost like quicksand. That screeching roar grew louder, moving me faster than I wanted to go. With no other choices left, I grabbed the next branch, the next root, the next rock, slowly climbing down the hill toward the hidden underbelly of the castle.

When I reached the bottom, I took a second to breathe, resting on a boulder as I craned my head to stare at the rough stone base of the castle. It was massive, and I really hoped I wouldn't have to climb anything because I doubted I could move another inch.

Trembling, I wiped at my tear-stained cheeks until I heard the roar of my name from Kian's lips.

"Vale," he thundered, so close it was as though he knew exactly where I was. "Stop where you are."

I flew to my feet, indecision pulling me in two. There was an opening in the castle wall, small, rough, but there all the same. I could go there, find my way to the king, plead my case, face the first trial.

Or I could let Kian and Xavier find me. Maybe we could get Nyrah together. We could—

"Come to me, my Queen. Move faster. They will be upon you too soon if you do not move."

Swallowing my fear, I ran for the rough cave-like opening, knowing that there was no way I could infiltrate the guild on my own. I also knew Kian and Xavier would never do it with me. There wasn't another option.

I ducked through the opening, crawling through the tunnel until it yawned into a colossal cavern, the ceiling lost to the darkness as a faint buzzing thrummed through my very bones. Shimmering spikes hung from the murky ceiling like the teeth of a great beast, and I worried if I had been too trusting of the voice in my head.

That faint buzzing grew louder, vibrating the slick ground beneath me. I took the dagger, slicing the delicate skin of my wrist just so I could get some light. My power bloomed, spilling out of me, illuminating the darkness like a torch.

"Almost there, my Queen. Closer. Let me look at you."

Fear drummed to the beat of my heart, the

wrongness of the voice finally registering. Idris hadn't sounded like this in my dream. His voice had been smooth, a gentle caress. This one was rougher, harder, louder.

"Vale," Xavier roared. "Get out of there."

"Vale, please. Please, turn around," Kian pleaded, but it was already too late.

Slithering in the darkness where my light barely touched was a great beast, its scales red as blood. And like the beacon I was, it drew closer, barreling toward me faster than I could blink.

And it wasn't until it rose up to its full height, did I realize just what it was.

A dragon—larger than Kian and Xavier by far—with fire rising in its throat, its wide-open mouth growing wider as it ate up the space between us.

And its gaze was set right on me.

CHAPTER 13
VALE

A thickly muscled arm wrapped around my middle and yanked me off my feet, placing me behind a broad back I'd grown to know well. Xavier had been putting himself between me and danger for the last two days, taking arrows meant for me, healing me when I was dying. Why had I even considered he'd stop now?

"Run, Vale," he shouted over his shoulder as he shrugged out of his coat.

The thick leather slapped the slick stone ground as white scales bloomed up his neck. His body seemed to double, triple in size. Then I got the bright idea to actually heed his order, stumbling back several steps as his body just kept growing. His shirt and leather pants split at the seams as his bones snapped and cracked, a moan of pain erupting from his throat that quickly turned into a roar.

That roar shook me to my very bones, the ground vibrating beneath me as the stalactites hanging from the ceiling began to crumble, falling to the ground around us like giant arrows, cleaving the stone ground in two. Blue fire exploded from his mouth as he stood his ground, but there was nowhere to run—not without being crushed by the falling debris. Xavier was enormous, nearly as big as the massive red dragon that hadn't once taken its eyes off me. Iridescent white scales shimmered against the light of my power. His thick tail flicked with irritation as he moved his body to block me from view.

The red dragon drew itself up, shifting its weight as that fire in its throat grew hotter, a deathly growl getting louder with each second that passed.

"Run, Vale," Xavier roared in my head, not realizing that I *couldn't*.

Then, like the shadow he was, Kian's dark dragon darted forward. Just as big as Xavier, just as vicious, Kian launched himself at the red dragon, barreling his full weight into it.

They rolled, slashing with their great talons, ripping into each other's flesh with their razor-like teeth. The red dragon raked its claws into Kian's side, and I found myself running into the fray instead of out the tunnel and to safety.

"*No*," I screamed, racing for the black dragon that had saved my life, that had pulled me from my own execution, that had given me a chance.

Then Xavier flew forward, his leathery wings knocking into the remaining stalactites, using them as projectiles to fight the red dragon off of Kian.

I gathered my skirts and sprinted for Kian, getting in between him and the giant beast as Xavier fought for our lives. But the great scarlet dragon was too vicious, too big, too fast. Soon, Xavier's gullet was under his claws, squeezing the life out of him.

Power swelled from my skin, and I launched a bolt at the red dragon, spearing his shoulder with an arrow of light. Snarling, it whipped its head back to me, Xavier forgotten, as fire rose in its throat once more.

Holding my hands wide, I roared at it much like I'd done on that mountaintop.

Light bloomed around me, shoving from my skin in a crackling dome that expanded by the second. That dome stretched wide, scorching his scales, forcing him back. Then it closed its mouth as it lowered its body, its massive golden eyes studying me intently as the fire in its throat died.

"You leave them alone. You want to kill me, fine, but you leave them alone."

"No, Vale." Kian's voice rang in my mind, sounding so tired, so hurt, as he crawled closer to me ready to do battle. *"He'll kill you. He kills them all."*

"I don't care," I shot back, accepting my fate. I'd already cheated Orrus more than once in the last twenty-four hours. Maybe it was just my time. But it wouldn't be theirs. "You're not dying for me. If this damn beast wants to kill me, then that's what it'll do."

An almost humanlike frown marred the red dragon's face.

"I do not want to kill you." His voice sounded much like Idris'. That gruff growl so different and so similar, I could see how I'd been confused. *"I guided you here, my Queen."*

That power surrounding me fizzled and died, falling in gossamer ribbons to the ground before fading away completely. "What?"

Its clawed hand shot out, surrounding me as it brought me to its chest, growling as Kian and Xavier rose to their feet.

"You will be my queen. My savior. I only wanted to keep you safe."

"Safe? Are you crazy? You nearly got me tossed down a damn mountain and almost killed my friends. You call that safe? Now put me down, or so help me, I'll figure out how to really hurt you."

A grumble of dissent vibrated its chest as it curved its gigantic neck to stare at me, its golden eyes narrowed.

"Are you threatening me, my Queen?"

"No," I seethed through gritted teeth, my power growing underneath my skin as my anger returned. "I'm warning you."

The faint snapping and cracking of bones drew my gaze to Xavier and Kian. Both naked and bloody, they exchanged a pensive expression I did not like one bit.

"Vale," Xavier called, his chest heaving as he stalked forward. "Are you speaking to that dragon?"

I blinked at him like he was a few turnips shy of a bushel. "Who the fuck else would I be talking to, Xavier? Do you think I'm yelling at this beast for my health?"

"No," he murmured, his voice pitched so low, I almost couldn't hear it. "I want to know if he's speaking to *you*. Inside your head. Like the way King Idris can, the way Kian can."

The way you can, too, dummy. But I didn't say that out loud. "Who do you think led me here? I didn't just stumble upon this place by accident."

Turning back to the dragon in question, I growled, "Put. Me. Down."

The sound rumbling from his throat was almost a purr, his big eyes softening. *"No, I don't think so. I think I like you right where you are. Nice and close and protected."*

His giant nostrils flared as he took in my scent. *"Maybe if you stay with me long enough, you'll lose their scent that's all over you. You should tell them that you're my queen, not theirs."*

Then the giant bastard curled his big body around mine, tucking me into the crook of his middle. Kian and Xavier started forward, but the dragon's spiked tail flicked in the space between us, discouraging their progress.

"For the last time, I am not your *anything*. I'm just here to break a stupid curse. Now, let me go."

He huffed an exasperated breath, almost rolling his big golden eyes. *"You have no idea what you're here for. You'll see, my Queen."*

"It's like talking to a wall," I grumbled, pinching

the bridge of my nose. "Do you have any suggestions on how to get this big lug to release me?"

Naked, bloody, and breathing hard, Kian stared at me for a solid minute before his gaze moved past me as his mouth stretched into a wicked smile. "Remember when Xavier told you that there were trials you would need to pass before you could break the curse?"

I crossed my arms as much as the dragon scales banded around my middle would allow. "Vaguely. Though the jerk hasn't told me what they are," I growled, my eyes narrowed on the strapping man staring at the dragon like he wanted to take a sword to him. "Please tell me I at least get to eat before I die a horrible death. I'd like to go out with a full stomach if you don't mind."

Xavier and Kian straightened, their nudity not even a consideration as a chuckle echoed from behind me. I tensed, but everyone else seemed to relax—even the dragon holding me. My feet touched the ground as his grip loosened, but he didn't exactly let me go.

Then Kian and Xavier dropped to one knee as a dark-headed man came into view, and when he turned to face me, I recognized him instantly. He was missing the crooked crown, but I would know those golden eyes and that sharp jawline anywhere.

Idris.

And still, my brain had not done him justice. Outside of my dreams, he was harder, harsher, more brutal, and also so beautiful it hurt. My heart, which had just begun to slow, picked up speed, fluttering in my chest like a hummingbird's wings. A dark cloak covered his shoulders, a golden pendant swinging in the opening. Its center stone matched the color of his eyes, both illuminated with more magic than I'd ever felt.

"There will be no dying today, my brave one," he murmured, his gaze glowing with a rush of power that I could nearly reach out and touch.

His voice was exactly how he'd sounded in my dream, in my head on the mountain. It was different from the dragon holding me but so similar it was no wonder I'd been tricked down here.

"You've just passed the first trial. Vale, meet Rune. My dragon, the other half of my soul, and my curse."

His *curse*?

And then I understood.

Kian and Xavier's dragon forms were under their flesh, under their skin. I wasn't sure how it worked

because we hadn't discussed it, but the basic funda-
mentals were plain as day.

The other half of my soul.

Idris and Rune were separated, cleaved. And that
was a very bad thing—especially if that had an
effect on all the magic in the kingdom. If magic was
dying, and this was why... My heart thundered in my
chest for a completely different reason.

How would I even begin to fix something like
this?

"I am not his curse," Rune rumbled, letting out a
huff of irritation. *"I am his punishment and his protection. I am his reminder he is only alive because I am
stronger than he is. That I can endure when he cannot."*

I chose not to disclose Rune's words, preferring
to keep my head right where it was. The last thing I
needed was to anger the one person who could help
me get Nyrah back.

"Fantastic," I groused, feeling like more of a
pawn in someone else's game the longer this went
on. "Do you happen to have a tutorial on how to get
him to let me go? He seems rather unwilling at this
point."

*"I am your protection, too, my Queen. It is not safe
up there."*

Personally, I thought anywhere else was a hell of

a lot safer than being held hostage by a giant fire-breathing lizard, but what did I know? He was probably right. Not a single Luxa had survived until now, and my survival was in flux at best. There was probably more than one cause of death around here just lurking in the shadows.

"I suggest you simply ask nicely," Idris offered, his smile both incredibly sexy and the most irritating thing I think I'd ever seen. "Rune doesn't often like being told what to do."

Simply ask him. I fought off the urge to roll my eyes. Though, it couldn't hurt to give it a shot. "Rune? Will you please let me go?"

Did I say that with gritted teeth and a death glare? Yes, I did.

Did the giant lizard seem to almost smirk at me in an almost exact replica of his human's expression? Also, yes.

"If I am forced to let you go, you must stick with the dragons. They'll look out for you. Do not stray too far from them, my Queen." Then Rune slowly loosened his grip, his talon-tipped hand falling away as his head bumped into my side. *"Remember what I said. Do not stray."*

First, he wanted their scent off of me, then he wanted me to stick with them. Which one was it?

Idris moved close to me, offering his hand as I minced over the end of Rune's tail. "See?" he said, his grin now a forced mask seeming to hide what he was really thinking. "He isn't as tough as he pretends to be."

Tell that to the dead Luxa, I thought, wondering if the giant dragon had gobbled them up for supper. I also wondered if anyone thought their sacrifices were worth it. If they were honored or forgotten, nameless women off to meet Orrus just like so many miners under the mountain.

At my tight expression, Idris' mask fell away. "To you. He will not be tough to you. Rune doesn't like anyone, but he's curled around you like a protector. That, my brave one, is just as rare as you are."

Somehow, it didn't make me feel any better.

I tossed a glance over my shoulder as I pulled my elbow from the king's grip. Kian and Xavier weren't looking at me. They were staring at the ground, and I hated it more than I could say. I wanted their eyes, and they weren't giving them to me.

It pissed me off. My hand tightened on the hilt of the dagger that was still somehow in my hand before I yanked up my skirt to slam it into the sheath at my thigh.

"I want to know why I'm here—and don't say

to break a curse because I already know that. What trials am I facing? What is expected of me? What am I getting out of this? I didn't survive a near execution to just get tied to the stake again. So please understand, if I don't like what you say, I will walk right back out that tunnel and disappear."

I had half a mind to do that, anyway. If facing down the dragon was the first trial, storming the guild would likely be a fuck of a lot easier.

Idris' mouth quirked up, something like pride in his assessing gaze. "The trials are secret, set that way to test the meddle of every Luxa vying to break the curse."

If that wasn't the dumbest thing I'd ever heard. I hadn't wanted the magic beneath my skin, and I sure as hell hadn't been vying for anything. I'd never been a volunteer. I'd been taken.

"You'd think after two centuries of utter failure, you'd bend that rule. Were you just going to toss me down here, and what? Hope Rune didn't eat me?"

Idris' eyes flared with power, his jaw set. "Something like that."

Unwanted betrayal hit me square in the chest. I shuffled backward toward the men I knew were a hell of a lot safer than the one before me. It wasn't until I felt the heat of their bodies pressing against my back, did I stop.

"And after so long without success, you thought there wasn't a better way? What's next? Tossing me off a cliff? Setting me on fire?"

Kian's arm banded around my middle as Xavier twined his fingers with mine. Rune took that opportunity to move his big body behind us, drawing up to his full height, surrounding the three of us in the space between his forelegs as he let out a growl that shook the very foundations of the castle. Their presence—their breath, their warmth—was a reassurance I needed more than anything.

"You want—no, you *need*—my help, and you show your thanks by trying to feed me to a fucking dragon? And I'm supposed to trust you enough for that sacrifice?"

Idris' gaze left mine to stare at the arm around my waist, the hand in mine. Then his golden eyes moved to glare at his dragon, *his curse*, before falling to me. His mask of geniality was long gone. Now all that was there was the searing truth.

"The trials are bound by secrecy because the curse that has plagued me for centuries demands it," he growled, moving closer to me as if I were a frightened animal that he was trying to trap rather than the woman with three dragons at her back. "If I could do it another way, I would. But this kingdom —this court—honors every sacrifice. We are not the *Perder Lucem*, Vale. We actually acknowledge our dead."

A tremble of fear nearly broke my composure. I hadn't so much as whispered about my grievances for the dead witches who came before me. The only time I'd said anything to that effect was in my thoughts.

I had to remember he was inside my head. None of my thoughts were safe—not from him.

"I didn't say anything about honoring the dead, *Your Majesty*. I merely expressed my displeasure about potentially being one of them. And still, you have yet to answer any of my questions, so I'll simplify my query down to just the one. What's in it for me?"

Because other than ensuring Nyrah never had to walk this path, the benefits weren't obvious.

Idris nodded as his eyes and pendant glowed brighter, hotter, rising with a power that seemed to race over my skin. "When you break this curse—and I do mean *when*—there is not a thing I won't give you. For as long as I'm breathing, all you will have to do is ask. Money, jewels, status. It will all be yours."

My chuckle was mirthless. "You know I don't want any of that."

A single finger lifted my chin as he brought his face to mine. "And that, my brave one," he whispered, his tone just as threatening as it was seductive, "is exactly why Rune didn't kill you instantly."

Then his grip closed over my elbow, light but firm as if it was a shackle I couldn't break.

Rune was right.

It wasn't safe up there.

Not at all.

I'd never been so pissed off and turned on at the same time.

The woman on my left barely looked at me as we traversed the nearly pitch-black caverns underneath the castle. Her jaw set, her mind buzzed like a hive of bees, her racing thoughts needling my brain. I couldn't hear all her thoughts, just the ones too loud for me to ignore, but it was safe to say my first in-person impression was not the best.

Vale did not give a single fuck that I was a king, didn't care that I had ruled a kingdom for longer than she'd been alive, that I had more magic under my skin than my body could contain alone.

She still thought I was scum, and honestly, I couldn't blame her.

In two hundred years, I had been helpless to watch as witch after witch died trying to break the curse that poisoned all of the magic in Credour. The same curse that hamstrung the dragons as a whole, that siphoned power from witches and vampires alike, that crushed shifters under its power.

It was my fault the curse was even a reality.

But under all my guilt, I seethed. White-hot jealousy raged under my genial smile and carefully crafted façade. Vale was supposed to be mine, and yet, it made perfect sense as far as curses went. The one woman who spoke to my soul, who was brave and smart and beautiful, wanted absolutely nothing to do with me and everything to do with the two men I counted as brothers.

Fighting over a woman was what got me cursed in the first place. Damn if it wasn't a bitter pill to swallow watching history repeat itself.

And still, I could not get the images of her running full tilt into a dragon fight out of my head. Zero hesitation, she just raced into the fray, not realizing that she would be as good as dead should Rune decide it was so. And then she stood in front of my men, protecting them with her magic, putting herself in harm's way to save their lives.

Never—not once—had a single Luxa earned the

respect and favor of Rune, had him defend her as if she were precious. Other than a handful of witches, very few even survived Rune at all.

She was unlike any before her, but if I couldn't convince her to give a shit about helping me, we would be dead in the water. Hell, I couldn't even unclench my own jaw long enough to tell her not to worry about the council members we were set to meet or the mob outside the castle gates.

Maybe it was better not to lie to her.

There were still two more trials for her to overcome, and yet, the most perilous thing she would face would be the council we were hiking toward. Then again, with the way she put me in my place, the poor saps would likely either fall in love with her or plot her doom.

Unlike any other Luxa before her, Vale didn't so much as take my hand as she hiked up the winding path toward the castle proper, her only moment of pause at the staircase. She swallowed hard as she stared at it for a second, but it wasn't I who was able to comfort her.

No, it was Kian, twisting the knife in my chest as he moved past me to get to her. He'd been my friend, my confidant, my right hand for centuries, and yet, she had so easily drawn him away with her light.

Frozen, I watched them climb, unable to understand how everything had gone so wrong so quickly.

"She's afraid of heights," Xavier whispered under his breath, remaining at my side.

That was definitely a problem, but not one I could think about right now. I was still pissed off Kian was walking with her, holding her hand, naked as the day he was born, without a shred of shame. Well, and the fact Vale hadn't so much as blushed at his nudity.

Growling, I weaved a pair of pants onto both of them from thin air, hiding their bodies from her gaze—not that she was looking. Her eyes were forward, her spine straight, her face blank, even though the scent of fear wafted from her very pores. The staircase was old, of course—everything in the castle was—but it was sturdy enough to hold us all, and the thick stone banister protected her from falling.

I had an inkling of what she had gone through and what kind of life she might have lived with the *Perder Lucem*, but the amount of steel in her spine astounded even me.

"Why?" I hissed, the word barely leaving my lips. Rune loved her, Kian and Xavier were licking her heels, I was half in awe of her. What did she have to fear?

"People fall, Sire. Her friends, her parents, perfect strangers. And under the mountain, she has been forced to watch as they die. And then life moves on as if their deaths meant nothing. Over and over again. Every day."

Kian and Vale continued on, but I didn't move an inch. "She told you this?"

Xavier didn't so much as look at me, his icy blue eyes so full of longing pinned on the woman walking away from us. He shook his head. "I healed her from the brink of death. That much magic passing between us? I likely saw more than she wanted me to."

No wonder she hated me. She saw me as a monster who let witches die for two centuries with no end in sight. And no wonder Kian and Xavier were half in love with her already. The way they were raised? They likely saw themselves in her.

"Anything else I should know?"

His gaze hardened as he actually met my eyes, something Xavier usually avoided at all costs. The resolve in his expression reminded me why I'd chosen him as my hand all those years ago.

"I will not watch her die. Do you understand? Neither of us will."

It was a threat and a promise all rolled into one, and I couldn't decide if I was proud, jealous, or pissed the fuck off. I figured it was a mix of all three.

"So noted."

The scent of fear wafting from Vale didn't dissipate until we reached the castle proper. Her heart was beating faster than a hummingbird's, but she didn't seem winded in the slightest. If it weren't for the death grip she had on Kian's fingers, I wouldn't have that first clue she was a hairsbreadth away from losing her mind.

I couldn't send her into the lion's den like that.

"You two, go get dressed. I'll prep her for the council."

My most trusted advisers, my closest friends in the world, stared at me like they were considering telling me no. Vale seemed to pick up on the tension because, just like she had with Rune, she stood in between them and certain danger.

"It's fine. I'd like to know what I'm walking into."

After a tense moment, the pair of them nodded and took off to actually put on real clothes to replace the illusions I'd conjured for them. I took that slight reprieve to survey her comportment, something the council would try to pick apart at the first sign of weakness.

Her spine was ramrod straight, the corset under her gown likely helping in that regard. The dark color of the fabric hid any filth from the caverns, and other than the drop of blood at her sleeve where she'd cut herself, she was the picture of perfection.

Then again, I was biased.

Gently, I took her elbow, guiding her to a small alcove where we could talk alone. She stared at my hand on her sleeve as if she would enjoy burning it off, but I didn't let her go until she was where I wanted her.

"Let me guess," she hissed, crossing her arms, "I'm about to walk into a room where I'm going to be picked apart by a group of old men who know nothing about me. Is that about the gist of it?"

The laugh that rumbled from my chest was just as foreign as it was welcome. I couldn't recall the last time I'd laughed, but it made sense that she was the one to do it. "You have it exactly right. There are twelve members of my council from all of the separate factions still remaining in the kingdom. They will ask you questions about your lineage, your abilities, and when your power is manifested."

She rose a single eyebrow that said, "That's it?" all on its own. "Those should be easy enough to answer. Why do you think I need to be prepped, then?"

"Because they are ancient and believe in the old ways of doing things. They will inspect your deportment, you're bearing, and judge you based on it."

Those gorgeous green eyes rolled as she shook her head. "This should be interesting. Any tips and tricks you want to share?"

Every other Luxa had come from money, from powerful families, from social climbers with less status than they wanted. Vale, coming from the heart of our enemy, was none of those things.

"You don't need my advice, Vale," I murmured, moving closer to her, wanting those beautiful eyes on me. "It doesn't matter what they think. It doesn't matter what anyone thinks. The only thing that matters is whether or not I believe you can break the curse, and I know you can."

Then she gave them to me, looking into my eyes for the first time since we got up here. "Then why do I have to meet them at all? Why shove me in front of some old fogies whose opinion means fuck all?"

"Because, unfortunately, this is the way it's always been done. If I want to keep the peace, it's the only way forward. Considering the mob outside my castle walls, you know more than anyone how incredibly fragile it is."

Her heart thundered so hard I could almost feel it in my own chest. "So if I go in there and they hate me on sight, what does that do for you?"

This was why Kian and Xavier were already in her pocket—had to be.

"Absolutely nothing. I'm not in charge of who Fate decides to show to me no more than they are in charge of who Fate decides should break this curse. I just have to show up and do my job the same as you."

Somehow, her spine got straighter. "Fair enough."

"I trust that if you can survive the guild, you can survive these assholes just fine."

She huffed as she shook her head. "I don't know why you sent Kian and Xavier away. You could have just as easily said what you needed to in front of them."

"Other than they needed clothes, you mean? Because I'm inherently selfish," I murmured, taking in her scent that was only slightly tainted by theirs. "In all of the futures I ever saw for myself, I never once considered that I might have to share. I find I don't like it much."

Those gorgeous green eyes flashed with ire, sweetening her scent to the point I was nearly mindless. "I am not a toy to be fought over or a prize to be won. I am only here to do a job, and that is all I am here to do."

Oh, how fun it will be to change her mind.

"Why come here at all, then?" I asked, stalking forward as she backed away, the wall halting her progress far earlier than she wanted it to. "Why allow them to bring you here?"

That question had been burning me up for an hour. If she hated me that much, if she didn't want anything to do with me, why allow herself to be taken?

"You're the one who can read my mind. You tell me."

My gaze dropped to those full lips. Oh, how I wanted to see if they tasted as sweet as they looked. But she didn't want me—of that, she'd made herself perfectly clear.

"I can't read your mind all the time. It's only when you're screaming at me that I can hear your thoughts. Once upon a time, that was considered a blessing. I'm guessing you'd consider it the opposite."

Her shoulder lifted in a gentle shrug. "I don't know. Hearing your voice on the mountaintop kept me alive," she admitted, her begrudging tone just as enticing as her scent. "Maybe it's not so bad."

I couldn't help it, I lifted her chin with a single finger, meeting those eyes. "And here I thought you hated me."

They narrowed to slits as the perfume of need wafted into my nose. She might dislike me, but she didn't hate me—not completely.

"Who says I don't?"

"Your scent does. But don't worry, I won't tell anyone."

At the sound of footsteps, I stepped back, allowing her to have her space before we walked into the throne room, only for the council members to fuck it all up.

"Your family name," Dorian demanded, sitting back in his seat as he surveyed Vale with a curled lip. He hated witches on sight, so getting his approval would be an impossible task—half the reason I hadn't told her just how hostile this meeting would be.

Vale's ire—her rage—made her far more formidable than she thought. And just like I expected her to, she latched that penetrating stare onto the vampire and took him to task.

"Tenebris. Though, I don't know what good that information will be to you, considering you've hated me since I walked in that door. Well, that, and the fact just about everyone in my family is dead."

Kian tried to cover his snort of laughter, but Dorian still heard him, removing his hateful stare from Vale.

"Tenebris is an older line but still just as formidable," Fenwick remarked, his ancient, crooked frame leaning forward in his seat. "We thought your family died out. Glad to see the scrolls were wrong. Do you recall how your family passed, child? I do hate incomplete records."

Vale appeared stricken for a second at the blatant—if unintentional—disrespect before she firmed her jaw. "If the guild leader of the *Perder Lucem* is to be believed, dragons chased them off a mountaintop, and they fell to their deaths rather than get cooked by dragon fire."

That had me sitting up. Not one memory I'd gleaned from her told me she blamed dragons for her parents' deaths. But it did explain why she wanted nothing to do with this kingdom. I wondered what other lies Arden poisoned her mind with.

"Though," she continued as light flickered from the healing cut on her wrist, "considering Arden also stabbed me and tied me to a stake to be burnt alive, it's completely possible he was lying. Sorry I can't complete your records for you."

The ancient mage was considered the head maester of the records and likely didn't catch her sarcasm, but Dorian did. And like the vampire he was, as soon as he smelled blood, he was as vicious as a shark.

"What makes you think you can break this curse, girl?"

The look she gave him could have melted iron. "I did help take out a whole conclave while covered in *Lumentium*, so I might be able to handle it. Or," she offered, holding up a finger, "it could be the dragon under your castle that really likes me. Other than that? Not much."

Her slow, sinister smile was a thing of beauty, but watching the council lose their minds? Fucking priceless.

"You've already passed the first trial?" Dorian scoffed, his sneer out in full force as he stood from his seat. "With no witnesses? And we're supposed to believe the word of a lying guild snake?"

Of course Dorian would be the problem.

"Who said she didn't have witnesses?" I asked, shutting him down before he fucked up and said something he couldn't take back. "I observed the trial personally." My words were laced with the power I so rarely set free as I waited for Dorian to try to impugn my honor.

"B-but how? When?" Dorian sputtered, the council buzzing around him with obvious affront.

This wasn't protocol, but nothing about Vale followed the rules.

"If you want," Vale offered, "we can walk on down to the caverns, and you can watch Rune curl around me like a kitten. But honestly, that staircase is a bit much if you ask me."

Another snort to my right reminded me that this had gone on long enough, but Vale wasn't done.

"Before you call me a liar again, remember that I didn't ask to be here. I personally don't give a single fuck what any of you think about me. My goal is to break the curse and move on with my life. If you want to stand in the way of that, fine. But remember, I've been living for years in the heart of a guild that would have killed me at the first hint of magic, and I survived."

Power bloomed from the healing cut on her wrist, her light so bright, it had Dorian, along with the rest of the council, shielding their eyes. It expanded in a dome around her, the magic growing until it swallowed myself, my throne, as well as Kian and Xavier. The walls of it crackled with blistering heat, and this was without even a hint of training.

What would she be able to do when she was at her full strength?

"If you're trying to scare me, you're doing a poor job of it," she hissed, her voice throaty with the threads of her power. "I've been keeping my magic under wraps for five years just to stay breathing. If you think a sneer and a bad attitude are going to intimidate me, I hate to break it to you, but you're going to have to step up your game, sweetheart."

Then, she dropped her magic just as quickly as she wielded it and winked at Dorian. Gods be damned, she was fucking magnificent.

"Vale has passed the first trial," I thundered, drawing the attention of the room back to the matter at hand. "She will reside here to hone her magic until I deem her ready for the next trial. And any disrespect to her will be considered as a slight against me. Is that clear?"

The chorus of "Yes, Your Majesty" was music to my ears.

"Then you are dismissed. Leave us."

It was only when the double doors closed, did Vale stumble. Before I could catch her, Kian was across the room, his speed one of the reasons he had always been my fiercest general.

He guided Vale to an empty chair, his expression darkening at the blood dripping from her nose.

"She's using too much magic," Xavier murmured, echoing my thoughts.

We'd seen this before, Luxa burning out before the trials could be completed, and it sent a spike of fear right through the center of my chest.

"Then you'll have to teach her how to use it properly," I hissed, fighting the urge to sweep her up and take her to the very healers who'd just stood there and called her a liar.

The only way she would survive any of this was if she could defend herself.

And the person teaching her couldn't be me.

My jealousy was about to bite me in the ass.

Despite the stares, I was in heaven.

Tearing into the roast boar with my teeth, I practically danced in my chair as the savory flavor exploded on my tongue. It was tender and juicy and unlike anything I'd ever tasted. I couldn't recall the last time I'd had fresh meat—if ever—and the experience was nearly as good as the orgasms Kian and Xavier had given me. My table manners may be atrocious, and I could make myself sick later from the sheer gluttony, but I would take focusing on the food over the matter I was purposefully ignoring any day.

Swallowing, I let out a quiet moan of pleasure before reaching for the candied carrots with a spicy honey sauce. I'd already sampled it, and the dish was absolutely divine. There were leafy greens and thick rolls, creamy sauces and roasted duck, fruits and pies and cheeses. Kian and Xavier had pointed out all the dishes, the sprawling feast meant just for me.

I wanted to try everything, and if I happened to burst at the seams, then so be it. The starving girl in me worried that so much abundance would go to waste, but I'd been assured that whatever I didn't finish, they would.

That said, both Kian's and Xavier's gazes had the potential to sear a pit in my cheek. Idris was wearing a hole in the plush rug in front of the wide windows of his *solar—whatever the hell that was*—and I did not care one bit. The only bit of pause I had was the redheaded woman sitting across from me, cleaning her nails with an impossibly sharp dagger.

Well, that and the dragon in my head, splitting my skull with his complaints about using too much magic.

"Do you think you're the first Luxa to burn out before you could even attempt to free us from the curse? How could you be so reckless? I thought you were smarter than this."

This refrain had been going on for about thirty minutes, and so far, I'd successfully ignored the dragon, the men, and the woman in my midst as I ate my fill. Okay, so it was tough to ignore Freya, but I was doing my best. The vampire had been introduced while I'd still been bloody, and while she hadn't lunged for my throat, I hadn't lowered my guard.

As soon as the blood left my nose, everyone acted like I was an inch away from death. Kian—of all people—treated me like I was spun glass, ready to break at any second. Xavier seemed to be analyzing me, eyeing me like I might explode at any second, and Idris...

Whatever magic he had, it was vast and volatile, reacting to his emotions in a way which had the entire castle shaking on its foundations. He only calmed slightly when Freya entered the throne room, a single look from her shining blue eyes quelling the worst of the earthquakes.

Those eyes were steadily trained on her manicure, not sparing me even the slightest hint of attention, and honestly, I preferred it that way. When they were trained on me, it was worse than the dragon vibrating my skull.

How was I supposed to know I could burn out? Yesterday, I'd fought an entire conclave of mages and mostly won. Today, I could barely pull off a stupid light show without bleeding and nearly passing out. Not only did it not make sense, but it made me think I was getting weaker, not stronger.

Was I worried about how the magic had affected me in the throne room? Absolutely. If I were to voice that, though, everyone would lose their minds. Again. It was bad enough that Kian and Xavier were hovering around me like bees, waiting for me to faint or something.

I'd messed up. In trying to prove a point to an asshole, I'd overdone it. I had to remember that a day ago, I was near death on a mountaintop. I wasn't completely healed from that yet, nor was I free of the magic-stealing ore that was probably still poisoning me at that very moment. I needed to remember that I'd been suppressing my magic for so long that letting it off its leash was *not* the best idea I could have had.

Before I could sample the gooseberry tart, I lost what was left of my patience. "Could you stop staring at me like I'm going to fall out of this chair at any second?" I growled, slicing the fork into the fruit tart and taking a bite. The soft, pillowy texture of the cream, mixed with the tangy bite of the fruit, exploded on my tongue, and my eyes rolled back into my head.

If this was how they ate all the time, it was no wonder they were so tall and broad.

"I don't know, *are you* going to fall out of the chair?" Kian growled, crossing his arms over his chest. "You were bleeding just from using magic, Vale."

As he'd said. Twenty damn times already. But at least he was treating me less like spun glass and more like he did yesterday. I'd take Asshole Kian over the worried one.

"Don't forget the fainting," Xavier grumbled, sitting back in his seat, his frown carved into his forehead.

This time, I did not fight off the urge to roll my eyes. "I did no such thing, but even if I had, why is that such a fucking surprise to you? Of course I *almost* fainted. Do you think the guild kept us fed and happy while we mined *Lumentium* for them?"

I shoved the tart away, so irritated, so scrutinized, so fed up, it was tough to keep a hold of the waning power beneath my skin. "Do you think they gave a shit about us at all? They didn't care if we died so long as the quotas were met. I have been starving for years, mining day in and day out with barely any food or water, just trying to survive.

Suppressing my magic, hiding in plain sight, stealing when I could. My. Whole. Life."

And that didn't even count the times I'd taken punishment for Nyrah or dealing with becoming her only parent while mourning my own, or trying to keep not only me but her alive, too.

The silence in the room was so loud, it grated against my skin.

"Of course my nose got bloody. Of course I nearly lost hold of my power. In case it was unclear to you, unless it's shoving it down so far no one can see it, I have no idea what I'm doing when it comes to magic."

Out of spite, I snatched the tart back and stuffed another bite in my mouth, trying not to remind the room at large that I'd almost died yesterday. And today. And likely would tomorrow because that was just my luck.

My gaze strayed to Idris, who had stopped his pacing to really look at me. His scrutiny was worse than Kian and Xavier combined because his stricken expression told me just how fucked he thought we all were.

His confidence in me was super uplifting.

And he'd thought I was some prize to be won. He

had no idea when he'd crowed my praises what he was getting into, now, did he?

"I'm sorry, my Queen. I forget you are nothing like the witches that came before you."

No, I wasn't, but I was tired of hearing it all the damn time. I was just a girl who'd grown up too fast in a world she knew nothing about. I was out of my depth, and if I didn't get myself together, Nyrah would end up paying the price.

If she hasn't already.

That insidious thought punched a hole in my chest as the doubt and fear crawled in to make a home there. While I'd been filling my belly with food, she was out there somewhere. And I hadn't so much as told anyone other than Kian and Xavier about her because I didn't know if I could trust them. If they wanted to hold something over me, it would be all too easy to use her as a bargaining chip.

And still, I worried every single second I was apart from her that she was starving or cold or...

Fuck.

Tears burned in my eyes, and I fought off the urge to run—fast and far so no one would see just how scared I was. Just how much I didn't know. I'd understood that it was important for the council to see me as formidable, but I'd been reckless. I knew that. I just didn't know how to fix it.

"So that is why you're doing this. You have a family," Rune's said, his tone so much softer now. *"A child. You do not want money or power. You want safety for your sister."*

Then, a thread of warmth filled my middle that had nothing to do with the food. My breaths came easier, my joints hurt less, my aches—even the ones I'd forgotten about—melted away.

"A gift, my Queen, but only temporary. Do not get used to it."

But it wasn't just the lack of pain that had changed. The light was brighter, sharper, the sounds louder, the scents...

And still, with whatever help Rune had given me, I felt their eyes pinning me to the chair. That power I'd been holding down? Well, now that it had been freed, it wanted to leak from my very pores all the time, and Rune's gift didn't help that problem at all.

I stood, backing away from the table as the meal turned to lead in my belly. How could I break a stupid curse if I couldn't even handle a single meal without losing my hold on my magic?

Xavier captured my fingers, threading them with his. "I'll teach you how to use it so it doesn't blow back on you. But tomorrow."

He brought my hand to his lips, and instantly, my thundering heart calmed. "Freya will show you around. Maybe then you can get some rest. We can start on the hard stuff later."

That's when I understood Xavier was giving me an out—letting me get out of this room before I lost my cool any more than I already had.

"I thought I told you to stick with the dragons," Rune warned, his voice vibrating through my skull.

But I needed to get out of this room, so I ignored him in favor of walking out the large double doors.

Freya easily caught up with me, appearing at my side in an instant. One second, I was by myself in the cavernous stone hallway, with its wide curved windows and delicate artifacts carefully spaced between the columns, and the next, her leather-clad body seemed to appear out of thin air.

I fought off the urge to jump. I had a feeling it would bring her far too much satisfaction. Luckily, her trusty dagger was nowhere in sight.

"Do you have any idea where you're going?" she asked, her bored tone telling me far more than I wanted to know.

She didn't want to be my shadow any more than I wanted her to be. So happy I could ruin someone else's day. I was on a roll.

"Absolutely not, but that room was stifling, and I needed an exit. I'd be happy to take any direction you have, though."

Freya stopped dead in her tracks. "I keep forgetting you are nothing like the snooty women who came before you."

"You mean the dead women?"

Freya gave me a blasé shrug. "We all die, Vale. It's just a matter of when and how. The witches who came before you came from auspicious means, vying for status or money or power. Which is likely why they never made it past the dragon under the castle."

"That's what Idris said. He said that Rune would have eaten me."

"Or burned you alive. It's really a toss-up if he's hungry or not whether he'll gobble you whole."

"If you are looking to inspire confidence in my current abilities, you are doing a shit job of it. Yes, I am aware I am very different from the incredibly cultured women who have come before me. And while I'm still alive and they're obviously dead, speaking ill of them just seems tactless. I've seen enough people die under the mountain to say that very rarely do we deserve the death we get."

"Are you going to be one of those pious, death-god-following witches?"

I thought about what kind of piety my night with Kian and Xavier qualified for. According to the guild, allowing magic-wielders to "defile me" was akin to giving the gods the middle finger. The joke was on them. I hated the gods more than they likely hated me.

"I curse Orrus on a daily basis, so I doubt it."

Freya snorted, her hand landing on the hilt of the sword at her hip. It had an ornate handle inlaid with gold and carved with runes in a language I didn't know. It was as long as her legs, and considering she was nearly a foot taller than me, that said a lot. She could take out whole armies with that sword and probably not blink an eye.

"I think I'm going to like you. How do you feel about books, little witch?"

I hadn't spent too much time with them under the mountain. The guild wasn't as fond of teaching people as they were far more interested in how much *Lumentium* they could mine. The only book I'd ever read involved my inherent doom, but Freya had piqued my interest.

"Books are nice. I haven't been around them much, but I do know how to read. My mother made sure I learned."

A frown pulled at her brow before she shook herself. "Right. Come with me. I'll show you more books than you can shake a stick at. Maybe one of the maesters will let you take a few of them."

Eyes wide at the prospect of reading something that didn't involve me ending the world, I readily followed her. The trip to the library had been a hike across the castle, but as soon as she opened the giant double doors, I was in love. Rows upon rows of books filled the cavernous room, the stained-glass ceiling letting in dappled light, casting the floor in its multicolored hues.

Books were lovingly placed on shelves that seemed to be stacked to the ceiling with little catwalks in front of each of them, all equipped with rolling ladders to get to the highest of shelves. I wouldn't be climbing any ladder, and those catwalks made me want to puke, but there were so many to choose from, I could have my feet planted on the firm ground and never run out of books to read.

I almost wished Kian or Xavier were with me just so I could hold one of their hands, pulling them from book to book and shelf to shelf. A quiet, sinister part of me also might have wished for Idris to be with me, too. I couldn't say I hated him exactly. The dashing, demanding man in my dream, the one who had encouraged me on the mountaintop, the one who'd had sworn revenge on my behalf, was harder to see in the light of day.

I wondered if the reality would ever live up to the dream and which one was the real him. I also wondered if I'd ever find out.

Much to the chagrin of the ancient maesters, I spent hours in the library, the calming environment easing my nerves. It only took a single eyebrow raise from Freya for the stingy one at the front desk to let me borrow one of the smaller tomes.

I'd picked it up at Freya's recommendation and fell in love with the writing. The story—as far as I understood it—was about an ancient pair of brothers in love with the same woman. Their love and jealousy spawned a war, and I really wanted to know how it ended.

By the time the sun fell in the sky, Freya had shown me around the castle a bit and directed me to what she called "my quarters." By that, she meant a section of several gigantic rooms in a tucked-away wing.

The ornately carved wooden doors led into a wide antechamber lit by warm magic lanterns that flickered and danced. The first space off the corridor was a lushly furnished receiving room with plush chairs and couches clad in fabric that seemed too nice to sit on. On the wall behind the largest couch was a painting of a dragon mid-flight, its blood-red wings flared wide.

Freya then pointed out a private dining room, the table already laid out with more food than I'd had in a year under the mountain. But the table was only set for one. I tried to ignore the faint ache in my chest at the thought of eating alone—of existing in this space alone. While Freya had endured my company all day, I could tell she'd rather be anywhere but showing me around.

The next space was a dressing room filled with wardrobes, bursting with exquisite gowns and leathers alike, jeweled hair combs and necklaces. Seeing all of it laid out and shining in the magical lanterns had me wondering if these items had been chosen for me or if they had belonged to every poor witch coming to break the curse.

And how ungrateful was I for wanting to know the answer to that question?

The nicest thing I'd ever worn was the dress I

was in. A day ago, I was in filthy, bloody rags, shivering in the snow in bare feet. I should be kissing Idris' boots for providing for me, and yet, I was horrified.

Were these rooms where every Luxa went if they survived the first trial? Was I surrounded by their failure, their greed, their avarice?

I tried to keep my thoughts off my face, but Freya could see through my mask, answering my thoughts as if she could hear them.

"No, every Luxa does not sleep here," she said, her sardonic chiding easing my nerves. "This space used to be for the dowager queen before Idris took the throne."

My fingers twisted together behind my back, a nervous habit I couldn't seem to break. "I didn't say anything."

Freya snorted. "Your lips might not have, but your face did. Granted, you're better at keeping your thoughts to yourself than most people, but your scent of revulsion did you no favors. Couple that with the grip you've got on your fingers, and that stoney expression you've got makes a hell of a lot more sense."

Swallowing hard, my lips pursed in chagrin. "I don't want to be ungrateful. It's just..."

"You don't want to wear a dead woman's clothes? I don't blame you. But don't worry. Idris made sure this room was stocked with all the latest fashions. The staff picked half the shops in town bare preparing for you."

"Oh," I whispered, wide-eyed, staring at the jeweled gowns and silks, each individual piece selected just for me. "That's... very kind."

Was it wrong that just the thought of someone doing all this for me made me want to vomit?

"Come on. Let me finish showing you around."

By the time she was done, she'd shown me the bedchamber, the bathing room, and a balcony solarium that overlooked the dark castle grounds. The sun had long since set, and the too-quick winter darkness had enveloped the world. All too soon, I was alone in the too-big space, wondering what to do with myself.

As much as I appreciated the opulence, a part of me missed Kian and Xavier. But more? I wished Nyrah was here to see all of this. There hadn't been a night I'd slept alone in my life, not a meal I'd eaten without someone with me. Nyrah had been my shadow for six years, but before then, it had been my whole family.

I used the book as a distraction and ate the still-warm food, filling my belly. Then I peeled out of the heavy dress and took a bath in the giant porcelain tub that dominated the bathing chamber. When I had nothing to keep me busy, the hurt set in, burning an aching hole in my chest. I gave up and went to bed, the silky bedlinens incredibly soft and oh, so grating at the same time.

Swallowing my tears, I curled under the covers, hiding in the darkness as I tried not to break down. I was safe and warm in a plush bed, and yet, I was the saddest I'd been since my parents passed.

"You're never really alone, my Queen," Rune murmured in my head, his soft rumble of a voice a comfort I didn't think I'd need but appreciated all the same. *"But I understand. It has been lonely here with no one to talk to."*

Startled, I tossed back the covers, sitting up as if I could look him in his golden eyes when he was floors below me.

"You've been alone all this time?" I thought, wondering if he could hear me. Then again, he could likely hear everything rolling around my head, the snoop.

"I'm not a snoop. You are simply bound to me. Just like I am bound to Idris. I can't tell you how long I've

been alone. Centuries with no one to talk to, no one to listen, forced to watch the other half of my soul find witch after witch with no business being in the castle."

Bound to him? What the hell did that mean? *"But can't you talk to Idris? He's the other half of your soul, right?"*

Rune let out a huff that could have been a dragon snort for all I knew. The derision, however, was noted.

"Other than forcing a few dreams here and there to tell him how stupid he is? No. The curse severed us. Splintering our bond. He knows part of the equation to fix it involves a Luxa, but the rest is a mystery to him. You, my Queen, are one part—the only Luxa to hear me."

It hurt my heart to think of his loneliness, of his silenced voice, of his isolation from everyone and everything, stuck under a castle with no one.

"Then talk to me, Rune. Say whatever you want to. It will help me fall asleep. I've never slept by myself before."

So, Rune talked, telling me about the history of this kingdom and of tales of Idris when he was a boy when their souls were still together. He talked until my eyelids grew heavy, and I settled into the pillows, drawing the blankets up to my nose as his soothing voice lulled me to sleep.

It wasn't until the searing heat of a blade sliced into my shoulder, did I remember Rune's warning.

The castle wasn't safe.

And I was about to find out exactly why.

CHAPTER 16
VALE

The light of the moon glinted off the silver blade poised to strike, the tip coated in the thick scarlet of my blood. Time seemed to slow to a crawl as a single drop splashed onto the pale coverlet, the fabric soaking up the blood like it was starved for it.

"*Run,*" Rune shouted inside my head, his voice so much fainter than it had been before. "*Run before I lose hold of him.*"

But I was nearly frozen, too. The shock of someone being here, of someone attacking me in the one place I'd thought I was safe, muddling my head. Or maybe it was what I'd been stabbed with. My blood sizzled and popped on the raised dagger as time seemed to slow to a crawl.

Lumentium.

The blade was poison, and I'd already been wounded. It was nothing like the rocks I'd used to hold, letting them gouge my palms to hold my power in. I could barely breathe through the pain as the shock and agony stole my senses. And yet, despite the magic-killing effects of the metal, I still felt power rise in the air, bombarding my senses as my brain finally caught up.

My left arm was useless, but I managed to roll away, the covers tangling around my legs as I fell out of the bed. Then I understood. Rune was doing this, keeping my attacker still so I could run, and he was using magic to do it.

Landing in a heap on the freezing floor, I scrambled to standing, but my limbs were sluggish and slow, my thoughts fuzzy.

My attacker was shrouded in shadow, his head hidden by a black cloak. Thick gloves encased his hands, likely why he could wield the blade at all. So many in Festia were magic-born, and that blade could and should hurt him just like it was hurting me.

"I'm losing my hold on him, my Queen. You have to run."

But I didn't know where I was supposed to run

or what would happen if I didn't run fast enough. I tried calling on the power that rested underneath my skin, drawing on the gifts I'd been given by Rune as well.

As soon as Rune's power failed, he would come after me. I needed to fight—to hurt him before he hurt me.

Didn't I?

"No, my Queen. You have to run. Get to the dragons. They can protect you."

A fat lot of good they'd be, considering I had no idea where they were. Still, I took his advice, racing for the door of the bedchamber like my life depended on it.

The magic in the room seemed to snap against my skin, and the world sped up. My feet were no longer stuck in molasses, which I couldn't help but think was a very bad thing. Before I could get to the door, a hand closed over my injured shoulder, bringing me to my knees. He pressed his thumb into the gaping hole of my wound, and white-hot agony raced down my spine. A strangled scream wrenched from my throat, and I kicked out, connecting with his knee. The squelch of the joint dislocating was music to my ears as hot tears raced down my cheeks.

"Get up. You have to get up, my Queen."

Couldn't he tell I was trying?

Blood poured from the cut, soaking my night-gown, dripping down my arm, and I slipped in the puddle it made. Gasping, I managed to crawl forward before climbing to my feet. The door to the bedchamber slammed open, and I had a shining moment of hope for a split second. Then, the looming figure yanked a dagger from the sheath at his hip.

He was on me in an instant, dagger raised, his steps so fast it was a blur. Blind fear and a spike of rage ignited in my belly, and a wave of light erupted from my wound as a scream raced up my throat. Power flew from me as if yanked by an unseen force, a bolt of magic tearing him in two.

Blood and viscera fell to the slick floor, and my bile rose. My skin steamed in the cold room as exhaustion weakened my limbs, and I nearly fell in the puddle of what once was one of my attackers. But that power didn't quit. It still poured from the wound, turning the scarlet blood golden as it dripped from my fingers to the floor.

It boiled against the cold stone, bubbling and popping as if my whole body was on fire. I wanted to run—I should have run—but there was another man in the room. If I left, he could escape, and then we'd never know who he was or why he wanted to kill me in my bed.

Rune roared his protest, his words rattling my skull as his voice got so much stronger than it was before. *"I'm coming to you. You must get to the balcony. Now."*

But I needed to know. Lunging forward, I latched onto his thick hood, ripping it off his head, the light pouring from my still-bleeding wound illuminating his face. Dead, milky eyes stared right through me, so at odds with his youthful face and full cheeks. He was just a boy, barely a man, and yet the person staring out of those eyes was ancient.

Slowly, he bent his injured leg back the right way before pulling it under him. There was no emotion, no cry of pain, nothing. If his skin wasn't pink with strain, I would have thought he was a revenant back from the dead.

Black magic flickered around his head, weaving through his hair and twisting into his ears and nose. He didn't so much as flinch as it slithered like a snake into his mouth, and then a dark, husky laugh vibrated from his chest.

"There is nowhere safe for you, little Luxa," he rumbled, his voice as if a chorus of men were talking at the same time. "We will end you and your whole line."

Not a revenant, but something else. I had no idea what kind of black magic was in his blood, and I wanted no part of it.

His hand tightened on the blade, telling me it was high time I actually listened to Rune before it was too late. Instead of running through the scattered body parts to the door, I changed course, heading for the paned glass doors that led to a private balcony I hadn't inspected yet.

The door rattled as I slammed into it, my bloody fingers slipping on the lock as I tried to open the damn thing. Then those hard hands closed over my shoulders, and he drew me away only to lift me up and toss me through the glass.

Shards cut through my skin as I landed on the stone balcony, the bitter winter wind tearing into me worse than the glass. Air left my lungs, the sound died in my ears, and through it all, my heart thundered as light poured from every brand-new cut.

A dark cackle tipped from blackened lips as he yanked me from the ground, his fist tangled in the front of my nightdress.

"Everyone said you were so tough, so powerful,

so protected. But how much could you mean to the king if he left you unguarded?" His head tilted to the side as he brought the dagger to my throat, the poisoned metal burning me with every second it rested against my skin.

"The curse will remain unbroken. No Luxa will unchain the beast. You will die like all the witches before you, and when your sister comes of age, we'll kill her, too."

Time seemed to stop again, but this time, I knew it wasn't Rune's magic at all.

The only people who knew about Nyrah were Kian and Xavier, and Rune couldn't tell anyone. I didn't think Kian or Xavier would betray me that way, so no one could know about her unless...

Someone from the castle talked to the guild. Nyrah was in danger. Rage mottled my vision, blinding me as a roar shook the very foundations of the castle. But that sound only echoed what was pouring from my own lungs. The glaring light poured from my skin as a dome of power shoved him back.

A coppery tang filled my mouth, but I didn't care. No one threatened my sister and lived.

No one.

"Stop, Vale," Rune snarled, his words punctuated

by his very real and very close roar that rattled my chest.

I glanced at the nearby turret, not as fazed as I should have been that there was a giant red dragon perched on it not fifty feet away. Fire rose in his throat, and I fought off the urge to scream.

"Let me end him before you burn yourself to dust."

"Not before I can question him," I hissed, ignoring the blood dripping from my hands, my nose, the cuts on my legs. Pain tried and failed to make itself known, but all I cared about was finding out who sent this poor excuse for a puppet to kill me and what connection they had with the guild.

My would-be assassin's magic flickered against mine as he stared beyond me. The black surrounding his head sputtered as light returned to his eyes for a moment. The milky haze left his irises for a solid second as he stared at the dragon, his mouth agape.

Rune's roar thundered through the air, deafening me as my own magic flickered. The milky cast to my assassin's eyes clouded his vision once more, and he bared his blackened teeth at Rune. Then he turned on his heel and ran, darting through the broken doors.

I moved to follow—except every bit of strength

I'd been relying on seemed to leave me at once. Glass cut into my palms as I fell to my knees, gasping as the air seemed to thicken in my lungs.

But for Nyrah, I would move forward.

Crawling, I trudged on, allowing the glass to slice into me if it meant that he wouldn't get away.

"Stop, my Queen. Please stop."

"I-I can't. He knows about Nyrah. I have to catch him."

I barely made it inside when the double doors to my quarters burst open, blue fiery magic coating the floor and the walls, stopping my assassin in his tracks.

Three figures darkened the door as Kian, Xavier, and Freya stood in his path. Sighing in relief that was way more of a whimper than I would have liked, I fell to my hip on the cold tile, praying they got the answers I needed.

They raised their weapons to strike, but before they could take his head or I could tell them to stop, the assassin plunged that poisoned dagger into his own throat and ripped it wide. He was dead before he hit the floor.

"No," I whimpered, sliding in my own blood as I collapsed on the glass-covered ground. A wet cough racked my body as a bitter pain settled into my very bones.

The world around me darkened, my light sputtering, dying. Shadows surrounded me as their shouts faded away to nothing.

My eyelids closed.

My breathing stopped.

My heart...

*I*T WAS AS IF LIGHTNING WAS STRIKING MY CHEST.

White-hot fire dug its fingers into every part of me, through my middle, down my limbs, through my head. I opened my mouth to scream, but no sound came out—or at least no sound I could hear. It felt as though I was underwater, begging for air as I suffocated on the coppery blood in my mouth.

I wanted to open my eyes, wanted to yell at them to stop, but I was locked away inside my mind as pain ravaged me. The blackness fell away, and a faint flickering of firelight drew me from the darkness.

"We have got to stop meeting like this," Idris said, his dark chuckle mirthless as he knelt at my side on the

floor. Glass was everywhere, and I was just as bloody as I'd been before, but this was different.

"Am I dreaming this time, or am I dead?"

Gentle hands pulled me from the cold ground, their warmth soothing as another wave of pain rocked through my body. I tried to relax into them, but it hurt too much.

"Neither, my brave one. At least not yet."

Understanding dawned. "They're trying to save me —trying to keep me alive. For you."

Because that was the only reason I was here, wasn't it? To survive, to endure, to break a curse when I didn't even know magic. To hide away in my corner of the castle, waiting to be used like a weapon.

"Not for me. For you. They refused to watch you die, and I cannot blame them. You are too precious to lose."

And despite his warmth easing some of my pain, I still ripped my hand out of his. "Is that why you left me unprotected? Unguarded? Why you allowed someone to come into my room and try to kill me in my sleep?" My laugh was mirthless. "No wonder every Luxa dies as soon as they come here. You couldn't care about us if you tried."

"I didn—"

"How many of us were there?" I hissed, despair

crawling up my chest. "A hundred? A thousand? Two hundred years and no one survived?"

"Fifty-one. Not including yourself." His golden eyes flashed with pain as he reached for me. "I remember all of their names. Every. One."

His warmth surrounded me as another wave of agony shuddered through me. "And you were not unprotected. Your guards were murdered, killed defending you with their last breath."

But where was he?

Where was Kian or Xavier or even Freya?

Why was I all alone?

"It's not their fault. They were trying to ease some of my jealousy by staying away from you."

And that made it worse. "You made them take me here and then abandon me? The only people I trusted to watch my back, and you rip them away, for what? If you wanted me so much, then where were you? Am I just a toy to you? Something you only want when someone else is playing with me?"

The ache in my chest had nothing to do with the healing and everything to do with Idris.

"No, Vale. I didn't ask them to abandon you. I didn—" Firming his mouth, he plucked me off the cold ground, pulling me to his chest. Fiery warmth filled my body, easing the worst of the pain.

Some of my ire melted with the relief, but not all of it.

"I didn't expect you to affect me like you do." The admission thawed me more. "My magic—it reacts to you, and my mind is scrambling to keep up. In the council chambers, you were so easily hurt, and—"

He shook his head, those golden eyes pleading for forgiveness. "I didn't know if it was my magic changing you or if it was them. I just wanted you to heal. I didn't mean for any of this to happen. I—"

I placed a calming hand over his mouth, gently shushing him as I rested my forehead against his. I had to stop thinking the worst of him. It was getting us nowhere.

"I misunderstood you. I'm sorry."

He pulled away, his face stricken. "No, Vale. I'm sorry. You-you're hurt because I could not protect you."

While that was true, I didn't believe it was his fault —not anymore.

"I will make this right. I swear to you."

His voice faded as the light from the moon fell away. Darkness surrounded me, but his warmth remained.

"You will be protected. I promise."

Sweet words.

But he could only live up to them if I survived.

CHAPTER 17

VALE

The last time I woke from a dream with Idris, it had been much more pleasant. Blearily, I cracked my eyelids, wishing for death to take me. My throat aching, my body on fire, I tried to assess myself. I wasn't on the glass-covered floor of my quarters, so that was a plus, but I could do without the coppery tang of blood in my mouth.

Amber eyes met mine, so much concern etched on Kian's face, it was as if it had been carved there by my blood alone. His head rested on a plush pillow, his body curled around mine, and the welcomed hint of safety had my breaths easing just a bit.

Had he been watching me sleep?

Waiting for me to wake up?

And why was that a balm to my battered soul?

"I've seen enough of your blood to last a lifetime, my beautiful witch." Pain ravaged his voice, twisting my insides into a knot. "I'm going to need you to stop doing that."

"Doing what?" I croaked, trying and failing to push myself up from the plush mattress that seemed to be doing little to ease the aches in my body.

"Almost dying in front of me," he murmured, slipping his thick arms under my body and pulling me to his chest.

Just touching his skin had me sighing in relief as his words twisted the knot tighter. The fear that was still clawing at me seemed to melt a little as tears burned my eyes.

"I can't handle it," he admitted, and I wanted so much to ease his fears. "I thought I was doing the right thing leaving you, but I shouldn't have. I should have been there."

Yes, he should have. But we couldn't change the past.

"Was I guarded?" I asked, unsure whether I should believe my dream conversation with Idris or not.

His nod was solemn. "Four on the door, four in the corridor. Standard royal formation. Idris insisted, but Xavier and I were going to do it, anyway."

Gods, it hadn't been a dream at all, had it?

"They're all dead, aren't they." It wasn't a question, and I didn't phrase it like one. None of it had been a dream. Not one bit of it.

"How do you know that?"

I didn't have the desire to hide anything from him. I was too damn tired. "Idris told me."

Kian looked around like he was searching for his king in the shadowed corners of the room. "When?"

"In my dreams, but I don't think they're dreams. Not really. He was trying to ease my pain. I think you were trying to bring me back, but it hurt so bad I wanted to die. Just like on the mountain, he kept me alive. I was so mad that I'd been left behind."

I swallowed down my tears, knowing they would do no good—not right then.

"He said that my guards were all dead, that they fought with their last breath to save me, but they failed. He said it was his fault that you weren't with me. That you were just trying to do the right thing."

Kian rolled his eyes before tilting his head to the ceiling. "Fucking martyr. Always falling on his own damn sword. You'd think after two hundred years, he'd learn his lesson."

The way he'd phrased it, it finally dawned on me that Kian and Xavier had been with Idris this whole time—through everything. Two hundred years of watching witches try and fail to free him from his curse. Two hundred years of finding new Luxa only to watch them die. I'd never considered that they were just as old as the king. It reframed the pain etched into his face, the light in his eyes, the ancient ache that seemed to pour from his skin.

"I think it hurt him," I murmured, brushing my fingers over the thick scar on his jaw, "taking my pain away." I wondered how he'd gotten it or if he even remembered, and I fought the urge to kiss it.

Kian's eyes closed tight, his jaw like granite, and I wondered if just that light touch hurt him as well.

"I'd hate for all his efforts to be wasted. Do you think I'm going to live?" I jabbed, trying to get those amber eyes back.

Kian snorted, his mirthless chuckle vibrating through my chest in an almost pleasant way. "It took vampire blood, all of Xavier's strength, and magic from Rune, but yeah, you're going to make it. Though, if you happen to grow fangs, Freya said not to give her shit about it."

My hand flew to my mouth, but all my teeth

were exactly the same as they had been before I'd nearly been killed in my own bed.

His chuckle that time actually held some humor. "No fangs just yet, then? Good. Witch magic goes wonky once turned. I'd rather Xavier not have to worry about teaching you and dealing with a baby vamp at the same time. Priorities, you know?"

I didn't want to be a vampire. The guild told stories about the blood-drinking monsters, and as much as I knew little of what the guild said was true, the taste of blood in my mouth proved I wouldn't be a very good vampire. I could barely handle being a Luxa.

The curse will remain unbroken. No Luxa will unchain the beast. You will die like all the witches before you, and when your sister comes of age, we'll kill her, too.

The memory of the assassin's words hit me like a hammer.

"They knew about Nyrah," I whispered, fresh tears filling my eyes. "The man—the assassin—he told me that they would make sure I didn't break the curse. That they'd kill my sister when she came of age."

Kian stiffened. "They were from the guild, then. We figured as much. No one here knows about her. Xavier and I haven't said a word. And I take it you're keeping it from Idris to make sure you can trust him."

Fear—real fear—filled every part of my body. "But he did know about her. And someone was talking through him. Like he was a doll or a puppet. But he was holding *Lumentium*. I—"

"I know. Freya smelled it as soon as she stepped into the corridor. That form of magic carries a certain scent. It's grave magic, and only dark mages use it—mages darker than the ones we met on the road. Their magic doesn't react the same way to *Lumentium*, probably because of how it was created. As soon as Freya is rested, she's going hunting. She'll find them."

"They knew where I was, they knew the formation of the guards, they know about Nyrah. I have to—"

"Heal. He said they'd kill her when she came of age, right? That means they don't know where she is. Meaning she can't be in the guild—not if Arden is still alive. He'd take her out before she could ever be a Luxa if he knew she came from the same line. It wouldn't matter if she was a child or not. Trust me."

Cold dread filled me as I remembered Arden's eyes flashing gold. "He's not human, is he?"

Kian's gaze bore into mine, the truth of it churning in my gut. "No. He isn't."

"If he isn't human," I whispered, "then what is he?"

But the puzzle pieces were falling into place. Dragons terrorized the mountain, but it couldn't be Idris because he and Rune were separated. Kian and Xavier wouldn't kill innocents, so that just left...

"He's a dragon. The worst of us."

This wasn't a war between two factions. This had always been a war between the dragons. And if Arden wasn't human, that meant that when he'd come to tell me my parents jumped rather than burn, it had been a confession.

"He killed them, didn't he? My parents. He told me they ran from the dragons, jumped in the chasm to avoid the fire, and this whole time, it was him."

Kian pulled me closer, lending me his warmth, his comfort. "When you said one of our kind killed your parents in the throne room, I knew it had to be him."

A little piece of my heart cracked, knowing he'd lied to me the whole time. It only made me want to break the curse more, if only to watch him meet his end.

"When it comes time for him to die? Promise to make it slow."

Kian gently squeezed me. "That's my girl."

Then he swung his leg over the side of the bed and stood. Only then did I notice the dark brocaded walls accented the same amber of his eyes.

"Is this your room?"

Kian snorted, truncated humor and derision all at once. "Like I would let you sleep anywhere else. Xavier is in the medical wing, healing from over-using his power. Freya is finding someone to snack on to replenish the blood you took, and Idris is trying not to bring the entire castle down on our heads. I'm all you've got, sweetheart."

Sweetheart. I didn't think anyone had called me that in a very long time, and certainly no one like him. A faint flush of warmth filled me at the small epithet, and my lips turned up, even though my body wanted to crawl into a hole and just perish. Xavier was hurting because of me. If Kian didn't seem so blasé about it, I was sure my heart would thunder out of my chest.

"I'm not complaining," I whispered. "It suits you."

"Glad you like it. Now, I suggest a bath and rest,

and maybe a nice breakfast. Then maybe you can convince the giant dragon on the turret outside to calm the fuck down."

My eyes widened. "Rune?"

"He nearly clawed his way into the castle trying to get to you. If Idris hadn't stopped him, he likely would have ripped you away and eaten us all as punishment for letting you get hurt."

"Rune?" I mentally called, not trusting my voice not to crack. He hadn't left me.

The dragon's presence flared in my mind, digging comforting claws into me. *"My Queen."* He sighed, the faint scent of smoke filling my nose. *"You wake."*

Was that his relief or mine? I didn't know, but it eased more of the pain in my joints.

"I'm okay. I'm sorry I didn't listen to you. I should have run when you told me to."

The grumble was slightly passive-aggressive, but I'd take it. *"Stay with the dragons, my Queen. Do not forget again. Yes?"*

I doubted Kian would let me out of his sight again, but I'd appease the giant dragon who'd done his best to save my life. *"Yes. Go get some sleep. You sound tired."*

The damn dragon grumbled again, but I almost felt it when he lifted from the turret and returned to his caverns. He was so much more present in my mind, his emotions more vivid, more tangible.

He'd given me more than just "a little" of his power. He'd flayed himself open for me.

"Thank you for saving me."

If dragons could smile, Rune would be just then. *"Thank you for staying alive."*

If I could have hugged a giant dragon, I would have. "Rune says to stick with you, and he's going to rest."

Relief hit Kian's expression as he carried me out of the bedchamber and into a bathing room. The tub was in the process of being filled from a metal spout in the wall, the heavenly scented water steaming as it fell in a gurgling rush.

"Like you'd be anywhere else. By the time this is all over, you might get sick of me."

He set me on my feet and held me against his body as he pulled the tattered, bloodstained gown over my head. I tried and failed not to blush as the throbbing ache in my shoulder made itself known. Despite the pain, I still remembered the last time I'd been naked with him. That reminder was punctuated by the heat of his body filtering through his tunic and into my bare skin.

Kian hissed as he set me away from him and surveyed the damage, but I was too scared to look. I'd been scarred before, and I found that not looking worked just fine for me. But the ravaged expression on his face twisted that knot in my chest so tight I had to look away.

"I'm so sorry I left you alone, Vale."

Then he pulled me in, wrapping me in his arms as he pressed a kiss to my damaged shoulder. "Never again. I swear it."

I didn't say anything—I couldn't. Not because I didn't believe him. A part of me did. But the other part wondered if any of this was real, if I was dreaming again.

No, your shoulder wouldn't be on fire if you were dreaming.

With a steadying hand, Kian helped me into the water, the surface reaching the underside of my breasts as the heat worked its magic. I was just settling in, when he yanked his bloody tunic from his shoulders, revealing acres of chiseled golden skin decorated with a mishmash of thick scars and swirling black tattoos.

A bath and a show? If I had the energy at all, I

286 ♦　　　　　　　ANNIE ANDERSON

would have said something, but as it was, with the water leeching the pain from my bones, I was too tired to move. My eyes popped wide when Kian dropped his pants, and I openly stared at his muscular thighs, lightly dusted with dark hair, his thickening cock standing at attention.

Mouth dry as a desert, I tried and failed to swallow. I was half-dead and considering just what I could do to rally. If this were a dream, I needed to make the most of it, and if it wasn't, dying soon hadn't been knocked off the table yet. That said, if he wanted to do naughty things to me, he would likely have to do all the work.

Kian urged me to lean forward before slipping behind me in the tub, the water rising to my collarbones at his bulk. I eased for a second before remembering what he'd see if he looked at my back, and I couldn't help but stiffen. It was one thing for me not to look at my scars, but I sure as hell didn't want him to see them.

Loosening my braid, I guided my hair over the worst of them.

"I know already," he murmured as he kissed the base of my neck. Brushing my hair back over my shoulder, he pulled me against his front. "I saw them."

Shame filled me because I knew what brand was on my skin. "I-I'm not—"

"A heretic? If I know Arden, you're no more a heretic than I am." He curled an arm around my middle, his thumb brushing my hip bone in a soothing caress. "I bet he branded you himself and for something small, right?"

Tension flooded from my body. Stealing food wasn't small, but I hadn't done it at all, so...

I barely nodded, but it didn't matter. The shame of that brand was fading. "I took the punishment for my sister. She got caught stealing food, and I'd told Arden that I'd put her up to it so they'd spare her. She was only nine. She wouldn't have survived it."

A finger found my chin, and he turned my head and tilted it back so he could look me in the eye. "You're the bravest woman I've ever met, you know that?"

At the time, I hadn't felt brave. I still didn't.

"She's my sister," I whispered, giving him a painful, one-sided shrug.

Hissing, I vowed not to do any shrugging for the foreseeable future.

Too bad Kian had other plans. His jaw hardened as his eyes flared with a hint of rage. He blamed himself for not protecting me, and he would set about rectifying it immediately.

"You get today to rest, to heal. Tomorrow, we start your training. Combat, magic, the works."

My eyebrows hit my hairline, the act alone hurting every muscle in my face.

"You're getting the Luxa crash course."

CHAPTER 18

KIAN

Vale gripped the dagger in her hand tighter as her brilliant green eyes lit with the faintest hint of her magic. She had tried and failed to score a hit off of me for the last three days, and I had a feeling it was pissing her off.

Good.

She needed to be pissed off.

It was a fuck of a lot more useful than her being frightened. The last few days had been filled with magic lessons and combat training—each new maneuver she learned making the scent of fear only grow. She was realizing how little she knew, how deep into this world she had been thrown, and it scared the shit out of her.

Join the club, my little witch. Join the fucking club.

I was scared out of my fucking mind because I'd seen her covered in blood, breath stopped, heart stopped, glass stuck in her skin, her wounds pouring blood, and I hadn't known how to help her. Xavier and Freya had flown into action, but me? I just stood there watching them try and put her back together, unable to do a damn thing to help her.

I'd never felt so helpless, so incompetent, so worthless as I had in that moment, cursing Orrus for trying to take her from me. And I begged. I begged every god and goddess, every deity I could think of, just so she would breathe, so she would live, so her heart would continue pumping.

Rune had perched himself on the stone railing of the balcony, nearly clawing his way into the castle to get to her, and honestly, I couldn't blame him. And if she'd have died, I would have begged him to kill me, too.

And when she lived, when she drew that very first breath, I promised myself that no one would touch her, no one would harm a hair on her head. Not ever again. But she had to learn how to take care of herself. Because if the gods forbade me from protecting her, she *had* to know how to protect herself.

She had to live.

Not for the curse. Not for Idris, not even for me. She had to live for herself because this world deserved to have her light in it. And it would be a cold, dark place without her.

That wasn't to say she wasn't a quick learner. She was. She picked up knife skills better than most young soldiers. It was the implementing them with finesse part she lacked. I supposed that made sense. She had been more accustomed to an axe for more years than she'd ever had with a dagger. But her arm was still too weak to use the axes we had, so we'd stuck with daggers for the time being.

"Are you going to come at me, or are you going to flit around like a bird? If you want to hit me, then hit me," I taunted, trying to get a rise out of her.

Those brilliant eyes flashed again, the only tell before she feinted to the left and struck, flipping the knife in the air as she darted past me. She plucked it from the meager inches right in front of my face as she twisted right, bringing the knife down in a move I didn't think she had in her.

Had I not managed to back up a step, she would have sliced through my forearm all the way to the bone. As it was, a thin line of blood welled from my skin, collecting into a single drop before the flesh healed over again.

"*Yes*," she crowed, losing every bit of composure she had as she jumped up and down. "I did it!"

I fought off the urge to tackle her to the ground. For the last three days, her scent had been driving me insane. Sharing a bath with her had been a mistake, but I couldn't have stopped myself if I wanted to. Which I didn't. I didn't want to stop touching her. I didn't want her scent to fade from my nose.

I wanted her in my bed and under me. I wanted her moans in my ear and her cream on my tongue. But her healing had taken priority, and she still had more of that to do. I'd been just as happy with holding her until she fell asleep and then staying awake to make sure no one harmed a hair on her head.

Once he returned from the med bay, Xavier and I slept in shifts, each of us taking turns teaching and protecting her while Freya hunted the culprits down.

And each night with her in my bed, in my arms, it was a struggle to forget the night we'd had before coming here. Back when she was still safe. Back when no one knew about her. Back when her shy kisses and soft moans had turned into her screams of pleasure as she melted my brain with her wicked tongue.

Had I known what was to happen, I would have never told her that we were stealing her away until we were already on the ferry. If I would have known...

I smacked the flat end of my wooden spear against her tight ass, reminding her we were in the middle of a fight. Encased in buttery soft fighting leathers from neck to ankle, she was fucking magnificent. Every move she made in them had my cock harder than a rock and aching to get free.

"Get your head in the game, Vale," I growled, crowding her as I plucked the bloody knife from her loose grip. "You think a fight is over after one hit?"

Was that an asshole remark? Yes.

Was it also true? Also, yes.

A frown marred the joy on her face as she lost her beautiful smile, but I kept going, even as she snatched the blade back.

"You think they will stop and let you celebrate as they're trying to kill you? That they'll put down their swords and let you breathe?"

Abashed, she dropped her gaze to the floor, her jaw tight.

Fuck.

"You're right, Kian," she whispered, throwing the dagger down with so much force it embedded into the wooden floor right next to my foot.

An inch to the left, and I'd be missing a toe.

"Any other vital information you need to impart, or can I quit for the day? We've been at this for six hours. If I wanted to be worked to death, I would have stayed in the guild."

She didn't so much as let me say a word after that crippling parting shot as she spun on her booted heel and marched to the training room door without a backward glance.

I snatched up her dagger, the same one I'd procured for her in the town and stowed it in an empty loop at my belt. She now kept it under her pillow as she slept and in the sheath at her hip when she was in leathers. For her to throw it at my feet meant she was really pissed off.

Yeah, I'd been more than an asshole.

Employing the speed I so rarely used around her, I managed to get between her and the door. Vale stopped dead in her tracks, glaring at me hard enough that fire might actually come out of her eyes.

"I'm sorry," I murmured, my hands raised in surrender. "I shouldn't have taken out my frustrations on you."

But that seemed just as wrong as it was right.

"But I'm so fucking pissed, I can't see straight. I knew what you would be facing when you got here. If it wasn't the gods-be-damned dragon under the castle, it was the council, it was the trials, it was everything." My chuckle was mirthless, and I fisted my hands in my hair, trying not to pull it out at the roots.

"Look what's already happened. I wanted to get you off this fucking continent so you would be safe, and now I'm so angry at you because you have no idea what it was like watching you nearly die. No, actually, not 'nearly' because your heart stopped, and you stopped breathing, and it took all of Rune and Xavier and Freya's strength to bring you back."

My throat nearly closed it was so clogged with tears I refused to shed. I wouldn't because she was alive now, and I was grateful. But damn if it hadn't nearly killed me. "You were dead, and there wasn't a godsdamn thing I could do about it."

"And that's my fault?" she demanded, those gorgeous eyes flaring bright, skirting around me and throwing the door open. "Because I wouldn't get on the damn boat? Your little plan to get me off the continent didn't once take my sister into account, nor did you even contemplate asking me what I wanted before you just put it in motion. You didn't *ask* me. You *told* me."

Shaking her head, she moved through my quarters toward the bedchamber, unfastening the clasps of her leather top and yanking it off her arms. Under it was a tight black vest that molded to her curves and did nothing to quell the ache in my cock.

After her attack, she hadn't so much as looked at the entrance of my wing, the carved wooden doors spelled with enough warding to deter nearly everyone. Confined to my rooms, there were only so many places for her to go and nowhere I wouldn't follow. Plus, this argument had been brewing for three damn days, and we were having it.

There was no escaping it now.

"I'm not sorry," I said to her back, her scars peeking around her swinging braid.

"Oh, trust me," she scoffed, throwing her leather top to the ground. "I know you aren't. And I knew you wouldn't be, which is why the first chance I got, I followed Rune's voice and got to the castle."

She slid through the bedchamber directly to the dressing room, where she sat on the stool to untie her boots.

"Breaking this curse is more important than my safety," she said, ripping her foot out of one boot before moving to the other. "It means that my sister will never have to stand in my shoes. It means that I can go back and get her with the full force of the crown. Breaking this curse is the fastest way to fucking save her."

Didn't she understand?

"Great. It's the fastest way to save her, but what about you?" I demanded, closing the distance between us. "Did you ever stop to ask that question? What good is saving her if she lives the rest of her life without you?"

I cupped her face in my hands, pressing my forehead to hers, kneeling before her like the queen she was always meant to be. "I've had you for less than a week, and I already know a life without you is meaningless. Can't you see that?"

"That's not fair," she said through gritted teeth, tears spilling down her cheeks. "I'm all she has in the world."

"Exactly, my beautiful witch. Which means you need to stay breathing no matter what. Understand?"

"I'm trying," she whispered, her breath hitching.

She was working so hard, and I was the asshole pushing for more. Gods, could I stop fucking up for five seconds?

"I know you are," I said, drawing away from her. If I didn't, her scent would drive me insane. I was already half-mad, one more second with my forehead pressed to hers, and I'd lose it and kiss her.

If I let myself kiss her, I'd end up devouring her whole. I'd give up anything, everything, I'd—

"Are you going to stop looking at me like I'm glass anytime soon?" she accused, wiping at her face. "I'm not going to break."

"You're healing, Va—"

"Bullshit. You and Xavier are scared. I almost died, I'll give you that, but you two won't even look at me anymore. I thought..." She closed her eyes tight before shaking her head. Standing in defeat, she let out a mirthless laugh. "It doesn't really matter what I thought, does it?"

Wait... Did she think we didn't want her?

Something inside me snapped. Before she could skirt around me, I had her in my arms with her back to the wall as I pressed my achingly hard cock against her center. Her small but strong hands rested on my bare shoulders, hanging on for dear life.

"Does this feel like I don't want you?" I growled against the tender skin of her neck, aching to sink my growing fangs into the column of her throat.

"I... I..." Then she moaned as she tightened her legs around my hips.

"Wanting you is not the problem. I want you every second of every day, even when I sleep, I want you. Every time I close my eyes, I see you sitting on Xavier's face, I hear you moan around my cock, I feel your mouth on me. I've been hard since you opened your eyes in my bed."

"But I've been in your bed this whole time. I'm all healed up. Why..." She trailed off, the hurt in her voice as if she'd driven her dagger into my chest.

Fuck it.

Fuck Idris. Fuck this kingdom. None of it mattered.

Nothing else mattered except for my mouth on hers. Unable to deny myself any longer, I captured those maddingly luscious lips with mine. Almost instantly, our kiss turned hard, fast, consuming. Her tongue met mine, her breaths stuttered, and I fell into the bliss that was my little witch.

I wound my fist in the rope of her braid, only breaking the kiss so I could taste the skin above her pulse point. She tasted like heaven, better than I remembered. A shiver vibrated through her, and it was all I could do not to rip off the rest of her leathers and fuck her right here in the dressing room.

But she needed to know...

"Because you're my addiction, Vale," I murmured against her skin, moving my lips to her jaw, her ear. "As soon as I have you, I'm going to want you all the time. I've merely had a taste of you, and I'm nearly driven to madness. What kind of feral creature will I become once I've had all of you?"

Her sweet moan was music to my fucking ears. And when she threaded her fingers into my hair and guided my mouth to hers again, I was a goner.

Vale's sweet scent surrounded me, invading my nose as her legs tightened on my hips. I needed her more than air, more than the blood in my veins or the promise of tomorrow. Reluctantly, I set her on her feet, the lack of her warmth invading my senses, a loss that speared at my soul.

But I never took my hands from her. No, my fingers were hard at work divesting her of every stitch of clothing she had on. I wanted to taste every inch of her skin, hear her gasps, her moans. I wanted her to beg.

On my knees, I yanked the leathers down her legs, tasting the delicate skin near her hip bone before pressing my tongue at the juncture of her thighs over her underwear. The fabric was soaked through already, making my cock pulse at the thought of taking her.

Vale's hips bucked as she let out a strangled moan, her fingers fisting in my hair. She smelled absolutely divine, and the animal in me wanted more of it. Talons sprang from my fingertips, the ache welcome as I shredded what was still on her skin. Her vest, her leathers, her underwear, it was all gone in moments.

Hooking her leg over my shoulder, I set about fucking her dripping cunt with my tongue. I drank her down as I flicked her pulsing clit, relishing every shudder, every moan as she scrambled to hang on to anything she could reach.

My little witch needed a seat while I fucked her with my mouth?

So be it.

Lifting her off her feet, I spun us, setting her down at the dressing table. Ass on the fabric stool, her elbows rested on the tabletop as those perfect tits shuddered with every gasping breath as she tried to get a hold of herself.

Well, I couldn't have that.

Yanking her to the edge of the stool, my grip was damn near punishing as I brought my mouth right back to heaven. Vale didn't care about my claws, didn't care about my grip. Her hips bucked as she moaned long and low, inciting my answering growl.

"Fucking beautiful," I rasped before attacking her sweet little clit, watching as each touch of my tongue made her tremble, made her flush, made her come undone.

Retracting my talons, I pet her tight opening, loving how slick she was, loving how her scent made me crazed. Vale's moans got louder as I teased her, and then I got exactly what I wanted.

"*Kian*," she begged, her hips bucking, seeking her pleasure exactly like I wanted her to. "*Please.*"

Then I thrust my fingers into her tight little hole, pumping them in time with my sucks on her throbbing clit. I knew she was untouched, and as much as I wanted to make her ready for me, none of that seemed to matter to her right then. Vale tossed her head back as her cunt strangled my fingers, squeezing them so tight I almost came in my pants at the thought of her doing that to my cock.

Then she let out a desperate sound as she rode my hand, her coming release punctuated by the delicate flush racing up her chest, into her cheeks, all the way to her hair. Hands gripping the dressing table, she was laid out like a sacrifice.

Head lolled back, mouth open, legs splayed wide, she was so fucking magnificent as she took her pleasure.

"Come for me, little witch," I growled, needing it more than anything. "*Now.*"

I felt it the instant her release hit her, almost like it was her hands racing down my flesh, touching me everywhere. When she screamed out her orgasm, I knew I'd give anything at all to hear her make that sound forever.

Boneless, her body wilted against the dressing table, sweat dotting her brow, her breaths coming in pants, her luscious breasts rising and falling with each one. And still, I hungered. Her taste was on my tongue, but it wasn't enough.

I needed more.

Lifting her off the bench, I carried her to the bedchamber and ripped back the coverlet, placing her gently on the soft sheets right where she belonged. Running my hands over her soft skin, I met those gorgeous green eyes, the ones that flashed and burned with unspent desire.

She wasn't done either, and I loved how sensual she was, how readily she took her pleasure.

"I want you, my little witch. Will you let me have you?"

Rising up on her elbows, she licked those luscious, full lips like she could devour me whole.

"I'm already yours, Kian. I thought you knew that."

Then she reached for me, unfastening my leathers, drawing them down my hips, freeing my cock. I gripped it at the base, giving it a rough stroke just to ease the worst of the ache. She looked up at me as her pink tongue swiped a drop of my need from the head.

If she did that again, I would unman myself down her throat. I backed away, toeing off my boots and yanking my leathers the rest of the way off. She bit her bottom lip, her expression ravenous.

Fuck, she would destroy me, and I would gladly let her.

I latched onto the back of her knees, dragging her ass to the edge of the bed. Breath hitching, eyes wide, she watched as I guided my cock to her slick opening and gently pressed the head inside. She was so tight, so hot, so fucking wet, I fought the urge to plunge inside her.

"You're so fucking *tight*," I rasped, my control slipping by the second.

A soft, surprised gasp gusted from her lips. "I want it. *Please*, Kian."

That was the only invitation I needed, taking that perfect mouth as I slowly thrust all the way to the hilt. I groaned against her lips, nearly lost in her as I fought for control. I held myself still, allowing her to get used to my size as I watched her face for pain.

A frown puckered her brow, but her walls contracted around my cock, her hips rocking against me. Her hands cupped my cheeks as those brilliant eyes met mine.

"More. I need more," she whispered against my lips, and I gave it to her.

Curling her leg over my hip, I pulled out slowly, her greedy cunt sucking at my cock like her mouth had. Then I thrust forward, burying myself once again.

Her hungry gasp filled my ears as her eyes went half-lidded.

"More, little witch?"

Groaning, she nodded, and I set about fucking her. It wasn't gentle. No, my little witch did not want gentle at all. The harder I thrust, the louder she got, her blunted fingernails digging into my shoulders as she took every single one. I'd thought she was tight, but as her pleasure rose, the walls of her sex only constricted around my cock like a vise.

She was going to come, and if I let her, I'd follow her over the edge.

Too soon.

I pulled out to a moan of protest and flipped her over. Then I brought my hand down on that lush, perfect ass as I climbed onto the bed behind her, loving the way her skin pinked before I thrust back inside.

At this angle, I filled her *deep*.

Eyes rolling into the back of my head, I set about fucking her in earnest, curling over her back as I took her pleasure for my own.

"Lean down, baby," I growled in her ear, and her chest hit the mattress, the switch in position making her claw at the sheets.

"*Ohhh, Kian.* Gods, please. Fuck me, please. *Please*," she begged, and my control snapped.

Gripping her throat, I nipped at her shoulder, her skin like a drug as my fangs lengthened in my mouth. My claws sprang from my fingertips, my scales raced over my body, and neither of us cared. I pounded into her tight cunt, her screams music to my fucking ears.

"That's it. Come on my cock, Vale. I want to feel it," I ordered, my fangs aching as I fought off the urge to sink them into her skin. "*Now!*"

My name fell from her lips in a hoarse, ragged cry as her walls fluttered around me, and I couldn't fight it anymore. My fangs sank into her shoulder as pleasure raced up my spine, and then I set out to follow her over the edge with her sweet blood on my tongue.

I'd never felt something so intense, the pleasure and pain melding together in my body. My balls tightened, my cock seemed to get harder, the ache radiating out and then the release hit, washing over me in a wave that threatened to drown me. Bliss flowed through every limb as I clutched Vale to my chest, our heavy breaths mingling.

Sitting back on my heels, I brought her with me, unsure whether I ever would want to be apart from her again. My cock throbbed inside her, my need rising as she melted against my body. Her chest heaved, her breasts flushed from her orgasm, her nipples hardened points as a smile curved her reddened lips.

She was perfection, and I would never get enough.

I wound her braid in my fist, tilting her head back as my hips shifted. "I need you again, *oroum di vita.*"

My life until death and beyond.

My fated one.

I knew it as soon as she'd screamed at me on that mountaintop. She was *mine*.

And I'd have to share her at some point, that Fate hadn't given her to just me. And as her hips began to rock in time with mine, I figured I'd be okay with that.

But later.

Right then, she was *mine*.

Only mine.

And I intended to have her.

Moonlight filtered through the sheer curtains, bathing the room in an ethereal glow. Warm, sated, and undeniably naked, I traced the dark swirls of Kian's tattoos with my fingertips. His large body was curled around mine, his arm hooked around my middle, holding me so close, his slow breaths tickling the skin of my neck.

Something told me I wasn't awake, but I wasn't exactly sleeping, either. It wasn't until golden eyes flashed on the balcony, did I realize what it was.

Or, rather, who it was.

Idris.

His dark-brown hair fluttered in the winter wind, his jaw flexing with his ire as he stared at the arm around my middle, at the man at my back, at the way we were curled around each other. I drew the sheets up, covering my chest.

No matter what we had between us, I didn't want him seeing me unclothed. He only would see that if I chose to show myself to him, not sneaking by into my dreams like a voyeur.

Idris' eyes glowed brighter, hotter, and he melted through the glass balcony doors, entering the room as if he owned it. I supposed he did. He owned everything in this place except for me, and I suspected that pissed him off more than anything.

That golden gaze latched onto my shoulder, the very same one that had been pierced through by an assassin's blade. It was also the same shoulder Kian had marked with his pleasure, but that had faded almost as suddenly as it appeared.

Now there was only the reminder of my attempted murder.

If the mirror was to be believed, the scar wasn't too awful. I had worse on my back. This new one was faded to a pale white of old wounds, the magic used to heal me taking most of the ugliness away from the flesh.

Why he was staring at it like he wanted to go to war was beyond me.

Silently, he approached the bed, head tilted, eyes flashing, his emotions bombarding me. Even though I *didn't know his mind, I just knew what I was feeling was coming from him.*

Jealousy. Rage. Envy. Need. Affection. Obsession. Each one was like one of my bolts, hitting me right in the chest.

"What are you doing here?" I hissed, pitching my voice low so as to not wake Kian. Then I realized just how ridiculous that was. Kian wasn't really here. I wasn't here, either. None of us were.

"Answering your call like always, my brave one. Why do you always call to me in your dreams?"

I sat up, clutching the sheet to my chest.

"I call to you in my dreams?" I scoffed. "No, you invade them."

A tiny bit of shame tugged at my heart. He'd helped me survive, of course, but this... This was him just being pissed off and nosy.

His eyes flared, his jaw clenching as his power blazed against my skin, his emotions flickering with his magic.

Want. Desire. Tenderness.

"Wrong, my brave one. I cannot come where I am not summoned. A part of you pulled me here. Why is that? Why do you want me to see you in this bed? Do you want me in it?"

Okay, so I'd gone to bed worried about Xavier and Idris. I'd considered my time with Kian could anger them, but... Like with Kian, I felt a connection to the others. A tie. A need. I didn't understand it, didn't know why I needed them, I...

"I d-don't... I didn't... I didn't do it on purpose." *Scanning my surroundings, I tried to understand how I could have brought him here.* "Where is here, exactly? You never answer that question."

Naturally, he didn't answer me this time, either.

Instead, the room around us faded away. The blue and amber walls bled to red. The coverlet changed, the bed. Kian wasn't curled around me anymore, the weight of his arm long gone. Now, I was wrapped in burgundy sheets, the silky fabric sliding over my naked skin as my surroundings settled into a bedroom I'd seen before.

The four posts of the frame rose high around me, the drapes of them drawn back as a crackling fire hissed and popped in the grate.

And I wasn't alone in this bed.

Propped up on the pillows, his back to the headboard, Idris sat shirtless. A golden medallion hung from his neck, the glowing stone in the center throbbing like the beat of a heart against tanned planes of war-hardened flesh. Scars and tattoos swirled together over the chiseled muscle, the firelight making his skin almost glow.

The silky sheets pooled around his hips, obscuring his

lower half without leaving anything to the imagination. Not only was Idris just as naked as I was, but he was also aroused.

Desire. Need. Need. Need.

"What is this? What are you doing?" I demanded, probably not as offended as I should have been. It was as if those emotions were invading my senses, bending me to his will.

"Making it fair." His voice was a sexy rasp akin to honey over hot coals. "Now I'm just as naked as you are." His mouth quirked up into an almost grin, the impish quality almost boyish for someone his age.

Tucking the sheet around me, I caught the flare in his eyes as they zeroed in on my tight nipples. That grin grew wider, the bastard, and naturally, they puckered under his gaze, practically begging for him to touch them.

Taste them.

"You and I both know this isn't fair." Was that my voice? That breathy, needy whimper? And why did he affect me so much? "What do you want, Idris?"

His eyes went heavy-lidded as he turned toward me, sliding to his side in the sheets. "I like the way you say my name. Do it again."

Shit. As much as his voice and body were lulling me

into some very bad decisions, I needed to keep my head about me.

"You know nothing about me, and based on the last week, you don't care to."

His lips pressed together into a firm line. "It's harder for me to be with you than I thought it would be. Here, it's safe."

Funny, it didn't feel safe. Nothing with him did.

"I'm not a toy for you to play with when it suits you."

Idris closed the distance between us, his fiery skin almost but not quite touching mine. If it weren't for the silky sheets, he would be able to feel my heart thundering in my chest.

"You are not—nor have you ever been—a toy. But I still want to play with you." His voice was calling to me, pulling at a thread I couldn't place.

The tip of his index finger traced my lower lip, his eyes focusing on my mouth. "Will you let me play with you, Vale? Will you let me touch you?"

Every time we were like this, he would lull me into his arms, igniting the flames of my need before flitting away. Either that, or he was apologizing for his idiocy. But he never really answered my questions, and I hated it.

I'd have to strike a bargain.

"I will give you one kiss if you tell me where we are.

Tell me how you can speak to me this way. Tell me something, Idris. How did you take my pain away? Why—"

Idris dipped his head, his lips almost touching mine. "That's at least three questions, my brave one. That means three kisses, correct?"

Rolling my eyes, I prayed to the gods for patience. "Fin—"

Before I could even get the word out, Idris' searing kiss branded my mouth. There was no other word for it. He didn't just capture my lips, he owned them, laying claim like the king he was. His arm was an iron band around my back as he tucked me under him, his hard body pressing into me, lighting me on fire.

"I can make you forget them, Vale," he murmured against the tender skin of my neck. "I can make it so you want only me."

It was as if he'd dumped me into a frozen lake.

Without trying, I shoved him from me, knocking him off the bed and onto the floor. He wanted me to forget them—forget Kian and Xavier?

The men who'd saved me.

Who'd stood between me and certain death.

Who'd cared for me.

Who'd stolen me from the clutches of Orrus himself.

Drawing the sheet around me, I yanked it from the bed, holding it to my breasts as I pushed off the mattress.

Idris was tangled in the coverlet, shock stamped all over his face.

"No. You can't. And until you get it through your thick skull that I will never choose only you, you will always be on the outside of that balcony looking in."

And unlike every other time, Idris didn't fade away with me hanging onto him. No, I shoved him away, taking back the section of my mind that he'd occupied. He did not rule here. I did. I changed the scene, returning to Kian's bedroom.

Only then did I notice Xavier resting on the floor on the side I'd been sleeping on. He was on his side, his white hair fanned out on the floor, his head resting on his biceps.

I didn't know if this was a dream or if this was reality. I didn't know if I would wake up next to him or in bed with Kian. But none of that mattered. I pulled a pillow off the bed and gently put it under his head. Then I drew Idris' sheets around me and curled into the crook of his hips, fitting my back against his chest as I fanned the sheet over us.

Idris thought he could make me forget them?

Never.

I SHOULDN'T HAVE WOKEN UP ALONE.

For the last four days, I'd woken with either Kian or Xavier by my side, their presence a balm to my soul after the attack. They'd taken shifts, teaching me combat and magic, royal protocol, and the histories of Festia. Unlike Credour as a whole, Festia had its own set of customs.

After living under the mountain my entire life, the intricacies of castle protocol made my brain hurt.

More, I'd have thought Kian would be with me. But what worried me wasn't that I was completely alone in the room, the fading light of the day drifting through the sheer curtains. No, it was the familiar burgundy sheet wrapped around my body and the scent of Xavier, Idris, and Kian on my skin. I'd gone to bed in Kian's arms, and I hadn't seen Idris in days. There should be no reason this sheet was around me and his scent was on my skin, and yet...

We had already established that in those

dreams, we spoke mind to mind, but never did I think that I could actually take something with me when I left them. The fact that Idris' sheet was actually here only proved those dreams weren't dreams at all. Stomach in freefall, I tried to understand.

That kind of power, that kind of... It just didn't make any sense.

And worse?

It scared the absolute shit out of me.

I flinched as the doors to Kian's bedchamber flew open, my fist closing around the hilt of a bejeweled dagger. Freya waltzed through the entrance while she popped a grape into her mouth. Her single red eyebrow was her only tell that she knew exactly what Kian and I had been up to for the last day and a half. And if I could smell Idris and Xavier on my own skin, I knew for a fact she could, too.

Who knew what she thought?

She fanned her face with an embossed white card. "At least someone is getting lucky around here. All I've had for the last few days is stonewalls, road-blocks, and fuck all to show for it. I don't know who's trying to kill you, girlie, but damn if they don't cover their tracks like an expert."

Of the things she could have said to me, that was just about the least comforting thing I could think of. Then again, I hadn't spent the last few days scouring the continent for my would-be assassin and she had, so maybe I should just be grateful that she was still alive to warn me.

I shuddered at the memories that I'd tried so hard to forget. His milky white stare, the black magic that had swirled around his head, filling his mouth, those blackened teeth. And those voices coming out of his throat...

"I'm sorry," I said stupidly, unsure how I could apologize for wasting her time. I doubted Freya actually enjoyed hunting people on my behalf, but she'd done it.

"Don't be sorry. I don't like it when someone breaks into my home and hurts people under my protection. And you weren't the one who covered your tracks so well, even I couldn't beg, borrow, or steal answers out of the lowest of the lows. Though, when I find whoever it is, I will gladly drain them dry. So, if you're keen on revenge, you're shit out of luck. I call dibs."

The snort that came out of me was wholly inelegant, but it did make the ancient vampire smile so, at least there was that.

"Do you happen to know where my previous guards are?"

"You mean your dragon boy toys?" she teased, a wicked smile curling her lips. "They're off using their noses to do what I can't. Hopefully, they'll be back before night falls. Then maybe they can entertain you while you go to this."

She handed over the fancy white card, and I clutched the sheet tighter to my chest to avoid flashing her while I took it.

The invitation was sickeningly formal with my name scrawled at the top in swirling calligraphy.

It would be my greatest pleasure to have you join me in the royal dining hall for dinner this evening. I eagerly anticipate the pleasure of your company and the opportunity for us to get to know each other better.

Yours respectfully,

Idris

When I looked up from the invitation, Freya was covering her mouth with her surprisingly delicate fingers, attempting not to fall down laughing.

"Is he kidding with this?" I asked, flinging the stupidly expensive cardstock away from me as if it burned.

"Unfortunately, I don't think so," she said on a

chuckle, her humor wholly unhelpful. "But at least he's making an effort to be sociable instead of staying the broody asshole we've all come to know and love. Trust me, little Luxa. He could most definitely be worse."

I had no idea what he expected to accomplish with this dinner. He didn't want to get to know me —not really. He wanted something to play with. Something to pass the time until this curse thing got figured out. And as soon as it did, he'd flit off to parts unknown.

I trusted that Kian wanted me, that Xavier did, but Idris? He wanted to be free more than he wanted anything else.

But I didn't think I could refuse—not without looking like a fool.

I wrinkled my nose at the white paper. "What the hell am I supposed to wear?"

IF IT WERE POSSIBLE TO KILL FREYA, I WOULD HAVE. I didn't know the first thing about murdering a vampire other than the ramblings of the guild, and after everything, trusting the guild was plain idiocy.

"I'm pretty sure I hate you," I muttered, pulling at the collar of my cloak, the only thing that was keeping the castle at large from seeing me in this damn dress.

"You're the one who said I couldn't show your back," Freya said on a sigh. "That left me with limited options. If I can't show your back or shoulders, then you get this."

She was right: I wasn't revealing either my back *or* shoulders. The first, because I had no intention of discussing the heretic mark on my back, and the second, because of the memory of his burning gaze on my shoulders. Instead, she'd dressed me in a confection of a dress with a neckline so deep that it was holding in my chest by a wing and a prayer, the gossamer fabric one wrong move away from ripping in half.

"Had I known this was my only option, I would have picked something else," I hissed, fighting off the urge to cross my arms over my chest. I'd been starving for years, but the sudden influx of food had given me padding where there had been none before.

"What's the problem?" Freya asked on a

whisper as we passed three members of the council in the corridor. "You look beautiful. If Idris manages to keep his hands off of you, I'd be surprised."

I shot her a glare. "You are too old to play that stupid. Him keeping his hands to himself is the problem."

Freya's devilish eyebrow rose as her lips pulled into a grin, the door to the royal dining hall nearly upon us. "Is it a problem for him or for you? I know whose sheets you were wearing when you woke up. The nose doesn't lie."

That was just it, wasn't it? His scent shouldn't have been on my skin. His sheets shouldn't have been around me. I'd pulled them out of a dream— one I didn't understand at all. How could I just walk in there and talk to him after that?

"What if I told you that I've never *physically* been in his room, but I managed to take those sheets with me when I woke up from a dream?"

Freya's grip on my arm was nearly bruising as her gaze drilled into me. Red flooded the whites of her eyes as scarlet veins crawled up her neck. "You dream walked? With Idris? How many times?"

I swallowed hard, my mind blanking. "Th-three? I think?"

"That's all? And you managed to take something with you when you woke up?"

Nodding, I yanked my arm out of her hold. "Why?"

Freya's smile was in direct odds with the scarlet veins and red eyes. "No one else besides Idris has been able to do that in two hundred years. No wonder they want you dead." The hushed laugh that came from her was three parts relief and two parts hysteria.

"You're the curse breaker."

Freya looked around, pulling me to an alcove similar to the one Idris had what felt like years ago. "In case it was unclear to you, keeping Luxa alive has been kind of a problem for us. If they don't die the first day, they definitely do during the second trial. But you? They didn't wait for you to die on your own, so they know something we don't. You have to watch your back, understand?"

Hesitantly, I nodded.

"You're armed, right?"

"Of course. After the assassin—"

"Good. You should be safe around Idris. They won't mess with you around the king but don't drop your guard. Desperate people are sloppy, and desperate, power-hungry people are reckless." She grabbed my hand, guiding me back toward the dining hall. "And finish that book I gave you. It's important."

Frowning, I wondered what that had to do with anything, but she didn't give me a chance to tell her I had no idea where the damn book was. She wrenched the door open and practically shoved me through the thing.

Standing near the giant fireplace, Idris looked up from the flames. His gaze flicked from me to Freya before the vampire gave me another little push and slammed the door shut behind me.

A man in a formal tunic seemed to appear at my left, making me jump. I nearly reached for my dagger before he held his hand out.

"Your cloak, Miss."

My gaze went from the man to Idris and back as my whole body tensed. Reluctantly, I removed my cloak, passing it off to him. The mostly nondescript man winked out of sight, seeming to vanish before my very eyes, my cloak in his hands.

What in the—

Before I could wrap my brain around a man just disappearing into thin air, Idris approached, his presence so familiar, I could practically feel him cross the room to me, ramping the heat of the room up one degree at a time.

With nowhere else to look, I finally lifted my chin and met his gaze. Those golden orbs seemed to spear me right in the chest as he held out his hand. And just like in our dreams, I could feel his emotions as if they were my own.

Contrition, hope, optimism, desire.

"You look beautiful. Every time I see you, it's like I've forgotten just how exquisite you are, and then you appear and remind me."

Dammit. How was I supposed to keep my head when he said things like that?

"Thank you for meeting me. I know after how I behaved last night, you might refuse, but I'm glad you didn't."

This was why I didn't want to be anywhere near him. It clouded my brain, muddling everything. How could I watch my own back if I was losing myself to him?

"I can't very well scold you for not getting to know me and then refuse when you try, now, can I?"

His full lips quirked up, his almost-smile appealing in a way I absolutely hated. It made him seem almost caring, but I was still mad at him for being a stupid, jealous idiot.

"Please, come sit with me."

"Go on, my Queen," Rune muttered, his voice so close it nearly made me jump. *"How will you break a curse without knowing the person beneath its weight?"*

I fought off the urge to roll my eyes at the damn dragon inside my head. Childishness wouldn't serve me here any more than rage would serve me in the guild. And dammit, if Rune wasn't right. If I wanted my sister back, I'd have to actually get to know the man I'd have to ask for help, wouldn't I?

But it wasn't just that. I actually wanted to get to know him. I just didn't think he'd let me.

"And I was hatched yesterday," Rune muttered. I had no idea he was so well-versed in sarcasm. Honestly, if he had an eyebrow to raise, he'd be doing it. *"If you'd just admit you kind of like the idiot, this would go a lot smoother."*

"I would, but he keeps being a possessive jerk and assuming he knows what I want instead of asking me."

"And you actually know what that is? Could have fooled me."

Did I? I'd been pulled in so many directions, I felt out of place and off-balance. People were trying to kill me, and I...

Idris pulled out a chair close to the head of the table, and I sat, staring at the extravagant place setting, trying to remember what fork I was supposed to use and when. Rune was needling me just because he could, the jerk, and he knew I wouldn't ignore him.

Not after what he'd done to save me.

"You could be nicer about it. Damn."

"And you could get your shit together. Looks like we're both screwed."

Never mind. Shutting him out was the only solution to his sassy ass.

"I'm ignoring you for the rest of the night."

Idris sat on the chair next to me at the head of the table, his expression wary as he stared at my hand. That's when I noticed the faint glow coming from my skin, even with no cut in sight.

Embarrassed, I pulled my hand under the table.

"Great. Look what you made me do. He's going to think I'm mad at him now."

"Aren't you? I thought he was being a high-handed asshole?"

Clearing my throat, I grasped for the first question I could think of like a lifeline. "Do you have any siblings?"

It was dumb. I could have asked him what his favorite color was or if he had any hobbies, but everything seemed too trivial. None of it was what I wanted to know.

Idris quirked his head as a frown marred his brow. "They really do keep the guild in the dark, don't they?" He huffed a mirthless laugh, his shoulders straightening. "Do you really know nothing about me? Nothing at all?"

And while I'd caught that he was answering a question with a question, his was a good one, so I answered it. "No, actually. Other than all magic-users being evil and you being the beast of them all? You're more of a mythical, never seen but always feared kind of thing. Plus, they worked us so hard, thinking about who we were actually at war with was secondary to staying alive."

He paled slightly, his jaw tightening, but he gave me a solemn nod. "I do—have a sibling. A brother. But you could say we're not close. And you have a sister. Nyrah, I believe."

Dread and fear made my chest ache. I hadn't told him about her on purpose. "How do you know that?"

Idris' was gaze assessing but kind. "The first time we dream walked. You were trying to save her. That was your sister, right? She was tied to the stake like you were. Cut like you were. But she faded away in your hands. Does she still live?"

Hot pricks of tears hit the back of my eyes. "I don't know. We got separated. I hope she made it out. It's pretty much the only thing keeping me going."

Well, that and I didn't want her in my shoes.

"That's it. That's why," Idris murmured, his smile almost sad. "She is why you stay. She's why you risked the caverns, even though my closest friends wanted to steal you off the continent. Why you faced Rune. Why you remain, even when you've nearly been killed. Why you train like your life depends on it."

His laugh was mirthless, his shoulders drooping in defeat. "I'm a fucking idiot. Rune didn't kill you because you don't want anything but your sister alive."

Before he could continue, a pair of those nicely dressed men popped into the room from nowhere, holding silver-domed platters. In tandem, they set them at our place settings, removed the covers, and then winked back out of sight.

The scent of the food was heavenly, and my poor stomach chose to make its hunger known, growling so loud it echoed around me.

I could be sad and still eat, dammit.

The faint scent of almonds combined with a sweet, candied aroma filled my nose as my mouth watered.

"Do not eat that," Rune warned, his voice so loud I winced.

"But I'm hungry," I protested, lifting my fork.

"I didn't wait two hundred years in silence for you to die on me. I said, don't eat that."

Then, as if the dragon in my head was controlling my movements, my hand flung the fork and plate from my grip, slopping the dish across the table. It slid off the wood before falling over the edge, crashing to the floor.

Then the scent registered, and I finally understood.

Shock had Idris' fork poised in front of his open mouth, and I flew out of my chair, slapping the utensil full of death away from his face. I splattered his shirt with the vile stuff but luckily stopped him from doing what I almost let myself do out of spite.

"What the fuck, Vale?" Idris sputtered, but I only whispered one word in answer.

And that one word was enough to send a thread of fear through him that I could feel myself.

"Poison."

CHAPTER 20

IDRIS

Wide green eyes blazed with her rising power as she trembled in front of me. Chest heaving, heart thundering in her chest, she was magnificent, even if she was completely bonkers.

"What the hell do you mean, poison? *What* is poison?"

This woman had just thrown her plate and fork and slapped food right out of my hand. There had to be a good reason for it. Sure, she was almost always mad at me—usually justified—but Vale wasn't crazy. If she actually thought it was poison, I appreciated the assist, but I'd scented nothing on my plate other than the candied almonds on top of the fig and brie tartlets.

Tartlets I'd gone to the head chef and specifically selected just for her because she'd loved the cheese when she'd dined in my solar. Included in the limited information I'd managed to glean from her, Vale loved food. Having starved as long as she had, she enjoyed every morsel that passed her lips, and she absolutely hated waste.

She wouldn't throw food just to spite me. Right?

She straightened, fisting her hands on her hips. Yes, they were glowing with her power just like her eyes were. "The food, you idiot. Can't you smell it?"

Was she implying she could smell poison? Only shifters could do that. Maybe a vampire if they were old, but not Luxa.

"Of course I can smell the food, Vale. But what makes *you* think that you can sniff out poison? You aren't a dragon."

"Technically, neither are you," she growled, the barb hitting home. "But one of us has a dragon inside their head, and one of us doesn't, and we both know that's not you."

Gods, the woman was talking in riddles. "What the fuck do you mean by that?"

She really needed to start talking sense.

"Don't you know already? Didn't they tell you?" she whispered, confusion clouding her expression. "Rune speaks inside my head. He told me the dish was poisoned. He's the one who flung the plate away, not me. I didn't want you to be poisoned, so I slapped the food out of your hand."

I stood so fast, my chair tipped back in a great crash. Hands planted on the table, I steadied myself as my magic threatened to drown me, the puzzle pieces finally fitting into place.

When she'd finally told me about her sister herself, I'd just assumed that Rune hadn't killed her because she was honorable, because she'd stood in front of my men, because she was kind. That it didn't matter what I wanted or what I thought she was. She wasn't the curse breaker. She was just a beautiful, smart woman who'd tugged at the shattered pieces of my heart.

And I was starting not to care whether she could break my curse or not. Because being with her was the most I'd felt alive in centuries.

Now to find out that Rune spoke to her, I almost couldn't let myself hope.

"Rune. *My* Rune? He speaks to you."

"Yes. He led me to the cavern. He called to me, demanding I come to him. I thought it was you. I thought you were calling me. But when I got there, I figured it had to have been a trick. That I would die, but then Kian and Xavier stood in the way..."

I'd always wondered how she'd found the cavern entrance. I'd assumed it was Kian or Xavier who'd brought her there, but now it made so much more sense. Her power had called to me that day, summoning me to the caverns. When I saw her stand in between my oldest friends and my dragon, I'd known she was the one.

Somehow, after her attempted assassination, I'd almost convinced myself the opposite.

"He slowed the assassin down to help me get away," she admitted. "I would have died had he not intervened. And then afterward, I was so close to death that he shared some of his life force with me —to help me live. I thought..." She swallowed, eyes wide, stepping away from me. "I thought all Luxa could do that. Like the light, I thought..."

I lunged forward so fast, she flinched, but I would not let her go, her small wrist swallowed in my grasp. I couldn't. I needed her answers more than air. "I believe you," I whispered, "but I have to be sure. Tell me what he's saying to you right now. *Please.*"

She tugged at her wrist, but my grip was iron.

"Tell me," I insisted, needing to know if this was

it or if two hundred years of searching was just the tip of the iceberg.

"You won't like it. He's not very pleased with you."

He never was. My dragon had often called me a bumbling idiot when I was being one, but if he could talk to her... if he could... if I could... "*Tell* me."

Vale winced, her beautiful face scrunching just a little as she tried to word whatever she was hearing into a more palatable version. Then she rolled her eyes and broke the seal.

"He says that you couldn't find your ass with two hands and a map, and that the only reason you were still breathing is because he's stronger than you. And it's your fault you and him are like this. And if you let me die, he will kill you himself and then go find your brother and finish the job you should have two cen—"

Without thought, I captured her lips with mine. She could hear him. She was the one. She was the only one. Lifting her off her feet, I spun her in a circle, so relieved, so pissed off, so...

How long had my dragon been in silence?

How long had we been severed?

And how long had there been someone in my castle plotting to keep us that way?

I let her go, circling the table to her far-flung plate, and lifted it to my nose. I caught the scent of bitter almonds disguised heavily under the sweet, candied figs.

It was poisoned.

I was sure of it.

I moved back to my plate, sniffing the same dish. There was nothing, not that it would have mattered if it was poisoned. Cyanide wouldn't kill me. Not much would.

"My dish isn't poisoned, but yours is. Rune saved your life." And to hear her tell it, this wasn't the first. My dragon had been saving her this whole time. He could talk to her. And a part of me was jealous as hell.

The other part of me?

It was a possessive, crazed animal that wanted to rip the men who'd tried to take her from me wide open and bathe in their fucking blood.

"So much for eating," Vale lamented, collapsing back onto her chair. "And here I thought being in a big fancy castle would mean I wouldn't starve. Joke's on me, huh?"

I knelt at the side of her chair, cupping her face in my hands.

"You will be protected," I vowed, resting my

forehead against hers. "No one will touch you. No one will harm you. I promised you anything before, and I'd meant it. I owe you everything. My kingdom. My life. I will owe you for the rest of forever."

She drew away, her gaze searching. "I can hear more than just you and Rune in my head. I can hear Kian and Xavier when they're in dragon form. They can speak to me."

Reality threatened to swallow me up. There was a reason she was so drawn to them. And it was one I couldn't deny, couldn't refute, and couldn't stand in the way of.

Fateborn mates.

There hadn't been a single set of them in two hundred years—not since the curse tainted the continent. Every curse had a remedy, and this one was designed by Fate herself to fuck with me in the only way that would teach me the lesson I should have learned two centuries ago.

Vale was born to be not just my mate, but all of ours. *Ours.*

My gaze fell to the shoulder with Kian's mark. The skin was pristine, but the glowing magic hidden under her lace sleeve told a very different story. It was faint, barely there, not a full mating mark, but still...

She was not only mine. If she could hear not just me and Rune, but them as well...

And she had no idea. Why would she? Arden wouldn't tell his people, and they were so isolated in Direveil that it would be impossible for her to know.

She is ours. Ours.

And if I wanted to break this curse—if I wanted that peace that only she would bring, if I wanted her *at all*, then I would have to understand that my self-ishness, my jealousy, my greed would have to end.

It was a lesson I should have learned by now, but only she could teach me.

"Isn't this just like the dream walking? Can't all Luxa do this? Freya called me the curse breaker because of the sheet I took from your room in the dream. She—"

I didn't need to be reminded of her strength, but shock made it hard to keep my power in check, made it almost impossible not to let it out so it could answer to the call of hers. This was why us being together while I was still under the blight of the curse was dangerous.

The floor shook so hard, the candelabras toppled to the stone floor. The chandeliers swung violently as my emotions got the better of me.

Vale pulled away from me, leaning back in her

seat as her brilliant green eyes widened. "What's going on?"

"Freya was right. You *are* the curse breaker. And it isn't Fate or circumstance that is trying to keep us apart. It's someone in this very castle."

She shook her head, her eyes filling as her jaw firmed. "Not necessarily. The man who tried to kill me had been spelled. I saw it. Someone was using him like a puppet. They might not know what they're doing."

That theory had merit, but there were too many things wrong with the timing. How could someone know about a dinner I hadn't decided to put on until this morning? How did they know Vale would be with me if they weren't in the castle watching? How would they know which plate was hers if they weren't in the kitchens themselves?

Someone could be a puppet, but they were someone with a fuck load of information and the means and opportunity to get the poison right on her plate.

I didn't want her to see what I was about to do, but leaving her alone just wasn't an option.

"Come with me." I latched onto her hand, pulling her out of the chair and sneaking behind the tapestries that led to the servant hallway to the kitchens. This was faster than going through the main corridor. If someone was waiting for her to keel over and die from poison, they would likely be in the hallway, prepared to make a scene because yet another Luxa had dropped dead.

A part of me thought it was complete idiocy that I hadn't realized what was going on before now. Maybe it was because Rune had killed so many of the Luxa himself that I didn't put it together.

Someone really didn't want me to break this curse, and other than my brother, I couldn't think of another person who needed me brought low that much.

There was a small office outside the main kitchens where the only person left in this castle I trusted spent most of her time. I didn't trust the council, Kian and Xavier were gone, and Freya had that look in her eyes that said that she was in the middle of a hunt when she dropped off Vale, so that only left Briar.

Fist pounding on her office door, I vibrated with rage as I tried to get myself together.

"Where are we? What is going on?" Vale whispered, her gaze darting around, her dagger clutched tightly in her hand.

Before I could answer, Briar whipped the door

open, her silvery hair and ancient half-moon spectacles the only comforting thing right about then, aside from the woman to my left.

"Vale, I would like you to meet Briar. She has been with my family for as long as I can remember and is just about the only person I trust right now."

Briar was a brownie and had been the steward of this castle since before it was built. She originally served under my grandfather before the turn of the millennia, helped raise my mother, and kept this place afloat while at war. Her grandson currently ran an inn in the town proper, and her daughter owned one of the finest shops.

She looked Vale over, her genial face assessing in a way that made me straighten in pride. Vale was strong and beautiful and whip-smart, and Briar could sense it. A blind man could see it, and Briar was anything but blind. Despite her age, there wasn't much that she missed.

"We need your help," I began, gently pushing inside her office. It was a moss-covered alcove with a domed ceiling and plants growing in every available crevasse. Butterflies danced between flowers, jumping from petal to petal, and tiny pixies flitted from bookshelf to bookshelf.

"Of course, tell me what it is, child." Briar's gaze went from me to Vale and back. "I mean, my King."

I waved away her attempt at decorum. It would be pointless if I couldn't trust anyone. "Someone in the kitchen staff tried to poison Vale. Cyanide. If she hadn't smelled it, I—"

Briar's lined face—once genial and kind—hardened to stone. Her large hazel eyes narrowed to slits as a pair of gossamer wings sprang from her back, and she rose in the air to look me in the eye.

"*What* did you just say?"

This was like the time she'd caught me fighting with my brother in the garden when we were ten. We'd shifted and burnt down the topiaries, the arbor, and one of the outbuildings because we'd just learned how to breathe fire. She'd made us rebuild the arbor and outbuildings by hand with no magic and re-grow the topiaries ourselves. It had taken months, but Briar was not a brownie to be messed with.

At least this time, I hadn't done anything wrong.

"Poison in *my* kitchen? From *my* staff?" she growled, revealing her sharp, pointed teeth.

Brownies were a loyal species. By nature, they wanted to protect those under their care. It had nearly torn Briar in two to have my brother and I at odds for so long, but she'd remained with me because of what he'd become.

"Just her dish, not mine. Because of who she is, I have to think..."

Briar's eye almost started twitching. She snapped her fingers, and the door flew open. She zoomed through it, her fluttering wings beating so fast I could barely see them. It wasn't until she was outside the dining hall, did she return to the ground.

She pushed through the double doors and walked straight to the plate on the floor. Not even getting within three feet of it, she froze.

"Poison. In my house? My food? My people?"

Spinning in a circle, her hazel eyes darkened to black, her faint-blue veins bleeding to red as they crawled up her neck and down her frail arms. Her fingertips blackened as she reached for the sky, and every single kitchen staff, chef, server, maid, laundress, and attendant was pulled through space and time, landing on their asses on the stone floor.

"I will hold them here, my King. Do what you must."

I shot a glance at Vale, who was staring at the large group of staff as if she might be sick. The jeweled dagger fisted in her grip. Her gaze swept through the crowd until she froze on one attendant

—the one who'd delivered her plate to her. He didn't look any different from the other attendants, perfectly nondescript, but her nostrils fluttered like Rune's did when he was sniffing.

Her green eyes began to glow, and she pointed the dagger right at him. "Rune says to detain that one. He smells of death magic and poison."

The crowd backed away from him, his mousey brown hair and eyes, his hunched shoulders clouded slightly with a magic I couldn't quite see. I knew him. Geoff. He was a rather standoffish attendant, but he'd never shown me he couldn't be trusted.

Vale moved closer to me, her hand latching onto my forearm. *"There's magic coating him. He's been spelled, for sure, but if we don't keep him breathing—"*

Shock had me staring at her anew. She was speaking inside my head like she was born to it, like she had known of her powers since birth.

"Quit staring at me like that. The last assassin killed himself before we could question him, which is probably why Freya couldn't find anything."

Out of all the things she could have said, that got my head back on straight. Before anyone could move, my magic shot out, latching onto the attendant and wrapping around him like a snake. I drew him to me, scenting the death and poison for myself.

As he got closer, he started struggling, his powerful glamour melting away. His irises turned milky as black magic curled around his head, so much like my own power. But where I was life, this was worse than death, worse than the grave, worse than a putrid afterlife.

He wasn't undead or a revenant, but the magic that had consumed him could only be accepted willingly by its host.

"Tell me who sent you, and I will let you live," I growled.

Almost instantly, he began foaming at the mouth, and it didn't matter what I tried, I wouldn't get anything out of him. The spell clouding his eyes had its own self-destruct sequence. I knew the magic well enough. I dropped my power and watched the attendant convulse on the ground, his life ending before my very eyes.

"Raise the wards, Briar. No one in or out until I say otherwise."

Briar's power shimmered over my skin almost instantly, and not a moment later, the dining hall doors slammed open. Kian's amber eyes were brimming with his power as Xavier's magic crawled like blue flames over the ground.

I pulled Vale to me, whispering into her mind.

"Stay with them. It seems like every time you're apart, someone tries to fucking kill you."

Shame warred with determination in my chest. I needed to get a handle on my kingdom, or the whole fucking thing would fall down around my ears. I met Kian's gaze. He knew exactly what I wanted, offering a small nod of acknowledgment.

I pressed a kiss to Vale's forehead as Kian reached for her. "I'm going to protect you, Vale. And when it's all said and done, I'm pretty sure you're not going to like how I do it."

Reluctantly, I released her, knowing before the night was through, there would be more death.

"What does that mean?"

I couldn't answer her—not now.

I had a promise to keep.

"Is this really the best time to be throwing a party?" I grumped, staring at the selection of dresses deemed fancy enough by Freya for the ball Idris insisted on hosting less than a day after someone tried to kill me.

Again.

Xavier pulled me to his front, wrapping an arm around my chest. The comfort was wonderful, but he was about to say something I did not want to hear. I just knew it.

"We need them to think that we believe we've caught the culprit. That we're celebrating, that we're resting on our laurels, *whatever*. Because when they try to hurt you again—and they will—we'll be ready for them. Idris is working with Briar to test everyone who comes through the gates for death magic to help weed people out."

He'd meant it to be soothing—the way he was pitching his voice, the way he wouldn't let me go, his warm heat attempting to lull me into a false sense of safety.

I called bullshit.

"So I'm bait, then. Fantastic. Can I be bait *and* be fully clothed at the same time?" I gestured to the selection of dresses, hating every single one of them. "What is this?"

It wasn't that they weren't pretty, they *were*. Some were beaded with intricate patterns and beautiful detailing. Others were in gorgeous colors and ornate stitching. They had everything I could ever possibly ever want in a certified confection of a dress.

The problem was that every single one would expose the brand on my back—a particular brand that in any other society would ostracize me and get me tied to a tree and burned alive.

Arden had told us stories.

And while I knew he was a lying shell of a man who used fear as a weapon, a part of me always worried that some of them were true. I supposed that brand was the reason it had taken so long to leave the guild. How could I subject myself and Nyrah to the world outside if it meant certain death?

Had I known I would be screwed either way, I probably would have left sooner.

"Oh, come on. What's wrong with these dresses?" Freya growled, sipping on a glass of wine that I was a thousand percent certain was not wine. "You bitched about the one from yesterday. You're bitching about these today. What's the problem?"

Freya had been in a bad mood since finding out I was likely the curse breaker. I chose to believe it was because we hadn't found the parties responsible for trying to kill me, and there had been another attempt on her watch.

"I don't want to show my back. We discussed this."

She snorted into her cup. "You think you're the only one with scars? Plenty of us have battle scars, little Luxa. Nobody's going to pay any attenti—"

Okay, so maybe there *was* booze in there with the blood that she was not-so-discreetly drinking. "I don't give a shit about the scars, Freya. I care about the brand."

Freya curled her lip, staring at me like I was pulling her leg. "What brand?"

I pinched my brow and gave her the highlights.

"After my parents died, we were starving. My sister stole food from the guild, and so they wouldn't whip a nine-year-old to death, I said I put her up to it. I took her punishment, and then Arden branded me as a heretic."

"Are you fucking kidding me?" Freya set down her cup, her face a little green. "That little shit-stain of a man *branded* you?" Understanding dawned. "And because it's a heretic mark, it can't be covered by a glamour. What a fucker."

That was exactly the response I was looking for, and I sort of loved that she was pissed on my behalf. "Essentially. Though, I had no idea it couldn't be covered by a glamour. I didn't even realize that was an option."

Kian pulled me out of Xavier's hold, pressing a kiss to the top of my shoulder where he'd bitten me what seemed like ages ago. The kiss felt possessive, and I hated that I really freaking liked it. "You know you'll look beautiful in anything you put on."

"Again," I protested, elbowing him lightly in the stomach, "I don't care about that."

Okay, so that was a total lie. I actually cared quite a bit that he thought I was going to look beautiful, but it was the mark that was the real worry.

"Honestly," Xavier mused, scratching at the

shadow of scruff on his jaw. "That brand—at least around here—will instill more fear than it will anything else. No one will burn you at the stake. They will be scared shitless of you, though."

And as foreign a concept as that was, it still sent a little thrill through me.

This *wasn't* the guild.

I *wasn't* powerless.

Not anymore.

If someone wanted to try to burn me, they would not only have me to deal with, but three dragons and an ancient vampire. Okay, so the vampire might be drunk off her ass before the night was through, but I figured she'd rally.

I crossed my arms, a tiny sliver of hope softening my resolve. "Fine. The silver one."

Freya's eyes lit up with glee. "Perfect choice."

THREE HOURS LATER, MY STOMACH WAS A MASS OF SNAKES. Everyone had given me a rundown of the protocol expected of me, but I feared I would mess everything up. I didn't like that I was bait, nor did I enjoy worrying about every single morsel that passed my lips.

I never wanted to starve again, but I feared I might.

"I'm not going to let you be poisoned," the dragon in my head grumbled. *"I saved you the last time, didn't I?"*

Of course Rune would take that personally.

"And I appreciate everything you've done, but it's still very frightening considering the circumstances. I feel like there's a target on my back—and considering the brand—I mean that literally."

At least I was a pretty target.

The silver dress I'd selected had a tight, strapless bodice encrusted with clear jewels and heavy metal beading, which laced up into a corset at my back. The neckline dipped just a bit at the center of my breasts, and I didn't know what magic it was using to prop them up *and* stay up, considering how heavy the wide skirts were.

The fabric shimmered in the candlelight, but it wasn't even the real showstopper. No, that was the gossamer cape draped across my shoulders, the beaded epaulets glittering like diamonds in the low light. The fabric was as thin as a butterfly's wing, and every time I moved, it sparkled like magic.

"You ready for this?" Kian asked on my left, his arm linked with mine as he guided me to the open double doors.

We waited behind a processional line, the herald's voice calling out their names and titles echoing through the hallway. Xavier squeezed my right arm, lending needed comfort as my emotions ran the gamut between pissed off and scared out of my mind.

"Have we told you how stunning you look yet?" Xavier asked, his blue eyes flaring as he looked me over. "Because I think they're going to have to invent new words for you soon. None of them do you justice."

Freya shot a look over her shoulder, her black and gold gown showing off her every curve. "Gods, Xavier. You keep talking like that, and I might forget I like women."

Even though she'd just established her preference for the ladies, I still kind of wanted to kick her. Xavier and Kian were *mine*, dammit. Sure, I may feel like I was being greedy and selfish. But...

They'd felt like mine since the forest, and I couldn't explain why.

"I'm fine," I murmured, swallowing the lie as I tried to calm the thundering of my heart. The people at our backs were already whispering, and I'd heard the word "heretic" passing more than a few lips in just the few minutes we'd been in line.

Kian leaned down and kissed the side of my neck. "Liar. But don't worry, I won't tell."

My lips curved into a smile, his words easing the worst of my nerves.

When it was Freya's turn, the herald nearly burst my eardrums, his magically amplified voice carrying over the giant hall. "Her Grace, Grand Duchess Freya Elowen Ashbourne, Duchess of Fierkeep, Countess of Gravesend."

I was trying to listen past the ringing in my ears as I watched Freya walk down the steps into the belly of the ballroom.

Ashbourne.

Freya was an Ashbourne.

Freya was an Ashbourne, and I'd killed her blood when I'd taken Thane's life.

Oh, shit. Oh, shit, shit, shit.

I was still reeling when Kian's title was thundered from the herald's throat. "General Kian Blackheart, Commander of the King's Forces, Defender of the Realm." And then Xavier's. "Lord Xavier Silverthorne, Hand to the King, Keeper of the Royal Seal."

But I was frozen to the spot when the herald

took one look at me, gave me a knowing smile, and then announced a name that had never been spoken aloud.

Not by anyone.

"Her Grace, Duchess Isolde Vale Tenebris, Lady of Shadowmere, Light Bringer, Curse Breaker, Grand Luxa of Tarrasca."

I was almost glad I hadn't eaten anything, or else I would have vomited all over the polished marble floor. The herald tilted his head, confusion coloring his face, but it almost felt false. Swallowing, I whipped my head forward and tried to wipe the fear from my face.

"Why are you frightened, my Queen?" Rune's voice in my head was a balm, helping me walk down the steps behind Freya, with Xavier and Kian practically holding me up. *"Do you need my help?"*

I almost shook my head, though I knew the giant dragon couldn't see me.

"No. I don't know. I don't think so." Squeezing my eyes tight for a second, I managed to pull myself together. *"No one knows that name, Rune. Not even my sister. It's never been said out loud. Not ever."*

Uncertainty followed by a boatload of anger flowed between us, proving Idris' little plan had already gone sideways. Whoever was against him was already in the castle, already in this room, already...

There was only one place where that name was written. It was in a very special book tucked away in our sleeping chambers under the mountain. It was the same book with a record of our entire family line, the *only* place. It was common for my family to only go by our middle names as a way of protecting what my mother called our "sovereign name." She'd told me names had power and no one should know it, that it would keep me protected.

I hadn't understood at the time, but now I did. The only person able to supply my name lived under the mountain. Which meant someone in this castle had a direct line to Arden.

And they wanted me to know it.

I took stock of the great hall as I got my breathing under control.

The soaring arched ceilings mirrored the night sky, glittering with glowing stars. Multicolored stained-glass windows depicted the gods and goddesses of old, their battles lost and won. Grand tapestries covered the stone walls, depicting dragons in flight, the images so intricate, I expected the beasts would break free from the artwork at any second. Thick wooden tables were piled high with food, the guests picking at the fare while we waited for the party to really start.

Iron chandeliers, with their glowing mage lights, cast an ethereal glow over the entire hall, even illuminating the small balcony filled with stringed instruments that seemed to be playing themselves.

Kian and Xavier led me to a raised dais, and Kian pulled out a giant, intricately carved seat at the center. I knew not to sit, though, because of who would be coming in last. Rattled, I hung onto the high back of the seat for dear life.

"What's wrong?" Xavier whispered, his gaze searching for a threat as Kian's grip on my hand tightened.

I shook my head, unsure of how I could tell him about the subtle threat of my sovereign name without causing a scene. They would want to shut this whole place down, and I had no idea if the rest of the attendants had been scanned by Briar's wards.

Then, the herald pounded his staff on the ground three times, signaling the grand entrance of the king.

"His Majesty, King Idris Ashbourne, Sovereign of Credour, Protector of the Realm, Lord of Tarrasca."

Oh, gods.

I should have put it together before now. Idris hated his brother. Arden was a dragon. Direveil had been at war with Credour for years.

Idris was Arden's brother.

I'd killed his nephew.

Oh, gods.

My breath wheezed through my lungs as Idris strode through the room, taking the seat to my right. I practically fell onto the chair, my shaking hands hidden under the table so they wouldn't draw attention when they started to glow.

"You look green, Vale," Idris whispered in my ear. "Are you—"

"I'm fine," I said, cutting him off as I pasted a smile on my face. "Everything's fine."

"Tell that to your thoughts, my brave one. Your mind is screaming at me."

I wanted to stay neutral—to be calm—but my mind wouldn't let me. *"You're brothers,"* I accused, trying to understand why. Was it a game to see how long it would take me to figure it out? Was it shame? *"Why didn't you tell me the man who tortured me, who nearly murdered me, who murdered my parents, was your brother?"*

Anger was my driving force. I'd saved Nyrah from that bastard, and I'd do it again. I wouldn't be sorry for killing him, not one second, not one minute, not one day. He deserved to die for what he had done.

"Because he is my greatest shame," he replied, the hurt and truth in that statement drawing my eyes to his in shock. His were burning into mine, pleading for me to understand. *"Everything he has been allowed to do is because I couldn't kill him when I should have. Two hundred years of misery because I failed to do my duty to the realm."*

My anger faded slightly, replaced with my earlier fear. *"You should know your herald announced my sovereign name. The only place it could be found is the Luxa history book where all our family names are written. Whoever told him the name knows Arden personally because that book is still under the mountain where I left it."*

Idris' face turned to stone, his jaw clenching tight as his golden eyes took on a red cast.

"Remember when I said you wouldn't like how I would need to protect you? I need you to act like what I'm about to say is not a surprise to you. It's important. Promise me."

I sucked in a quiet gasp when he grabbed my hand under the table and rose to his feet, taking me with him.

"Do you promise?" he murmured as a hush fell over the crowd.

I braced for impact as I gave him a reluctant nod.

"Please remain seated," he thundered, his voice louder than the herald's magically amplified one. "Esteemed guests of Credour, I have summoned you here from far and wide to share a momentous announcement with you all."

Dread filled my belly at his formal words, and I didn't know if it was his, Rune's, mine, or all of ours. This was going to end badly, and I braced, pasting a pleasant—if completely fake—smile on my face as I waited for the punch line.

"It is with great joy that I declare my engagement to the gracious Duchess Isolde Vale Tenebris, who has captured my heart and soul with her loyalty, her strength, and steadfast determination to bring peace to this realm."

I should have won an award for my facial expression alone because my heart stuttered in my chest as I fought the urge to punch him right in the throat like Kian had taught me. And through it all, Idris continued his little speech like he wasn't highhandedly changing my entire fucking life.

"Our union will not only bring prosperity and unity to our beloved continent, but she will bring light to an era of darkness. So, please, raise your glasses and celebrate with me in this joyous occasion, and may blessings shine upon us all."

Cheers rose from the crowd, the guests standing as they clapped and shouted their congratulations.

I, however, plotted murder.

"You're not going to have to worry about your brother coming down the mountain to kill you because I'm going to do it myself."

Idris brought my hand to his lips and kissed it before clutching me to his chest. *"Stay strong, my brave one. I'm about to kiss you in front of all these people. Make it look real, please."*

Then he pressed his lips to mine, and as much as I wanted to kill him, as much as I wanted to knee him in the balls and stomp on his chest, I let him kiss me. And damn if it didn't look real.

He cupped my face in his hands like I was something precious instead of something he'd stolen with a lie. He touched his forehead to mine, breathing me in before his lips brushed my mouth.

Once.

Twice.

And then he laid his claim.

Just like in the dream, he didn't just kiss me, he owned me. His thumb massaged my pulse point before he clutched my throat in earnest, sweeping his tongue into my mouth in a carnal, needy kiss.

And as good as it felt in the moment, it was a lie.

It was all a lie.

When the kiss broke, the crowd was thunderous, matching the beat of my heart. But I saw none of it. No, I saw Xavier's stoney expression, Kian's blanched face. I saw Freya's worry. None of them knew what he'd planned. At least there was that.

"Please, carry on with the festivities. We will return very soon."

Idris drew me away into a hidden, deserted hallway. My breaths came in panicked pants, and he pulled me into a dark room with a fire burning in the grate.

His arms wrapped around me, and I finally just fucking lost it. Magic burst from my skin, knocking him on his ass to the floor, a barrier surrounding me in a tight bubble where *no one* could get in.

Flat on his back, he still held up his hands in surrender. "I know you're mad—"

"You fucking think? Of course I'm mad." I ripped the cape from my shoulders, the tight collar on my throat a not-so-subtle reminder that he thought he owned me. And "mad" wasn't the right word. Furious was too tame for the rage I felt right then.

"You just put a target on my back. What the fuck were you thinking?"

He stood, towering over me, though he couldn't get through my shield. "I was thinking my status, my crown, could show them you can't be messed with without consequences. That you were completely under my protection."

There was no way, as old as he was, he was just that naïve. "I have been in your house this whole time and nearly killed twice. They already know I'm under your protection, and they. Don't. Fucking. Care. Why would you think telling an entire hall full of people I was your fiancé was a good idea?"

Red flashed in his eyes as a faint tremble rattled the castle. *Oh, he wanted to be mad now?* Well, too bad.

"Because it needed to be done. Because they can't just come in here and take you away from me. They fucking can't, okay?"

I dropped my shield just long enough to punch him right in the gut. I took pride in the fact that he doubled over, shock coloring every facet of his expression.

"I'm. Not. Yours. When are you going to get it through your thick skull? I have never been yours."

His smile was pure knowing, and doubt filled me

as he rose to his full height. "You sure about that? We speak mind to mind, Vale." He said it like it was some big thing.

I rolled my eyes. "It's not special. I do that with Kian and Xavier. Rune, too."

"Exactly. But only mates do that. In all our histories, only fated mates speak mind to mind, and there hasn't been a fated mate—pair or otherwise—in two hundred years. Not since the day I was cursed."

I stepped back from him like the distance would make his words less true.

"The mark on your shoulder? From Kian? I can see it—every shifter can—even through your clothes. He marked you as his. It's not complete, but it's there all the same."

I shook my head. No, Kian would have told me. He would have said. "I don't believe you."

Idris' expression was resolute, firm. He wasn't lying. "Ask them—ask Xavier. They'll know. Hell, if you really want a straight answer, why don't you ask Rune. He knows what's going on, even if he won't tell you."

But Rune was silent in my head, which was answer enough. "So, this is just your stupid curse, then? I have no say? None at all? I'm drawn to all of you, but it's not real at all?"

I'd been drawn to them since the beginning— needing them, wanting them, and I couldn't explain it. Did they even care for me? Or was it just a bunch of magic? And why did it feel like my heart was breaking?

"Of course you do. It isn't a death sentence. Think of it more like extreme attraction with an added communication benefit. Yes, the connection is there, but it is our responsibility to forge it, to strengthen it. You have a choice. You always have a choice."

It sure as hell didn't feel that way. By announcing the engagement, it was like he'd just ripped it all away.

"I don't love you," I hissed, aiming to hurt him like I was hurting, and the barb struck true when he flinched.

His jaw firmed, his gaze burning into mine. "You think I don't know already? You don't have to love me to marry me, Vale."

I knew that. It happened every day. I just thought... I had no idea what I thought. I'd never planned for myself past getting out of the guild. What did it matter if I was engaged to him?

"I won't give them up. Kian. Xavier. I won't ignore them and favor only you. I *won't*."

Something like hope hit his features until he masked it. "No one asked you to. With who they are to you, it's a losing battle."

A part of me was clinging to a precipice, knowing I would fall.

"I don't want to marry you," I whispered, fear settling in before I could stop it. What if he was right? What if this was the only way to stop them long enough to break the curse? What if this bought us the time we needed?

His chuckle was mirthless, and it struck me, too. "I know that, too. But I'll give you what you seek if you agree to marry me."

Gods, he was a complete idiot. "What are you going to offer me now? Jewels? Riches? Castles? You know I don't want any of it."

"Your sister." He reached for me, his fingers sliding through my magic like a blade, latching onto my hand. "I'll help you save her if you agree to marry me. I will expend every ounce of power of the crown to get her back to you."

My laugh was half-crazed as I dropped my barrier, the damn thing no good against him now. "So, bribery. That's what you're going with?"

His finger found my chin, lifting my gaze to his. "If it's what it takes to keep you safe."

I had to remember that he only wanted me to break his curse. He didn't care for me. He might be attracted to me, but just like he'd said, it needed to be cultivated. And Idris had no plans for that.

"There's something you should know," I said, aware if I waited to tell him the truth, it wouldn't work out well for me.

He adjusted his grip, closing me in the circle of his arms, his towering body filling me with as much safety as dread all at the same time. "I'm listening."

I swallowed, my resolve wavering, but I forged ahead. "The reason I was tied to that stake? It was for murder. I killed Arden Ashbourne's son—your nephew."

His brow puckered, his eyes gleaming in the low light, but his hold didn't so much as loosen. "I assume you had a good reason. Unless you regularly go about slaughtering people?"

"He tried to rape my baby sister. I made sure he never touched another woman again. Gulping, I tacked on the rest. "I'm not sorry. I'd do it again in a heartbeat."

Idris pursed his lips, nodding. "As was your right. Though, I wish you would have told me sooner. It explains his tenacity in trying to get to you. Why he was so brutal on the mountaintop. He wants blood."

I thought of my parents. "He's not the one who is owed blood. I am." My smile could have cut glass. "So when you make promises, be sure to take this into account. I've killed for her once already. I won't hesitate to do it again."

A faint hint of pride touched his smile. "Noted, but it doesn't change a thing for me. Do you accept my offer?"

If it meant getting my sister, how could I not? "I accept."

As soon as I said the words, it felt as though my heart was trapped in a vise. Idris brought my hand to his lips before plucking a ring from his pocket and slipping it on my finger. It was a large onyx jewel with a blood-red center, the colors swirling in a near-constant state of movement.

It was beautiful and foreboding, and as much as I wanted to take it off, I couldn't. And though it was just a simple stone, it seemed to weigh a thousand pounds.

Because if I didn't play this just right, all our lives would be on the line.

CHAPTER 22

Xavier

The familiar circular room barely contained my rage as I stared at the side of my king's face. He had been one of my closest friends for more years than I could count, and yet, just looking at him made me want to smash his skull in and spit on it.

Then again, I might just be jealous.

Kian's mark on Vale's shoulder was a near-constant reminder that the pull I felt toward her was nothing more than a wish that would never come true. And after the impromptu proposal masked as an announcement, I wanted to shift into my dragon form and let my animal eat him.

"You can't still be mad at me," Idris murmured, sitting on his throne as he'd done for so many years.

"And you can't still be this stupid. You took her choices away. How could you do that after everything?"

He leaned to the side, his haggard face the only consolation in all this. "It was the only way to keep her safe."

Nope. No consolation. Just idiocy. "Bullshit. You did what you wanted and fuck everyone else. Have you learned nothing in all these years?"

Idris stood, fury etched on every line of his face, and still, I did not care one bit. "That's not fair. She agreed of her own free will. I agreed not to stand in the way of you or Kian's claim on her. She demanded it. The engagement is to put her under the banner of my protection."

Most of it didn't make one bit of sense. "She was already under the banner of your protection, and they tried to kill her twice. No, you wanted to publicly lay your claim and maneuver her into a situation she couldn't get out of. This is Zamarra all over again, only this time—"

His eyes flashed as the room shook. "Zamarra has nothing to do with this. I care for Vale, yes, but this time, I actually know when the woman I love doesn't love me back. Arden and Zamarra were after my throne. Vale doesn't want it. She only wants her sister, and I will happily oblige. This curse made me a pawn, and sometimes what you need is a queen to right what has been wronged."

He took his throne, his face far more haggard as the minutes stretched on. "She will be my queen, she will break the curse, and I will help rescue her sister. Maybe then—" He shook his head, chagrin twisting his lips. "Maybe she'll see me like I see her."

Oh, what love-sick fools we made. "You're lucky it's me here for this and not Kian."

And the only reason he wasn't here was that he was begging Vale not to murder him for not telling her what the bite on her shoulder meant. Granted, the begging had quickly devolved into moans I couldn't listen to, but at least one of us was getting some.

"We both know I wouldn't even see him coming," Idris muttered, pinching his brow. "Did the council say why they wanted this meeting? It's too damn early for this. You'd think after a ball, they would sleep in for once."

I swallowed down my jealousy for a moment. "No, only that the events of last night were concerning and needed to be addressed."

Idris snorted. "How much do you want to bet they think she's ill-suited for the throne? Like she isn't a Duchess in her own right with higher standing than them."

"It's not her title that they take issue with. It's what she is—the power she has. They see it as an end to their own power and influence. They think once this curse is broken, it will be worse than it was before. It will be like under your father's rule, where no one took into account the other factions. The writing is on the wall."

And that was the part I didn't think he understood. People wanted Vale dead because she represented the end to their power, not just the end to the war. She was the end of their ability to profit off of the strife. Desperate people did very stupid things when they were backed into a corner, and with her mounting power, it only signaled the loss of theirs.

"Why do you think I wanted to put her under the banner of the crown? This is the only real way to protect her." He let out a long-suffering sigh. "Let them in. Let's get this over with."

Twenty minutes later, I considered whether or not murdering the entire council would be a better idea than listening to them trash Vale one more time.

"She is a backwater nobody raised by our enemy," Dorian roared, his decorum lost in the weeds of his argument. "Not only can we not trust her, but she has yet to complete the second trial. We all know the curse breaker is meant to be your mate. She must complete the trials or else—"

Golden power shot from Idris' fingers, wrapping around Dorian and raising him in the air so fast the ancient vampire could do nothing but hang upside down, his pale face now as red as the blood he drank.

"Or. Else. What?" Idris growled, eyes flashing, ground shaking, his patience long gone. "I know you weren't about to threaten my intended, Dorian. You wouldn't be so stupid, now, would you?"

Dorian's face purpled. "N-no, Sire. I-it's j-just—"

I drew my swords, fitting them at his neck. "I suggest you spit it out."

"T-there is talk," he wheezed. "That she has be-bewitched you. G-given where she came from, it will quell t-the unrest at the gates if she completes the next trial."

Swiftly, I withdrew my blades from his neck, retaking my position next to Idris.

"Disrespect her one more time, and I will take your head and put it on a spike as a reminder to all on this council who the fuck you're dealing with." His gaze left Dorian as he addressed the council as a whole. "Vale is under my protection. *Mine.* A threat to her is a threat to me, and I take it as such. She will be your queen. Act like it."

Then he dropped Dorian, the ancient vampire scuttling back to his chair like the whipped boy he was. The council took the opportunity to kneel, which I thought was smart. But it wasn't until Fenwick stood, wringing his hands, did the reality of it all come crashing down.

"Your Majesty, if I may? While we can acknowledge the discourse here today has been less than ideal, it is important for the facts to be heard. If we want the unrest to be quelled, your intended must complete the trials, and soon." Fenwick stepped forward, his face tight with worry.

"There is talk amongst the townsfolk of civil war. No one wants to see this great kingdom fall. We must have her complete the trial, and soon, and it must be above reproach. Just like with all other Luxa, she must not be told of the trial beforehand. It is imperative to the success of our kingdom."

But I knew what the second trial was, and there was no way she could complete it—not without help.

"How soon?"

Fenwick's beard shivered a bit as he winced. "As

soon as possible. A day at most. We cannot wait any longer, I'm afraid. Merchants are being looted, farms robbed, it is imperative strength is demonstrated in a positive way or—"

Idris raised his hand to stop his ramblings. "Set it up. As with all other trials, I will not tell her of the details, however, you will soon find she is everything needed in a Luxa and more. You are dismissed."

"But, Sire," Fenwick sputtered. "How can we be sure you won't—"

Idris' eyes blazed. "The bonds of the curse prevent me from saying a word of the trials to anyone. That information has been passed down from council to council for two hundred years. Are you claiming even the bonds of the curse are not above reproach for you?" Idris stood, and the council fell to their knees.

"This curse was designed by a witch determined to teach me that only my true mate can break it. I have watched thirty-five women fall to Rune's flames, thirteen fall to their deaths on the cliff, and three burn up from their powers. Fifty-one women have died—some I've cared for and some I have not. Not one of them has been told beforehand. Do you think after that much death, I would break the streak now?"

A chorus of "nos" filled the room.

"Set up the fucking trial and get your loyalty in check. Or I'll check it for you. *Dismissed*."

As soon as the council left the room, Idris turned to me. "You know everything I just said? None of it applies to you. Prepare her, do you understand? You swore to me you would not watch her die. Neither will I."

On that, we finally agreed.

Without looking back, I stole through the hidden tunnels, racing through the castle to get to her before the council could. We needed to get out and we needed to get out fast. By the time I got to Kian's room, I had formed a plan.

I just needed her to go along with it.

Bursting through the doors, I passed Freya with her feet up on the dining table, half-dozing. She cracked an eyelid, saw me, and then went back to snoozing. Her help was out. Kian was likely monitoring his soldiers, if I had a guess, and disruption would cause a stir.

So that just left me.

I moved directly to the bedchamber. Naked, wrapped in a sheet, and fast asleep, Vale was curled around a pillow, her hair a mass of waves tangled around her shoulders. She looked so peaceful, and I was about to shatter it completely.

Before I could touch her, she woke with a start, a dagger in her hand and to my throat in an instant. She was getting faster. And fuck if she wasn't the most beautiful thing I'd ever seen. My cock thickened with her warm naked body against mine.

"Xavier?"

I had to focus. Now was not the time to let my dick run the show. "I need you to get dressed, and we have to leave. Now. They are holding the second trial tomorrow, and you must be prepared. Move quickly before someone on the council gets the bright idea to sequester you."

Eyes wide, she flew into motion, racing off the bed to the dressing room. "Leathers, please. And a cloak. It'll be cold where we're going."

Ten minutes later, she was dressed and braiding her hair into a queue down her back, following me through the hidden corridors to the south grounds away from prying eyes. I'd already grabbed my spare pack, and soon, she'd learn the rest of the plan.

This was where it could get dicey.

Before we exited the tunnel, I pulled her to a

stop. "You have two choices, and you aren't going to like either of them."

"You're scaring me, Xavier. Tell me what's going on."

"We need to go to the mountains and return before morning when they come get you for the trial. That means we have to—"

Eyes wide, she backed away from me. "F-fly? No. No way. Why—"

"The trial has to do with heights. If we don't work on it now, you'll die tomorrow, and there's not a damn thing I can do about it. Now, here are your choices. I can magically put you to sleep, and we can travel there quickly, or you can fly with me and start getting over your fear now. Choose."

Her heart thundered in her chest, her pulse point trembling with each breath. "Are you sure this is the only way?"

"I wouldn't put you through this otherwise."

Steely resolve straightened her spine. "I want to fly with you."

The faraway shouts of guards meant her absence had been detected. If we didn't get out unnoticed, we'd be dead in the water. "After I shift, I'll lower myself. Climb on my back. At the base of my neck is a deep indentation behind the last fin. Sit there and hold onto the spines. Got it?"

Those shouts grew closer. We didn't have any more time left.

"Fin, spines, got it. Shift. I have your pack."

I peeled out of my leathers, and she stuffed them in the bag as I walked into the open space of the grounds before my bones snapped and cracked, the shift taking me over. I was still recovering from the pain of the transformation when Vale climbed onto my back, seating herself exactly where I told her to. Her body was so much lighter than I expected, and I worried whether she'd be able to stay on my back.

"Please hold on tight."

Her grip tightened, and I launched us off the ground, darting into the low-hanging clouds, my white scales blending easily. I had hope no one saw us leave, and as soon as I could, I broke west, heading for the cliffs where her trial would take place. The path by carriage would take hours, but this way, it was only minutes. The sharp cliff face already in view, the falls cast prisms even in the low light.

"Almost there."

In minutes we landed, and Vale leapt from my

back, her whole body shaking. Falling to her knees, she gulped in air, her fists curling in the shore of the winding river that led to the falls. The water here was freezing, mostly mountain runoff, but it pooled at the bottom of the cliff into a natural hot spring. It was one of my favorite places despite the horrible connotation.

My shift was quick as I gave her the information she needed to know now that no one could hear us while throwing on a pair of pants.

"The trial tomorrow is supposed to test your connection to Rune. The curse breaker has to be able to speak to him mentally for this work. You're the only one who can do that, so there is no problem there."

Shuddering, she stared up at me like I had two heads. "Why do I need to be able to talk to Rune, Xavier?"

It was more accusation than question, and I had a feeling if she could stab me, she would have. I did not like the odds for my balls after this.

"The trial is you walking off this very cliff blind-folded. To complete the trial successfully, Rune has to catch you. The only way you will survive this is if you are mentally bonded to him. That's not what

I'm worried about. I'm pretty sure it's the heights problem that might screw you over."

"You're pretty sure?" Her laugh was half-crazed, but she stood straight and tall. "And how is taking me up here going to cure my fear of heights, exactly?"

She had a good point, but it was all I could think of on short notice. Maybe if she tried it and didn't die...

"Now, this plan needs some work, but I was considering blindfolding you and having you walk like you would in the trial. Because I'll already be shifted and nearby, I will easily catch you just as Rune will. It'll help prepare you for the—"

"Sudden fucking drop?" she offered, and then let out a hysterical laugh that chilled me to the bone. "Who came up with these trials? And why... why me?"

"It's not as bad as it sounds."

"Says the man who's never fucking done it. It would be like asking you to jump off a cliff and shift mid-jump. Are they *crazy*?"

Yes, but the council didn't come up with the trials. Zamarra did. It was as much a punishment for him as it was a way to never release him from his curse.

"Crazy or not, this is still what they're going to make you do. As soon as we return to the castle, they will sequester you, take you up to this very cliff, blindfold you, and make you walk off of it. By knife point if necessary. You wouldn't be the first one who doesn't want to walk off a mountain to almost certain death."

"Great. Fantastic. I love this for me. It's not my worst fear to fall off a mountain or anything."

I reached for her, knowing she'd hate it, but my instinct was always to comfort her. Reluctantly, she let me pull her into my arms. "I'll catch you. I'll always catch you. Do you trust me?"

She rested her forehead against my bare chest, clutching me tight. "With my life, apparently. Do I have to do it blindfolded the first time?"

Twenty minutes later, Vale was finally walking toward the edge, her pale face and shaking legs moving at a turtle's pace. A sudden gust of wind had her crouching on her hands and knees as the wind whipped at her tears.

"I'll catch you, little Luxa. I promise. You can do this."

Even though she couldn't hear me, I hoped she still managed to get the message. Her head darted up, meeting my gaze almost like she could. Heaving a breath, she stood, determination stamped on every line of her body.

And before I could say another word, she launched herself over the edge.

I managed to land before she could pass out, but it was a near thing. She slid from my claws to the ground at the edge of the falls, tears streaming down her face.

"It's okay, my little Luxa. You're safe."

She let out a little mirthless chuckle, the spray from the falls coating her leathers and hair almost instantly. "What about any of this is safe, Xavier?"

It felt like I was hallucinating. Had she just answered me? Shock made me freeze, my brain working overtime to catch up.

"Tell me you can hear me, Vale. Please. Gods, please don't let this be a fluke."

She stood on shaky legs, confusion stamped all over her face. "Of course I can hear you. I heard you in the caverns. I hear you now. What are you freaking out about?"

My shift back to human form was painfully slow, but I took every bit of agony and swallowed it down so I could wrap her in my arms. Lifting her off her feet, I did not care that I was naked as the day I was born or that the water from the falls was damn near freezing. I didn't care that the rapid shifts had left me starving and weak.

I needed to kiss her more than I needed air.

Sliding my mouth over hers, I captured those luscious, full lips with mine and tasted her with my tongue. She let out a soft, surprised sigh, kissing me back like she'd done at the inn, falling into me as if she never wanted to come up for air. It was like coming home. Her arms wound around my neck, her legs around my back, and I didn't want to know anything but her.

My kisses drifted to her neck as I nibbled her fluttering pulse, aching to have her carry my mark. She was my mate, too, and the peace it gave me nearly brought me to my knees.

"Xavier," she moaned, her little pleas making me want to devour her until she screamed for me. "What's going on? Why—"

I still needed that mouth. I'd answer her in a minute, I just needed a little more.

More kisses, more moans, more of her. Needed it so bad, I didn't know if I could come up for air. She reached between our bodies and gripped my cock in her tight fist. It wasn't hard enough to hurt, but it did get my attention.

Breaking the kiss, I let out a needy groan but managed to focus on her.

"Xavier. I need you to answer me. What is going on?" She gently stroked me as she asked the question, and I fought off the urge to thrust in her hand. Gods, this woman had me wrapped around her finger.

"You can hear me," I whispered against her mouth, relishing the tight gasp that came from her. "Only mates can do that. I thought with you hearing Kian and Idris, I would be on the outside looking in for the rest of my life—always wanting you, always needing you, and never having your light again. I thought—"

This time, it was her kiss that shut me up. And when it broke, I knew she was mine, really mine.

"I thought you knew in the cavern," she murmured, clutching me tighter, closer. "I never wanted you to feel excluded. I thought after the inn, maybe you didn't want me anymore. You'd been keeping your distance... I should have just asked you."

I gripped her tighter as I captured her lips again, directing my feet around the warm pool to the hidden cabin situated at its shore. One of these days, I wanted to fuck her in the water, lap at her sexy pussy on the shore, but for now, she needed no clothes and a warm cabin.

Waving my hand, the wards cocooned us in their protection, and we entered my one oasis away from the castle. It wasn't as lush or comfortable, but it was quiet and safe, and a part of me was kicking myself because I hadn't brought her here days ago. With a flick of my fingers, the fire burned hot in the grate, warming the room almost instantly.

But even as curious a being as she was, she still wanted me more. Her fingers flew to the fastenings of her leathers as she yanked them off her arms, and I set her on the small wooden table to help her take off the rest. Each stitch of clothing removed made my cock harder, my need higher, her scent surrounding me as it mingled with mine.

Her shirt went first, her perfect tits fuller since I'd seen them last. Tipped with rosy nipples, I closed my lips over them. The moan that came out of her made my cock ache, the urge to make her do it again nearly overwhelming. And when she was completely naked with her perfect ass on my kitchen table, I decided to make her my breakfast.

Latching onto her hips, I yanked her to the edge and knelt at her feet, draping her lithe legs over my shoulders.

"Your taste is burned in my brain, my little witch," I growled against the skin of her thigh, my fangs lengthening as I ached to mark her. "I've been dying for seconds."

The first taste was heaven, better than I remembered, and damn if that memory hadn't gotten me through some lonely nights without her. Her scent filled my nose as I licked her slick little pussy, her need coating my lips. Curling my tongue around her clit, I sucked her little bud into my mouth, and the sounds she made drove me past ravenous.

I set out to make her scream, knowing what she needed. Sucking her clit until she was writhing on the table, I thrust two fingers inside her wet, greedy pussy. Hips bucking, she rode my fingers and my face, gripping my hair in her fists as she took her pleasure. I curled my fingers, adding a third as I stretched her, getting her ready to take me.

Her tight little hole clamped down on my fingers

as her release hit her, light bursting from her skin as she rode out the wave of her orgasm.

Fuck, she was magnificent. Eyes bright, skin flushed, the tips of her rosy nipples so tight they were pebbled points. Golden power shimmered across her skin, reaching for me as her fingers beckoned me to her.

"Take me, Xavier. Fuck me. Mark me. I need you."

I didn't know if she'd actually spoken or if our powers melded our minds together.

My magic answered hers, coating us both in the blue flames as my need nearly drove me to madness. Our powers twined together as I yanked her up in my arms, crossing the room to lay her down on the plush mattress. I wasted no time, spreading her legs wide, guiding the head of my cock to her slick folds.

She shivered in want, her mind calling to me.

"Please. I'll be so good, I promise. I need it. I need you."

I slid into her in one rough stroke, her mental pleas driving me insane.

"You want to be my good girl, huh?" I growled, capturing her gasp with my mouth as I stole a kiss. "Show me what kind of good girl you can be."

Eyes rolling back in her head, she guided my fingers to her mouth, taking the three I'd slipped inside her and sucking them clean one by one. I felt those sucks all the way in the base of my cock, and I fucked her in time with them, her heat burning me from the inside out. I fought off the urge to rut, to fuck.

"Next time, I'll have Kian fuck your pretty mouth while I'm inside this tight little pussy. Or better, I'll let him fuck your ass while I take you. Fill you up so full," I whispered in her ear, her answering moans telling me she not only wanted it, she needed it. She clenched around me, the flutters of her first orgasm reaching for her.

"But right now, you're mine, aren't you?" I growled, taking my fingers from her mouth and wrapping them around her throat. "Say you're mine." The vibration of her moan traveled up my arm and down my spine, tightening my balls.

"I'm yours," she whimpered, the needy sound nearly pulling me under.

I pulled from her, and her magic responded, lashing at me, nearly burning me, and fuck if it didn't drive my need higher.

I want you back. I need you.

Flipping us over, I draped her across my lap, her luscious ass in my hands, her legs on either side of mine, straddling me.

"Put me inside you, baby," I ordered, and gritted my teeth as she gripped my cock, too far gone to tease me.

Notching the head at her folds, she slowly sank onto me, her eyes widening as she bottomed out. Her breath stuttered, and a needy moan fell from her lips as she rocked to take more of me.

"You're so much bigger like this. So full. So good."

Helping her set the pace, I wrapped my fist in her braid, tilting her head back as I drove up into her. She whimpered so sweet when I pulled, exposing her neck to my teeth. Nibbling on her throat, the tops of her breasts, her nipples, I fucked her until her legs were jelly and her orgasm was so close she clawed at my shoulders.

Then I pulled out again. This time, her magic stung like a whip, and when I flipped her, I spanked her sexy little ass in response.

Once.

Twice.

Three times, her flesh pink and tender, and when I ran my talons over the raised handprints, she shivered and moaned.

"You don't come until I say, my little witch. Not until you beg for it."

Putting her on her hands and knees, I wrapped

my hand around her throat, pulling her back impaling, her on my cock. Setting a punishing rhythm, I fucked her until she was mindless, clawing at my legs, my arms, anything she could reach with her dull little nails.

"Oh gods, please. I'll do anything. Please let me come."

"That's it. Fuck, you beg so pretty. Do it again."

As much as I wanted this to last, her orgasm was bearing down on her. Sweat slicked her skin, her limbs trembled, her pussy sucked at my cock, squeezing me so tight I thought I might die.

"Please, Xavier. I—"

As soon as she said my name, I brushed her clit with my thumb, and she screamed, her release slamming into her so hard, her power lashed out at the both of us.

My fangs lengthened as her magic called to my dragon, guiding them to the same place Kian had marked her. As soon as I sank them into her skin, a fresh release hit us both. Her blood filled my mouth, drowning us as our magic mingled, mixed, tying us together so tight I didn't know where she ended and I began.

Clutching her to me, I got lost in the pleasure. Time and space meant nothing. The only thing that mattered was her. I didn't need food or water or air. I didn't need the sun or the moon. She was the only thing I needed.

As our magic bound us together, I knew I'd do anything, be anything for her.

I'd even cheat if I had to.

Boneless, we melted into the bed, twisted around each other as her golden light and my blue flames finally dissipated. And when they did, uncertainty filled my belly as I clutched her to me tighter.

"They're going to try to kill you again tomorrow," I murmured, the truth of it cutting through the haze of our pleasure.

The council, Arden, the guild. She was in their crosshairs, and I didn't know what to do to protect her other than running away.

"I won't turn and run," she whispered, gleaning my thoughts.

Determination replaced the uncertainty.

"Then we need to make sure you're ready for them."

CHAPTER 24

VALE

The council came for me in the middle of the night.

Hugging my knees alone in Kian's bed, I stared at the closed bedchamber door. Freya's voice thundered through the wood as she demanded that the council wait until I was properly dressed to sequester me.

"We do not answer to you," Dorian protested, his voice carrying through the thick wooden door.

"They don't, but you *do*, my progeny. Remember who you are speaking to, Dorian, before I make sure you cannot speak at all." Freya's voice was dark and deadly, her part to play just as important as mine. "It is not proper for you to enter her bedchamber—"

"Don't you mean the *general's* bedchamber?"

I didn't know who was ballsy enough to say that to Freya, but the unsettling squelch coming from the other side of the door was not comforting at all. If I had a guess, it was body parts landing on tile, but I didn't want to know for sure.

"Does someone else want to impugn the Duchess' honor, or do you want to allow me to get her dressed? You forget there is always someone more amenable to take your place on the council, good sirs. Preferably someone with more sense."

"Rune?" I'd relayed the plan to the linchpin of it, knowing it was all too easy for the whole thing to fail.

"I'm ready, my Queen." His voice was a small comfort, proof this might work.

"I'm scared. What if they try to keep you in the caverns? What if they try to hurt y—"

"They can't. I left the keep hours ago."

It wasn't much to calm my nerves, but it was something. The ways all this could be sabotaged were endless, and I hated we didn't have more time to iron out the details.

In the hours I'd spent with Xavier alone in his cabin, we devised a plan of action that would keep me alive. Acting surprised and afraid that I was being sequestered by a bunch of men who likely wanted me dead wasn't the hard part.

No, the hard part was making sure Freya remained my chaperone. It was imperative I had someone I trusted with me for this to work. Though, it might be less of us convincing them and more of Freya just saying it and it being so.

She was talented like that.

When the door opened, she noted the dagger clutched in my fist and gave me a small tip of her lips. Then she slipped through, locking it with a snap of her fingers.

"Let's get you ready."

Thirty minutes later, Freya and I were flanked by eleven of the twelve members of the council as we strode through the corridor to the throne room. The twelfth needed to go to the infirmary to put his intestines back inside his body, and I wondered why Freya couldn't have taken a few more out before we walked into this obvious trap.

She'd helped me into a dress meant for battle, the unsuspectingly warm leathers covering me completely from neck to wrists all the way past my ankles. It was almost completely black, the thickly scaled bodice protecting my ribs and stomach. But that wasn't the only defense. The underside of my arms and the top of my shoulders were scaled as well, and the split skirt revealed sturdy leather pants with that same reinforcement on the thighs.

The outfit was a smaller, dressier version of the leathers she typically wore, making me feel almost prepared for whatever they would throw at us. But when we entered the throne room with its wide columns and giant arches, real fear took hold of my middle and refused to let go.

Idris sat on his throne with Kian and Xavier at his flanks, his expression so closed down it was as if he was protecting himself from me.

"It's just a mask, my brave one. Nothing to worry about."

I almost wilted in relief. We were on shaky ground, he and I, but a part of me still trusted he would fulfill his promises, trusted he would honor the agreement we'd made.

Idris stood, and based on protocol, everyone but me knelt. The giant ring on my finger meant that only I stood, dipping my head to show my deference.

"It has come time for the second trial. As with all trials, they shall remain secret until they are to be performed. As is custom, you will be blindfolded on the journey so you may react to the events in a true testament to your power and connection to the Ashbourne line."

"You can do this, Vale. Rune is with you. I am with you. And no one will let you go into this alone."

"Do you accept this test of your will, your connection, and your loyalty to this crown?" he asked, and I thought of saying no for a split second. My gaze went from him to Kian to Xavier and back again.

Nyrah. Remember who you're doing all this for.

"I accept," I whispered, my fear of what was to come selling it more than anything.

Then, without another word, a blindfold was slipped over my eyes, and the trial began.

THE CARRIAGE RIDE SEEMED TO TAKE HOURS, THE BACK-and-forth rocking making me sick to my stomach. Or maybe that was the nerves. Freya sat shoulder to shoulder with me on the bench, her attempts at making me laugh fruitless, but I appreciated her trying.

When we stopped, the familiar sound of the falls signaled we were in the right place, but when hard hands practically yanked me out of the seat, my relief crumbled to dust.

The sound of a sword unsheathing had my breath coming in panicked pants, the urge to rip off my blindfold almost too much to take.

"Touch her like that again, Dorian," Freya hissed, "and I will take your hands along with your tongue. With silver no less, so neither will grow back."

"You're not even supposed to be here," he grumbled, his hand gentling on my shoulders as he guided me closer to the roar of the falls.

"And you're supposed to treat the intended of the king with more respect than you'd give a sack of grain, but here we are. Is this how you've treated every Luxa who has participated in the second trial? Given how much disdain you've publicly shown to Vale, should I look into the validity of their deaths? Should I encourage their parents, their families to investigate? Or should you just treat someone with respect?"

Dorian pulled me to a stop—gently this time—and turned me so the falls were to my left. "I would never. I want this curse broken just as much as you do. I would never—"

I could almost feel Freya's eyebrow mocking him. "Uh-huh."

He let out a gusting, long-suffering sigh. "I apologize, Your Grace. I sometimes forget my strength, and I let my prejudice of the guild taint my actions. Please forgive me."

Turning to his voice, I hoped he could see my raised eyebrow. It wasn't as good as Freya's, but she'd taught me well. "I know you don't like me. I don't much care for you either, truth be told. But we don't have to like each other. As long as you truly care for Idris, as long as you are loyal to him, you can hate me all you want."

A ball of light formed in my palm, bright enough I could see it through the blindfold. It was so hot, it was its own mini sun, burning like a beacon in the middle of the day.

"But if you touch me in anger one more time, Freya will have to gather your innards in a potato sack and send them back to your family because there will be nothing left of you. Are we clear?"

His gulp was audible over the rushing of the falls, and his hand left my arm like the leather had branded him. "Crystal, Your Grace."

"Fantastic." I let the light wink out, pulling the power back into myself before I overused it. The last thing I needed was to get a bloody nose and pass out, though, that had been happening less and less. "Then let's get this show on the road. What am I supposed to be doing here?"

"I'm sure Freya explained the process to you," a familiar voice said, but I was having trouble placing it.

Freya snorted. "I actually did nothing of the sort, Fenwick. Just as required, I have told her nothing of the trial. It is your job to explain it."

"Very well," he tutted, the exasperation in his tone almost comical if we weren't in the middle of a death-defying trial. "Your Grace, Duchess Isolde Vale Tenebris, Lady of Shadowmere, Light Bringer, Curse Breaker, Grand Luxa of Tarrasca, this trial—as King Idris stated—is an assessment of your connection to the Ashbourne line. Specifically, your mental connection to the dragon known as Rune. To complete this test, you must call him to you as you walk."

"*Already above you, my Queen. But dawn comes soon. I won't be able to hide in the clouds much longer.*" His voice in my head nearly had me wilting in relief, but I straightened my spine.

"And?" I knew the rest, but his instructions seemed a little circumspect for someone so keen on the details. Hell, the man had been almost apoplectic at the thought of completing his Tenebris scroll...

Oh. *Oh, shit.*

We'd been expecting Dorian to be the interloper. He'd been practically salivating at being in the carriage with us, making sure the trial was done to his standards and no one told me about my task beforehand. But according to Freya, no one liked Dorian—not the king, not the mages or Fae. He had limited connections except in the vampire community where he was revered, and he wouldn't have the first clue about the sovereign name business.

But Fenwick, with his scrolls and mage connections...

Fenwick *would*.

"You must not take off your blindfold or stop walking. To complete this task, you must allow the dragon known as Rune to either stop you from walking over the falls or catch you once you do."

Pursing my lips, I ripped off my blindfold and stared him right in his pale, watery eyes. "And that sounds like slow suicide."

The ancient councilmember leaned heavily on

his cane, his beloved scroll held tight in his fist. His expression was colored in surprise, but it was so false, I knew my math was right.

"What are you doing?" Dorian sputtered. "The trial is supposed to be completed blindfolded. Those are the rules."

Rules? "And how many women have died blindly following your rules?" My gaze landed on the mage, those eyes taking a milky quality I knew well. "What was your plan exactly?" I asked, tilting my head to the side as I drew the dagger at my thigh. "Break my neck while my back was turned? Stab me in the back? Or just hope I couldn't talk to Rune and walk right over the edge?"

"I-I don't know what you're talking about." He moved backward, his shocked mask slipping just a bit as his gaze darted to Freya and Dorian. "What is she talking about?"

"So far, I've been stabbed, thrown through a glass door, and nearly poisoned while I've been here, and I'll have to admit, you covered your tracks pretty well. You shouldn't have tipped your hand with the sovereign name, Fen."

Freya stared at Fenwick like he was a specimen on a slab, her blue eyes bleeding to red as scarlet veins raced up her neck, her nails blackening as talons lengthened to vicious points. "What have you done?"

Dorian shook his head, not in denial, but in disbelief as he stared at Fenwick and his tightly clutched scroll. "You have interpreted the scrolls for two hundred years. No one has touched them but you."

I knew the vampire was smarter than he looked.

"Arden was always your favorite," Freya murmured. "Your pupil. How long have you been a spy for him?"

Inky-black power seemed to burst from his very pores as the scent of death and decay filled my nostrils.

Freya and Dorian stood as my guards as Fenwick raised his hands to the sky. Then he brought them down in a tidal wave of magic, knocking us all off our feet. The ground all around us split into a perfect circle as bodies crawled from the earth, each in various stages of decay. By their dresses, they were all women, and by the golden lights at their middles, I had a feeling I knew who and what they were.

It was bad enough I was stuck on top of a fucking cliff. Now I had to deal with this?

"Freya, how many Luxa have died on this mountain?"

She shot me a worried glance before whipping her head back to the full coven of reanimated witches. "Thirteen."

Yep, this was exactly what I wanted to hear.

Fenwick was just on the outside of the death, his milky eyes and blackened swirls of magic sucking at their light. He was gathering power—stealing it— his dark chuckle chilling me to the bone.

"Two hundred years, and you never suspected?" He tutted again, the formerly grandfatherly gesture now malevolent. "Not one Luxa survived the trials? Surely not all of them could be morons willingly jumping off of cliffs to their doom. And yet, no one batted an eye. You really did make it too easy for me." He waved the scroll in the air. "All because you didn't want to read a slip of paper."

But over the course of his little monologue, Fenwick's voice changed, deepened, no longer masked by his deception, morphing into a voice that haunted me in my dreams.

You will die like all the witches before you, and when your sister comes of age, we'll kill her, too.

He sounded like the assassin who had tried to end me and nearly succeeded. But more, he sounded like Arden. Like the guild leader was speaking from his very mouth. And as I realized exactly who he sounded like, I was temporarily blinded as my vision left the top of the mountain.

As if I was seeing through Kian's eyes, I watched as members of the council pressed Lumentium daggers to his throat, the sizzling metal biting into his skin. Wrists in chains, he fought them, but it was a losing battle.

The scene changed, and then it was Xavier with his face in the dirt, a spear of that same magic-stealing metal poised at the base of his spine.

And then it was Idris watching his two closest friends being detained as he stood with a dagger poised right at his heart, the burning tip of the blade piercing his skin through his leathers. And all of them were surrounded by the same inky-black magic flowing from Fenwick's fingertips.

This wasn't a trial for me. This was a full-on coup.

"Rune," I screeched in my mind. *"They need you."*

My vision returned as fire streaked across the sky, the red dragon circling closer. *"You need me more, my Queen."*

And then the witches moved toward us, tightening the circle we were trapped in as Fenwick let out a gleeful laugh.

"Do you like their distress, Vale? Do you like

seeing their pain through their eyes? Your mates are just as trapped as you are, except when they die, you'll feel every second of it. Gods, I do love a good mate bond. Too bad yours will be your undoing."

Blackness nearly blotted out the coming dawn as Fenwick's power poured into the sky. "Consider this my formal resignation. It's time to crown a new king."

Freya glanced over her shoulder at the edge of the cliff, putting Fenwick's words together just as I had. We needed out of this circle, we needed to get down to the bottom of the mountain, and we needed to put an end to this bullshit council once and for all.

Freya gripped her blade tight in her fist as she tossed her twin one to Dorian. The vampire seemed shocked she'd give him a weapon, given the coup he'd unwittingly landed in the middle of. "Don't make me regret this."

With a tandem nod, they targeted the witches surrounding us. Freya slashed first, aiming for the golden light at the Luxa's center, her deteriorating ribcage bleeding the power like a war wound. As soon as the blade touched it, magic exploded from the long-dead witch in a dome of retribution, black tainted gold knocking into Freya like a giant's fist.

Freya flew back, landing flat on her back in the dirt, her skin mottled and burned from the sizzling power. Leathers singed, skin red and raw, the vampire sucked in a startled breath, blinking up at the sky.

This wasn't just a circle of witches—this was a prison.

Dorian hadn't even noticed Freya's instant defeat. He was too busy chopping at the legs of the least decayed of the coven, his slashes doing little except whittling her down to a more manageable size. It was the Luxa's magic that had burnt Freya, not the witches themselves.

And maybe I could fight fire with fire.

"Get back, Dorian," I yelled, even as the dragon in my brain roared for me to stop.

Allowing the power to rise within me, it shot from my chest in a dome of golden light, enveloping Freya and Dorian as it shoved against the barrier of the witches.

As soon as the power hit them, it was as if lightning had struck me right in the chest. My body burnt, smoldered, scorched from the inside out as I screamed. It was pain, yes, but it was more than that. It was the darkness of it, too. Like a bladed weapon, it tore at me as it drowned me in agony.

"Stop, my Queen. This is not the way. You'll burn up. You're already burning."

And he was right. All that pain, and I hadn't moved them an inch. No, instead, they stepped closer, nearly bringing me to my knees.

"I can't just stand here, and the council is hurting them."

"They can take care of themselves. Worry about you and get out of that circle."

"I'm trying."

Fenwick's milky irises met mine through the haze of it all, his gaze flicking from milky, to black, to Arden's gold, the guild leader shining from the old mage's eyes.

"I told you that you would burn. It's not how I wanted it, but I have to say it is much sweeter than watching you tied to a stake."

"And I. Told you. That you'd go. Down. W-with. Me."

Instantly, I dropped the dome, going for a more targeted approach. Bolts had worked for me before, right? In all my lessons with Xavier, we never managed to get me to draw power from myself, only from the rage I harnessed inside of me.

Sucking in a breath, I ignored the witches moving closer. Ignored the pain, the burning, the way my skin steamed in the cold air. Ignored every-thing except for forming a single strong bolt of magic as I imagined Nyrah's face perfectly in my mind. The image changed, and I saw Xavier on the ground with a spear pointed right at his spine, Kian with a blade at his throat, and Idris bleeding from the tip of a poisoned dagger pushing into his chest.

Rage banked the flames of pain, turning them into power. I formed a bolt of perfect magic, not aiming for the witches or the barrier but for Fenwick himself, the ancient mage a mere puppet for Arden's machinations.

And when that bolt cut through the barrier like a hot knife through butter, I relished the moment it hit Fenwick right in the shoulder. Shock slammed into his expression just before he flew back, knocking him into the jagged rocks of the shore.

But the witches around us did not fall. Their circle broken, they began to move, reaching for us as if they were defending their master. Freya drove a blade into the neck of one, taking her head as she moved to the next. The first witch fell into a pile of bones and decaying flesh.

I felt a ray of hope for a shining second before rotting hands ripped me off my feet, slamming me into the ground with enough force to nearly knock me out. My ears buzzed as putrid flesh reached for my chest, but before she could make contact, Dorian's sword cut through the top of her head.

The vampire yanked me to my feet, tucking me behind his back as he put himself between me and another Luxa. "If you plan on calling that dragon, Your Grace, now would be the time."

"I'm out of the damn circle."

"Oh, I know," he growled. *"On your right."*

I barely had time to turn my head before red scales zoomed over the top of the mountain. Talons extended, he snatched up two dead Luxa in his claws and crushed them to a pulp.

Swallowing a startled laugh, I set my sights on Arden's puppet. Cane gone, he crawled to the scroll he'd once clutched so tightly, his blackened blood pouring from the wound in his shoulder. He looked back at me, and golden eyes glowed with power as he set his sights on the scroll again.

Malignant magic flew from his fingertips, and the scroll burst into flames as he started laughing in between wet coughs that stained his lips black with his blood. The dark, maniacal chuckle grew as the paper withered in the inky fire. "Good luck figuring out how to break the curse now."

Dread pooled in my belly as that voice took on

the voices of so many, Arden's power flaring as Fenwick's body began to die. "You think we haven't been here this whole time? You think the unrest is just a fluke, that we haven't engineered it brick by brick? Magic isn't just dying—we're killing it one Luxa at a time. War is coming, little girl. Sooner than you think. And that incomplete mate bond won't save any of you. Especially not your little sister."

Then he reached into his cloak and removed a pulsing orb of purple magic. "If my little puppet has to die here, he'll at least do me the favor of taking you with him. He'd served his purpose, anyway."

The orb pulsed faster, a faint ticking coming from the glass as if it were a clock.

Whipping around, I shot out a wave of magic, knocking Freya and Dorian into the rushing falls, hoping they would land safely in the water at the bottom.

"Rune, I hope you're ready to catch me because I'm about to do something really fucking stupid."

The ticking got louder, faster, time rushing away from me faster than I could catch up. I took off at a dead run, racing for the edge I hoped I'd never have to see again.

"My Queen. Wait!"

But it was too late. I didn't have any more time.

My feet reached the edge long before I was ready, and I prayed that if Orrus was kind, he'd make my death quick.

For the second time in less than a day, I flew over the edge of a cliff, only this time, I didn't know if anyone would catch me.

CHAPTER 25

VALE

Blood-red scales slammed into my shoulder as I landed on Rune's giant back.

"Hold on," he roared, twisting in the air as the ground rushed to meet us.

I skidded, barely hanging onto the slippery spines as gravity threatened to steal me away. Wind whipped at my eyes, and then we crashed into the earth, the jarring impact loosening my grip. I flew, a scream tearing from my throat before his enormous talons plucked me from the air and clutched me to his chest.

Heart in my throat, I hung onto his claws as I tried not to throw up.

"You're bleeding," Rune whispered inside my

head. Or maybe it wasn't a whisper, it was just that my ears were ringing, and the world was fuzzy.

"I don't care. Let me down so I can get to them," I croaked, my voice a husk of what it used to be.

Rune gently set me on my feet, but I immediately wilted to the ground, my hands gripping the gloriously cold snow as my body burned. Too hot, too tight, my leathers suffocated me, and I ripped at the fastenings, sucking frigid air into my lungs as soon as I was free.

Staggering to my feet, I trained my glare onto the councilmember holding *Lumentium* on my men. Lip curling, my power shot out of me in a wave of protection, knocking them away before I fell to my knees. I barely registered them falling to the ground before Freya and Dorian flew from the water, swords drawn, prepared for battle.

Coughing, red spattered the snow, and I knew I was in real trouble.

The world around me shimmered and faded as I tried to get back to my feet.

"My Queen?"

"Are they alive? Did I make it in time?"

Strong hands plucked me from the snow, and I saw Xavier's white hair before a slash of healing magic nearly had my back bowing in renewed agony.

"Not this time, gods dammit. You cannot take her from me." Xavier's voice roared in my head, comforting me even though he was so sad.

The world tilted, swayed, but I still caught the flashes of blades clashing as the roar of two dragons vibrated through my chest. Golden power flew like vines wrapping around men, lifting them in the air, the council members losing their weapons as Kian and Rune circled them like prey.

I made it. They're safe. I did it.

"Stay with me, Vale," Xavier ordered, and I wanted to follow it.

I did.

But my body was heavy, and I was so tired. He ripped off the remainder of my leather corset, leaving my upper body in just a thin silk camisole. Snow sizzled against my skin as he rested me on the ground before his hot hand pressed into my middle.

Searing power filled me again, and I screamed at the brutal agony of it, even as it healed my lungs, my organs, my heart. His eyes glowed as his long white hair floated around his head, his nose bleeding as sweat dotted his brow.

"I won't lose you, Vale. You are staying with me one way or another. I will not watch you die."

I reached for his face, cupping his cheek. "I'm okay. I'm alive."

Blue eyes flashed in reproach. "You were coughing up blood. You nearly burned up."

He wasn't wrong, but there were more pressing matters at hand. "Help me up."

The roar of a dragon had us both freezing for a single moment before he plucked me from the snow, clutching me to his chest as he brought us to the impromptu execution of men desperate for power.

Black swirls of magic filled their mouths, their eyes, their faces flickering from normal to monsters and back.

"Can you see them? Can you see the magic?" I whispered, wanting to be nowhere near them. They were almost as bad as the dead Luxa up on the cliff.

"What magic?" Idris barked, fury stamped on every line of his face.

My gaze shot to Freya. She could see it, too. "Death magic, they draw on the dead Luxa. Like Fenwick. Like Arden."

Maybe it was because we were touched by their magic, but even Dorian's frightened eyes were on them like he'd never seen something so horrible in his long life.

Freya nodded. "They are covered in it. It's poisoning them from the inside out."

"It's like they're rotting," Dorian whispered before covering his mouth and nose like he was about to lose his breakfast.

Idris drew up to his full height, his chest bloody, his eyes hard. "That's all I need to hear. For the crime of high treason against the crown, you are hereby sentenced to death by dragon fire." His gaze cut to the four remaining councilmembers. "Any objections?"

The bowing men all shook their heads, but I knew this couldn't be all the rot in this kingdom.

Another roar shook the earth as Rune and Kian enveloped their darkness in flames. And the most unsettling part?

They didn't even scream.

THE ONLY PLACE THAT FELT SAFE WAS IDRIS' ROOMS, AND that was due to Briar's tight warding. Freya and

Dorian sat at the dining table, large glasses of blood in their goblets as I sat curled in a blanket on a large, comfortable chair. Kian sat on the floor to my left, playing with the ends of my braid, while Xavier sat on the ottoman, his hand not leaving my ankle.

Even Rune was nearby, perched on the turret like an overgrown pigeon.

"Take that back. I am, at the very least, an eagle or a falcon if you're insisting on making bird analogies."

I giggled into my wine, my fourth of the night, and I planned on drinking a whole barrel soon enough.

Idris stopped his pacing, his eyes glowing for a moment before his lips curled into a smile for a second. I felt him in my mind, reading me as he'd done over and over again these last several hours. Kian and Xavier and Rune did it, too, and I was getting used to it. I'd consider putting a stop to it once my buzz lifted, but for now, it brought them peace.

While Freya, Dorian, and I had been up on that cliff, the real coup had happened down at the falls. All three of them had been blocked from me behind a wall of Fenwick's death magic, and it scared the shit out of them collectively.

I, personally, was trying very hard not to freak

out. Over half the council was dead—either by their own hand, in Fenwick's case, or by execution. Dorian, of all people, was a good guy. The scroll Fenwick carried was gone, and now we had no idea how to break the curse. Oh, and nearly everyone I cared about was nearly killed, and there was a war coming.

This wasn't over.

Not hardly.

"Tell me what he said again," Idris asked, his paused pacing doing little to ease my nerves.

"She told you three times already," Freya griped into her goblet. "The curse has something to do with completing the mate bond. That's about it. Other than 'war's coming,' there is nothing else."

But he needed to hear it, even if I didn't want to say it again. *"He said that they've been here this whole time. That they've been tearing this kingdom apart since the beginning. And with every dead Luxa, we're losing more and more magic. He threatened you and Nyrah and..."*

"You have to move up the wedding," Kian murmured. "As soon as possible. Complete the bond and see if that helps break the curse. If it doesn't, if war is coming, you need all the protection you can get. A royal title will protect you. I didn't think so at the engagement, but even when you were fighting for your life up there, they still hesitated to hurt Idris."

But not me. They hesitated to kill him, but I was cannon fodder.

"And you think a title will save me?" I asked, staring at those burning amber eyes.

His nod was almost imperceptible, but it was there.

"Xavier?"

His hand squeezed my ankle. "It needs to be public and big. Invite the townsfolk as well. Have a feast. They need to see you, love you."

My gaze drifted to Idris. Hope was in his eyes, but also resolve. He agreed with them.

"The soonest I can get it put together is ten days, a week at a push," Freya mused.

I tilted back my cup, swallowing the rest of my wine.

"It is for the best, my Queen," Rune murmured, his tone the softest I'd ever heard.

He'd always called me "his Queen," and soon, it would be all too true.

"Let's do it then," I whispered, staring at my knees as I reordered my life in my head.

When I'd accepted Idris' proposal, I'd never

really considered that I'd actually marry him. It was a far-off concept, a fantasy, an ephemeral notion never to come true.

Now, we were getting married in a week.

I did not see that coming.

Not at all.

"I think I'm going to need more wine."

Thank you so much for reading Ruined Wings. I can't express just how much I love Vale, Kian, Xavier, and Idris along with their ragtag bunch of friends. And we aren't quite done yet!

*Next up is **Stolen Embers** and all the crazy, dragon shifter shenanigans that is to come. I hope you're buckled in to see Vale & company contend with their crazy mate bond, the coming war, and the curse chaining their king!*

*If you would love to see a special, NSFW deleted scene from **Ruined Wings,** turn the page! I hope you enjoy it!*

BONUS SCENE

Dear Reader,

I hope you enjoyedRuined Wings. Vale, Kian, Xavier, and Idris have a very special place in my heart, and I am absolutely ecstatic for you to read more about them.

I have an extra special NSFW deleted scene for you as a thank you for reading. All you have to do is click the link below, sign up for my newsletter, and you'll get an email giving you access!

SIGN UP HERE:
https://geni.us/ruined-wings-bonus

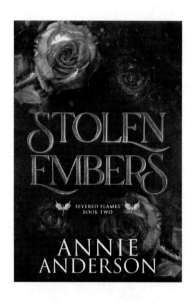

STOLEN EMBERS

Severed Flames Book Two

Light bringer. Curse breaker. Queen—*if she can live that long...*

Vale Tenebris never intended to honor the pact with the cursed Beast of a king, nor did she expect to fall so hard for the dragon shifters who saved her life. But when the ruthless Guild infiltrates the kingdom, this witch finds herself caught between an impending war and a promise she never meant to keep.

With the kingdom teetering on the brink of destruction and war on the horizon, Vale must uncover the secrets of the ancient curse before the men she loves are stolen from her forever.

And that is only if she can master the wild magic threatening to consume her.

No pressure.

Stolen Embers is a spicy dragon romantasy set in the Severed Flames universe. You can expect three sinfully hot, super growly shifters who will do anything to keep their woman alive. Mature themes will be present. Reader discretion is advised.

Preorder your copy today!

BOOKS BY ANNIE ANDERSON

SEVERED FLAMES

Ruined Wings

Stolen Embers

IMMORTAL VICES & VIRTUES

HER MONSTROUS MATES

Bury Me

SHADOW SHIFTER BONDS

Shadow Me

THE ARCANE SOULS WORLD

GRAVE TALKER SERIES

Dead to Me

Dead & Gone

Dead Calm

Dead Shift

Dead Ahead

Dead Wrong

Dead & Buried

Soul Reader Series

Night Watch

Death Watch

Grave Watch

The Wrong Witch Series

Spells & Slip-ups

Magic & Mayhem

Errors & Exorcisms

The Lost Witch Series

Curses & Chaos

Hexes & Hijinx

THE ETHEREAL WORLD

Rogue Ethereal Series

Woman of Blood & Bone

Daughter of Souls & Silence

Lady of Madness & Moonlight

Sister of Embers & Echoes

Priestess of Storms & Stone

Queen of Fate & Fire

JOIN THE LEGION

EXCLUSIVE SNEAK PEEKS,
GIVEAWAYS, BOOK DISCUSSION.
COME FOR THE BOOKS.
STAY FOR THE MEMES.

To stay up to date on all things Annie Anderson, get exclusive access to ARCs and giveaways, and be a member of a fun, positive, drama-free space, join The Legion!

facebook.com/groups/ThePhoenixLegion

Acknowledgments

A huge, honking thank you to Shawn, Barb, Jade, Angela, Heather, Kelly, and Erin. Thanks for the late-night calls, the endurance of my whining, the incessant plotting sessions, the wine runs... (*looking at you, Shawn.*)

Every single one of you rock and I couldn't have done it without you.

ABOUT THE AUTHOR

 Annie Anderson is the author of the international bestselling Rogue Ethereal series. A United States Air Force veteran, Annie pens fast-paced Paranormal Romance & Urban Fantasy novels filled with strong, snarky heroines and a boatload of magic. When she takes a break from writing, she can be found binge-watching The Magicians, flirting with her husband, wrangling children, or bribing her cantankerous dog to go on a walk.

To find out more about Annie and her books, visit www.annieande.com

facebook.com/AuthorAnnieAnderson

instagram.com/AnnieAnde

amazon.com/author/annieande

bookbub.com/authors/annie-anderson

goodreads.com/AnnieAnde

pinterest.com/annieande

tiktok.com/@authorannieanderson

Made in United States
North Haven, CT
09 June 2025

69677706R00266